Finding Theresa

Paul Baugh

Book cover designed and painted by Anna Fagin Larimer

Scripture passages have been taken from *The New American Bible,
revised edition* (NABRE) Copyright @ 2015. Published by the United
States Conference of Catholic Bishops, Washington, DC.

The Choice written by Nicholas Sparks (2007)

Bless the Broken Road co-written by Marcus Hummon, Bobby Boyd
and Jeff Hanna (1994)

I Got You Babe written by Sonny Bobo (1965)

I Do (Cherish You) co-written by Keith Stegall and Dan Hill (1998)

Everything I Own written by David Gates (1972)

Table of Contents

Finding Theresa

Under a moonless cloud covered night I dwelt,
adrift upon an ocean of pain felt.
With no compass or rudder to guide the way,
praying for a better day.

Into the darkness of the abyss I descend,
unsure if the fall will ever end.
Waters from which one day I would be saved,
Certain to become my grave.

In the darkness of my night,
you came to me and we took flight.
Beyond the clouds we flew,
to heights I never before knew.

Those days were ours to treasure,
beyond the ability to measure.
With the coming of a new dawn,
Over me swept the fullest calm.

Days turned into months and then into years,
In each other's arms we had no fears.
Once two desperate souls,
Through each other we had become whole.

But seemingly from out of nowhere returns the darkness of yesterday,
Determined and relentless to collect its pay.
The mightiest of all storms come it may,
On the horizon it approached ready to have its say.

When once it seemed as though we would always be together,
Now I fear you will be lost forever.
When once we were one,
Now I am alone.

Knowing what we shared it is hard to believe,
The thought that you would leave.
All that is left to do,
Is spend the rest of my life finding you.

1

Prologue

This is a story about a very special person in my life. I want to share it with you because it is a story that encompasses every emotion one might encounter. It is a story of uncertainty and hope, a story of loss and perseverance. It is a story that brings tears of joy and sadness from a single thought. It is also a story of pain as deep as one can experience and happiness beyond one's imagination. It brings smiles to one's face and provides warmth to the heart. Above all else, however, it is a story I want to tell because it is about God's greatest gift to us. Love.

At times difficult to describe but deeply felt. It comes in many forms. God's love for us and our love for Him. A love shared between a couple. A parent's love for their child. A child's love for his or her parent. Siblings' love for each other. The love shared between grandparent and grandchild. Our love for extended family. Love shared between friends. A love for our neighbor. Love for a stranger, particularly those living on the margins in our society. Each love just as important as the other but unique in its own way. A passionate bond that connects us as a community living in harmony and individually by seeking the best for those we love, notwithstanding our own needs.

An authentic and genuine love is the foundation for humanity in both communal and interpersonal relationships. We become complete when our life is full of love. Whether we admit it or not it is something for which we all yearn. Yet, on an interpersonal level, it can be all so difficult to find.

I have discovered over the course of my life I usually have the best results finding something when I'm not looking for it. This might be why I have been accused on many occasions of doing a 'man look'. You might ask what is a 'man look'? Well, a 'man look', as described to me, is what happens when a man is asked to go find something and after ten-minutes of unproductive and less than earnest searching returns attesting that the item is not where it is supposed to be or possibly doesn't exist in the first place. Upon the man's announcement, the person (usually a woman) who asked him to find the item goes to look for it herself and quickly discovers the item in the exact location she told the man it would be found.

To make matters worse the 'she' in the equation is usually the man's wife and the man's failed search adds to an ever-growing list of the dreaded "I told you so's". The ironic twist of the 'man look' is that if the man had not been asked to find the item, there's a good chance he would have come across it himself without looking for it. For some reason, genetics possibly, the pressure from the request to find the item causes the man's mind to go numb, making the quest unattainable.

For me, this phenomenon especially holds true for love. I have experienced love, a romantic love that is, twice before the story I am about to tell. At the end of each of those relationships I knew I wanted to find love again, a consummate love. A love waiting for me that would be everything I imagined about love. After my second love ended and I began healing from the heartache, I started looking for that perfect love we all yearn for. I just knew if I searched hard enough, I would find my perfect love. I looked everywhere ... well within reason I should clarify. I joined friends when they would have social gatherings. I opened up in a professional setting to allow myself to meet new people. I accepted friends' invitations for blind dates. I joined a few online dating apps. I 'met' many women whether it be by messaging, telephone conversations or meeting in person. Most of the women I met during my search were nice and were no doubt perfect for someone. But they were not perfect for me. As time went on, I felt my search was proving to be futile. Perhaps, I began to think, perfect love only exists in fairytales.

I had developed a mindset over the years that my happiness was dependent upon being in love. I discovered I had it all backwards. The elusiveness of that perfect love eventually gave way to a contentment with living life by myself. It was not the life I would have chosen for myself but it was one I learned could be satisfying.

An amazing thing occurred once I accepted this new lifestyle. I woke up one morning and realized I was happy. Not just an in the moment happiness. Rather a general happiness in all parts of my life. This new found happiness settled upon me. A new rhythm to life filled with happiness became normal. It felt right. It felt safe. I accepted it. The urgent search for love became a memory.

As I was soon to learn, however, with happiness we become different people. We grow closer to becoming the person we were created to be and as we become that person new possibilities arise. With the end of the 'man look' for a perfect love, the pressure to find it subsided. The genetics of the male species that caused me to go numb in my endless search for love eased its stranglehold on my mind.

The story that follows is about finding a love beyond any love I had previously known, when least expecting it. It is about a love that grew until it was perfected. A love so deep and so true that it felt as though it was a blessing from God Himself. But even with a love so deep and Godly, how far does it transcend? What can it endure? What are its limits? Does it end?

PART 1

Chapter 1: Tribulation Becomes Preparation

I have told you this so that you might have peace in me.
In the world you will have trouble,
but take courage, I have conquered the world.

John 16:33

Have you ever camped under a moonless sky in the middle of nowhere? Did you stay up all night or wake up before the first signs of daybreak? If so, you know that Thomas Fuller's quote that 'the darkest hour of the night comes just before dawn' would certainly apply during that last hour before the first signs of dawn arrive.

Staring up at the heavens you see nothing but black skies filled with a myriad of stars reminding us of the incomprehensible vastness of the universe in which we reside. The landscape around you is barely illuminated, if illuminated at all. It is impossible to see anything in the distance. The only thing that may be visible is directly in front of your eyes but even then what you are seeing is only vaguely familiar and your mind is uncertain as to what it is seeing.

Of course, in Fuller's case he was referring to a metaphysical darkness and dawn suggesting things will begin to improve when all seems hopeless. The darkness, however, is just as real in this metaphysical sense. When we are hopeless, everything appears dark and we are unable to see things around us for what they really are, causing uncertainty to creep into every aspect of our life. The possibility of an approaching dawn is unfathomable.

As we begin this story, I was in that darkest hour of the night. This story is about a woman named Theresa. She too was in the darkest hour of the night. We had both experienced love before (or a facsimile of love). In different ways, both of our prior relationships brought us to what was then the darkest hour of our lives. Both of our experiences, after those relationships ended, left us with no hope of finding love again. We had both reached that darkest hour before a new dawn.

Me

Born in Bloomington, Indiana and having lived in southern Indiana my entire life, I'm a *Hoosier* at heart. *Hoosier* in the sense of an Indiana native for sure but more to the point an *Indiana University Hoosier* (with *IU* being located in Bloomington). I grew up in Ellettsville, a small town just outside of Bloomington, and lived there for most of my life.

Ellettsville is your typical small midwestern town where everyone knows everyone, we all look out for each other, gossip travels faster than social media over the internet, and the town social life is focused around the events at the local schools – science fairs, school open houses, football and basketball games, band contests and concerts, and choir shows and contests. Of course, there is also the annual fall festival that lasts three days the third weekend of each September, including a parade that is attended by practically everyone in town and many people from Bloomington. It is Ellettsville's time to shine.

Growing up in a small town provided me with many opportunities I might not have had otherwise in a larger town such as Bloomington. With a relatively small group of classmates to compete with and being fairly athletic, it was a perfect opportunity for me to excel in sports, particularly basketball. Being a native *Hoosier*, like many other high school players in Indiana it was always my dream to play for Bobby Knight at *IU* but I discovered *IU* basketball was at a much higher skill level than what I possessed.

I was extraordinarily shy until well into my college years. So much so that I found it excruciating to speak to girls, similar to the selective mutism portrayed by Raj in *The Big Bang Theory* for those familiar with one of my favorite sitcoms. As such, I didn't socialize with the popular kids and didn't go to any of the parties many of my classmates attended. In fact, I didn't have my first drink of alcohol until I was in college.

I lived a charmed childhood, adored and loved by my parents with just enough discipline to know not to get out of line. I didn't excel in school not putting much effort into my school work, resting on my laurels of being the star of the basketball team to get me through with slightly above average grades. The only blip in my childhood occurred when I was riding a bicycle at the age of ten and was run over by a large truck resulting in life-threatening injuries that required several months of recovery. It was during times of tragedy such as my accident when Ellettsville united as a community as my family and I witnessed when the town rallied to offer us assistance any way they could during my recovery.

During my first two years of college, I approached my education as I did in high school and learned the lackadaisical approach was not working in an atmosphere where everyone was there competing for the best jobs in their chosen fields. As I entered my third year of college, I finally realized true adulthood was quickly approaching and it was time to set concrete goals for myself and work as hard as I could to reach those goals.

My education transformed into my passion overnight making me the ideal student, even forcing myself to come out of my shell to become that student who actively participated in class discussions. Because of this new dedication to school, I was able to graduate with a good grade point average, squeak into law school and eventually earn a law degree.

I had been in love twice before meeting Theresa, both times beginning under circumstances when I least expected it. My first love began in junior high and lasted until my sophomore year of college and, in my heart, well beyond my college years if I'm being honest with myself.

It started at a junior high school dance. I was not really the dancing type but school dances in junior high were the thing to do back in those days. My friends and I would attend them just to be able to hang out together. It was an opportunity to get away from our parents and feel like we had a little freedom. Actually dancing, however, was the furthest thing from our minds. We would stand in the corner talking about our recent football or basketball game and prod each other to go over to talk to a girl we might be interested in, who herself would be standing on the opposite side of the empty gym floor with a group of her friends. Over the course of the evening the gym floor would begin to fill with couples dancing but the unspoken understanding between my group of friends was that we would not be joining the others on the gym floor nor would we, under any circumstances, cave to the endless prodding from each other to go over to speak to the girl on the other side of the gym we were foolish enough to admit to each other we had a crush on.

During an early autumn dance in eighth grade, our evening was proceeding with this same ritual when the girl from the other side of the gym I had a crush on walked across the floor toward our group. Kathy was a year younger than me but I had been noticing her at the school football games the whole season. She was beautiful. She always had a smile on her face and she was always laughing and joking around with her friends. When I would pass by her in the hall between classes I would glance at her and she always seemed to catch me doing so and would smile. I would smile back but quickly look in a different direction to avoid the remote possibility she would try to say something to me.

As Kathy came closer from across the gym floor, she locked eyes with me and to my surprise walked straight to me and asked me to 'slow dance' with her. Kathy had obviously not received the memo about the 'no dance' clause in our rule book. Before I could collect myself, I heard myself saying 'sure', followed by cackles from my friends as I walked toward the gym floor. I have no idea to this day how I managed the courage to accept her invitation. In a daze, with my heart pounding in my chest, the next thing I knew I was slow dancing with the prettiest girl at the dance to Johnny Rivers singing *Swayin' to the Music*.

Adolescence is a difficult time in one's life to fall in love and many people would describe love during that time as 'puppy love'. Kathy and I did fall in love and I have no doubt it was more than puppy love. For the longest time it was my desire and belief that she and I would one day marry, have a family, and grow old together.

Unfortunately, I will admit, I was not mature enough at that time in my life for such a relationship and by the time we reached our college years we went different directions in our lives. Above all else, the pain experienced from this lost love taught me to fight for what I believe in, to always nurture what you love and to never give up on your dreams. These lessons resonate in my soul to this day as will become apparent in this story.

My second love produced a twenty-year marriage. My former wife, Tina, and I also fell in love when I was least expecting it the summer after my third year of college. I had borrowed a friend's motorcycle and was riding with another group of friends. We cruised out to a beach at a local lake and noticed a group of girls unloading their vehicle in the parking lot for a day at the beach. We stopped our

12

motorcycles behind their car and my friends took the lead talking to them.

While the girls and my friends were talking, Tina and I kept exchanging glances at each other and struck up our own conversation. To my delight, I noticed when my friends would try to talk to Tina, she would politely answer but turn her attention back to me when she was finished. I found myself wanting all of Tina's attention and was delighted that she seemed to want the same from me. As we finished up our conversations with the girls, my friends and I invited them to a party later that evening.

I was pleasantly surprised later that evening when Tina and one of her friends stopped by the party. Tina and I spent the evening getting to know each other while talking outside on a bench because the music was too loud inside the apartment.

After a long courtship extended by a temporary separation, we married while I was in law school. We had two children together, Brent and Misty. They were born five years apart with Brent being the oldest. I would like to think Tina and I were both good parents having made our children the foundation of our marriage, being there for them in every aspect of their lives as they grew to adulthood.

It's funny how two people can perceive the same life differently. I have a specific recollection of mowing the grass on a summer afternoon in 2008 and thinking to myself how happy I was with the life Tina and I shared with our children. I felt we had reached a point in life where everything was perfect and we could start looking toward a transition in our marriage after the children left the nest. The only thing I felt missing was God.

Later that same week I was driving to work listening to a gospel channel on the radio when I heard the announcer saying being saved was as simple as acknowledging Jesus as your savior and asking him to come into your life. The announcer encouraged his listeners to not wait if they were ready to make those declarations. I had never been baptized but an increasing urge to do so had been building in me for several years.

Although I knew the announcer's proclamation was not the same as being baptized, something was encouraging me to make those declarations and I complied during my commute, not really expecting anything to happen. What followed surprised me. A calm and peace immediately swept over me and it felt as though I had a new best friend sitting next to me in the passenger seat. Something began stirring in me telling me my life was about to change.

Change it did. It was not long after my memorable commute to work that Tina told me that she was unhappy in our marriage and wanted a divorce. Talk about a hard sucker-punch to the gut. My initial thought was she was playing some kind of cruel joke on me. We were a happily married couple, so I thought. Divorces happened to other people, not us, so I thought. No one in my family (parents, aunts, uncles, sister) had ever been divorced so it couldn't be happening to me, so I thought. I had always felt I lived a charmed life in which bad things didn't happen to me, so I thought. I quickly realized, however, Tina was serious and my hope she was playing a joke vanished. I was knocked off my feet.

How did I fail to recognize she was unhappy? I pleaded, I demanded, I became angry, I refused to accept it and I fell into a deep depression – all of the classic signs of grief were raging through me. My self-confidence was destroyed. My life with my wife was over. My life with my children would be changed forever. I convinced Tina we should attempt to reconcile a couple times but those attempts only prolonged the suffering experienced in a failing marriage. In the end, the only resolution was the end of our marriage. A deep depression was descending upon me covering me like a blanket, threatening to bring a darkness to every area of my life. The darkest part of the night had arrived.

Every relationship we have presents us with opportunities to learn something about ourselves, often times through the realization of our own shortcomings. I am sure I had many shortcomings in my relationship with Tina but the recognition of two in particular have assisted me in an inner growth that contributed to healthier relationships going forward and an ability to find a forgiveness that opened the gates to me finding happiness.

The first was a lackluster spiritual life. Faith was never something Tina and I put much effort into and is my biggest regret as a husband and parent. We would attend church occasionally for the big holidays such as Christmas and Easter, but even that was sporadic at best. The absence of a spiritual life in our marriage, although not the cause of our failed marriage, prevented us from having tools to rely on during difficult times.

The second lesson was the role my complacency played in our marriage failing. I fell into a routine over the course of our marriage. I assumed responsibility for chores in our relationship, completed those chores faithfully and left it to Tina to complete chores I had assigned to her in my mind. I didn't work on keeping our relationship fresh and failed to keep Tina and me at the center of our marriage. I foolishly allowed our children to become the totality of our marriage. Correcting these two shortcomings became an integral part of my psyche after my marriage to Tina ended.

As the shock of my divorce began to wear off, I thought I wanted to find love again. I knew in my heart I had more love to give someone. I wanted another shot at love and vowed to get it right the next time if the opportunity ever arose. But after the failure of a twenty-year marriage that I believed with all my heart was filled with love, I wasn't sure if I even knew what love was anymore.

If I didn't know what love was how could I hope to find it or get it right? I thought from my marriage to Tina I knew what characteristics I found attractive in a woman but would I find those characteristics attractive in someone else? And to be completely honest, I wondered if I actually found those characteristics attractive in Tina or had I just become comfortable with them.

It had been close to twenty-five years since I had 'dated' anyone other than Tina. The whole idea of 'dating' seemed a little adolescent at my age but that's where I found myself. The times were a lot different from when Tina and I were dating so, as odd as it may sound, I wasn't sure if I even knew how to date. How would I meet someone to be able to ask them out on a date? I didn't go to church. I wasn't involved in any activities outside of work. My life consisted of work, my children, and their activities. I had no interest in prowling around my children's activities for single mothers.

One major development that had occurred since Tina and I first started dating was the internet. The internet has brought a lot of changes to our world, good and bad. One of those changes offered me an avenue to meet women via dating sites. I know, I know … a lot of those sites have received some bad publicity over the years. But like a lot of things on the internet, if used correctly it can be quite useful.

I decided to use a few of the dating sites to give me an opportunity to meet women of my age in a safe atmosphere and to get to know them a little before deciding if we wanted to meet in person. My strategy with these sites was to meet as many women as possible online and, if they were interesting, meet them in person to see if anything clicked. I figured if only a small number of people who meet using a dating site actually fall in love, I would increase my odds by meeting as many women as possible.

The other thing meeting women on the dating sites did was allow me to start developing a mental checklist of the characteristics I found attractive and unattractive in a woman. Over the course of about nine months or so I became obsessed with finding my perfect match on these dating sites. That match never materialized and eventually I became exhausted with the whole process of dating sites and ended my online search for the perfect match.

It was around this time that Brent and I were travelling back from one of his *AAU* basketball tournaments in Las Vegas. We had just landed in Dallas to catch a connecting flight to Indianapolis. Upon landing we were informed our connecting flight would be delayed and our layover was going to be eight hours. We were anxious to return home making this news disappointing. What were we going to do for eight hours? Brent was heavily into gaming and had his laptop with him to keep himself occupied. I, on the other hand, had nothing to do to pass the time.

I went to the airport bookstore and browsed for something to read. I was looking for a novel to read when I stumbled upon a book that seemed interesting called *The Choice*. It was written by an author I had never heard of named Nicholas Sparks but the cover described it as a love story which is my favorite genre of literature. I thought the read would be a good distraction during the layover.

As it turned out I read the book from cover to cover during the layover and flight home. The storyline told of a deep love that developed between 'Travis' and 'Gabby'. At one point in the storyline Travis was driving Gabby home from a dinner engagement when he wrecked their car, severely injuring Gabby. The story culminated with Travis having to make a life-or-death choice to either let Gabby die or, against her wishes, keep the hope of their love alive.

As I returned home, the love Travis had for Gabby weighed heavy on my mind. I told my sister about the book and that I hoped to someday find my Gabby. She assured me that one day I would.

Theresa

Theresa was born in Baltimore, Maryland, the youngest of six girls. I'm not a statistician but I assume the probability of having six girls without a boy must be low. Interestingly, Theresa's father had eight brothers and no sisters so maybe it is a hereditary thing.

The sisters were essentially born in two groups of three with a sizeable gap of years between the two sets. Although Theresa is close to all of her sisters, the three oldest were approaching adulthood as Theresa entered her school age years. Theresa's parents were by all accounts wonderful people and excellent parents.

Theresa was quite the entrepreneur in her younger years, taking advantage of the gap in years from her older sisters. One of her older sisters was married when Theresa was in first grade and shortly after marrying was expecting her first child. When the older sister would visit during her pregnancy, Theresa would charge her school friends twenty-five cents to come to the house to see her pregnant sister.

As Theresa approached adolescence her parents moved away from Baltimore. The four oldest sisters had moved out of the home by then so only Theresa and her sister closest in age to her moved with her parents. The family settled in Virginia Beach and made it their home for the remainder of Theresa's childhood. Between Baltimore and Virginia Beach, Theresa grew up as an East Coast girl.

After graduating from high school Theresa married and had four children (Scott, Ben, Stephanie and Jeff). Initially, Theresa, her husband and the children lived in Virginia Beach. Theresa dedicated herself to her children, putting her own goals and education on hold to take care of them. She stayed active in their lives, enrolled them in Catholic school and served as a parent assistant in the school. She attended mass regularly and encouraged her older children to be altar servers at mass.

Theresa's marriage to her husband proved to be difficult, the details of which she did not talk about publicly, so out of respect for her privacy I will not do so either. After her fourth child was born, Theresa's husband moved the family to Indiana, away from all of Theresa's family, friends and everything she knew.

Indiana was a place that couldn't have been more foreign to her than if it had been Siberia. Theresa had zero connections in Indiana and she was not prepared for a midwestern way of life. She experienced culture shock after her arrival in Indiana.

Shortly after moving to Indiana, she was driving with her children along a country road when she abruptly brought her car to a stop. She instructed all of the children to get out the car and walk to a fence line alongside the road where a group of cows were gathered. Neither she nor her children had ever seen cows up close and personal and figured that was the perfect time.

Theresa also had to adjust to differences in interactions with people from what she was used to on the East Coast. Shortly after settling in their first home in Indiana there was a knock on her front door. Theresa was reluctant to open the door not knowing who was there or what they wanted. Mustering up courage she opened the door finding a neighbor couple she had never met before standing at her doorstep with a pie they had baked. The couple introduced themselves, welcomed Theresa and the kids to the neighborhood, gave them the pie and encouraged her to call if she ever needed anything.

Theresa also had to adjust to the change of pace in Indiana which was significantly slower than what she was accustomed to on the East Coast. She felt like everything in Indiana was moving in slow motion. Motorists, for the most part, weren't driving as if they were in a race. Shoppers at the grocery store strolled through the aisles as if they had all day. While taking walks in the neighborhood or walking on the sidewalks in town people took the time to say hi and initiate conversations rather than rushing by as if they were late for an important meeting.

Although her marriage had been going downhill when Theresa's husband moved the family to Indiana, the move accelerated its deterioration. It was quickly becoming an unhealthy marriage for both her and her children. With considerable consternation and after several attempts, Theresa was eventually able to extract herself and her children from the marriage and unhealthy environment. By this time, however, the children had settled into their new schools, made good friends and were participating in extracurricular activities making it hard for her to return to Virginia Beach.

Theresa soon found that being a single parent without any marketable job skills was much more difficult than she anticipated. To make matters worse, her soon to be ex-husband abandoned the children and she received no financial assistance from him. If her parents taught her anything, however, it was not to feel sorry for herself and when life throws you curveballs you find a way to persevere any way you can.

Theresa worked three jobs and attended college classes in her spare time, all while taking care of four active children. With a lot of hard work and sleepless nights, Theresa earned degrees as a registered nurse and nurse practitioner. She purchased a house for herself and the children. She became employed as a registered nurse in the emergency department of the local hospital and later became a nurse practitioner in the emergency department, eventually being promoted to the director of the fast-track area. It is hard to comprehend all of the intelligence and perseverance Theresa possessed or all of the sacrifices, hard work, tears, worrying and fatigue she experienced during this period but she was determined to make a better life for herself and her children.

Like myself, after a period of adjustment, Theresa began looking for love again but was uncertain if she knew what it looked like or if it was something that she could find. She had a couple of relationships after her divorce but they did not materialize to marriage. Theresa also turned to the dating sites in search of a perfect match. She accepted some invitations for actual dates but never felt any of the people she met were a match.

Theresa's online dating experience ended when she had a date with a man who, during the course of their date, proceeded to give her his psychoanalyses of everything he perceived to be wrong with her. Date over. Online dating finished. The darkest part of the night had arrived for Theresa.

Chapter 2: The Journey Begins

For I know the plans I have for you,
declares the Lord,
plans for welfare not evil, to give you a future and a hope.

Jeremiah 29:11

April 18, 2021

It's 5:00 a.m. The alarm clock doesn't ring. There was a time not so long ago when I wouldn't wake up before 7:00 a.m. without an alarm clock. Those days and the tranquility that existed with them have transformed like a calm sea giving way to an approaching storm. Now I am lucky if I can sleep to 5:00 a.m.

Like most nights recently, I must have woken up every half hour. I didn't go to bed until after midnight. Toss in a disturbing dream. I never remember dreams but for some reason this one is haunting me. I dreamed the receptionist at the hotel where I've made reservations can't find my reservation and I keep reading the wrong confirmation number to her from the reservation papers I printed. The restlessness and journey before me suggest the day will be long and tiring.

For more than eleven years life has been nothing short of a fairytale. Each day seemingly better than the day before. Sure, there were some minor bumps in the road along the way but overall, I couldn't have been happier in life. Personally, spiritually and professionally I felt fulfilled and satisfied. I recall having felt something similar to this in my marriage to Tina only to be knocked off my feet with an unexpected curveball. Nevertheless, for the past eleven years there was no doubt in my mind this time was different. I had never been surer of anything in my life.

Refusing to accept it, however, I know the winds of change began blowing this past August and seemed to increase in ferocity with each passing day. The restless nights were becoming an issue for the past couple months. The darkness of a distant past was returning and on April 1 the darkest hour of the night, of my life for that matter, arrived as my world was shattered when Theresa left me.

There has been too much on my mind since she left. Sadness, confusion, unhappiness and depression intermixed with the inability to avoid life changing decisions in the days to come. How did our fairytale come to this? But the thoughts racing through my mind this past evening have weighed heavier on my mind than all my other sleepless nights. This night was different. This night was mixed with a fear of what was to come in the next seven days and an anticipation and longing for the possibilities those days might offer. The journey before me was one I felt compelled to take. I had to find Theresa again. If I wanted to avoid succumbing to the darkness, I had no choice but to find her.

I wanted to pack the night before but I convinced myself I was tired and could get a good night's sleep and arise early and pack for the journey in the morning. That was a mistake compounded by the elusiveness of my sleep. As I arose, I found I was just as sleepy as when I laid down the night before and hoped my misjudgment wasn't a sign of more misjudgments to come in the days ahead.

The first order of business was packing for seven days. Thankfully, packing didn't prove difficult. It was my intention, after all, to avoid interaction with everyone during those seven days of searching for Theresa so it didn't require much thought to pack. I threw everything I would need into a suitcase, showered and grabbed something to eat for the road and was out the door by 5:30 a.m. My *Waze* app estimated the drive would take eleven-and-a-half-hours but I thought I could probably shave some time off the drive since I would be by myself and would be able to limit the time spent for pitstops.

I expected the drive to be uneventful. The search wouldn't begin until I arrived on Jekyll Island, the place I hoped to find Theresa. I would turn on my *Bluetooth*, listen to the songs on my playlist and just try to relax on the drive there. But as Theresa has often told me, you can't always expect the expected and the drive proved her words to be true. Almost as soon as I pulled out of our driveway my eyes clouded over with tears as I remembered the first time I found Theresa.

May, 2010

Tina and I had settled into a comfortable shared custody arrangement with Brent and Misty with our kids rotating between our respective homes. Brent had just finished his freshman year at *Indiana University* in our hometown of Bloomington. He and a few high school friends rented an apartment resulting in his presence in my home being less and less frequent. His new found freedom required an adjustment for me because he and I had always been close throughout his life. But he was enjoying his freedom and I had to accept he was now a man with his own wishes and goals.

Misty, however, had just completed her first year of high school and I was discovering her adjustment to high school had been much more difficult than Brent's. Much to my surprise I discovered raising a daughter carried with it a whole separate set of issues than raising a son. Misty's experience left me with the thought that adolescent girls could be painfully cruel to each other, much more so than boys. Misty is a beautiful girl which seemed to only amplify this cruelty fueled by classmates' jealousies. As a father, I did not respond well to providing her with comfort and guidance during her struggles but I did my best to be there for her in whatever way I could.

Unbeknownst to me something had changed in me since my divorce. After the separation with Tina, I knew I was angry and not happy. It was tearing me apart. Placing blame with Tina, I was angry at her for wanting a divorce. Whatever happened to "until death do us part?" I didn't want the divorce, Tina did. I was angry that our family was ripped apart. I was angry that our children would be from a broken home. I was angry that our children would not be sleeping under the same roof as me every night. I was angry that all of our hopes and dreams as a couple would not be realized. I was angry that just as the children were reaching adulthood our plans for a life together after they left the home would never materialize.

I knew I couldn't continue with this anger so one day, while taking a long hot bath, I allowed my emotions to spill out. Refilling the tub with hot water several times I cried for several hours until there were no more tears left. Eventually, however, when the tears stopped an epiphany came to me, or perhaps God spoke to me. I came to understand at that moment that my anger was hurting no one but myself and my children. My anger was making my life miserable. I had to let it go. For the benefit of my children for sure but just as importantly for my own sanity.

During his *Sermon on the Mount* Jesus told us if we are merciful, we would be blessed with mercy. Remembering these words, it came to me the only way to be released from my anger was to forgive Tina for all of the inequities I perceived she had committed and accept that I too was to blame for our marriage ending. It dawned on me that Tina's unhappiness in our marriage did not occur in a vacuum.

I finally understood that I had failed to give her what she needed in our relationship which contributed to her unhappiness. I finally understood Tina's decision to end our marriage could not have been easy for her either but was something she felt she needed to be happy. From that moment my whole persona changed.

I wasn't immediately aware of this transformation. Several months later while having dinner with Brent and Misty, they both made a comment about how much happier I seemed. I was surprised by their comments and upon further discussion they said they could tell I was not happy even before their mother and I separated. This revelation was a shock to a man who had believed he was in a happy marriage. Upon further reflection, I looked back at my marriage and realized there were many signs that confirmed their thoughts.

By May of 2010 online dating was a distant memory for me. Although I hadn't deleted my dating apps, I had stopped reviewing notifications from those apps that indicated a possible match had been found. In early May, 2010, I came home after a long day at work. Misty was with Tina for the evening so I figured I would use the time to tidy up around the house and then go to my bedroom and watch an *NBA* playoff doubleheader. I had just finished my chores and was watching the beginning of the first game when my phone dinged with one of those familiar sounds signifying I had a "new match".

I had learned to delete these messages without looking at them as soon as they appeared. But this time something compelled me to look at the message. It indicated someone named "Theresa" was a match and I reviewed her profile. "Hmmm", I thought. My interest was piqued but it was obvious from the profile "Theresa" was in a league way higher than mine.

I will admit that upon opening her profile the first thing that caught my attention was her profile picture.

Profile pictures are notorious on these dating apps for not being an accurate depiction of how someone actually looks when you meet them in person. The profile picture of this possible match for someone named "Theresa" showed the most beautiful woman I could imagine. She had a glow to her. Her eyes were stunningly radiant. Her smile was mesmerizing and offered promises of someone who liked to have fun and joke around like myself. She had long shining hair with one side tucked behind her ear. Her face was that of a movie star ... not the sultry type but rather the beautiful, down to earth, girl next door type. The picture had all the makings of one of those that would in no way resemble what the person actually looks like.

Who could this be I asked myself? I had to know more about this woman so I studied her profile, periodically looking back at the picture of whom I was reading about.

She lived in Columbus. Well, that's not optimal being an hour away from where I lived but I had travelled further to meet "matches". She was a nurse practitioner. I wasn't completely familiar with what a nurse practitioner did but I found the fact that she was a professional to be intriguing. She was involved in charity work. In my mind that meant she must have a compassionate heart. She was a member of *St. Bartholomew Catholic Church*. Interesting. I still had this lingering desire to grow closer to God. She was on The *Columbus Firemen's Cheer Fund Board*. I wasn't sure what that was but it suggested she was involved in her community which was appealing to me. She liked to travel. I did too and now that Brent and Misty were older I would have more opportunities to travel. She loved animals.

I could not imagine not loving animals, always having had a family dog in my life. Family was important to her. My family was the center of my life. She loved celebrating the holidays, particularly Halloween. I loved celebrating the holidays … wait, did I read that right, "particularly Halloween"? OK, whatever, I guess. I could learn more about that later but she would fit in with my mom in that regard. Her alma mater was *Indiana University*. A fellow *Hoosier* I concluded.

I looked at her picture again. I read her profile again. I looked at her picture again. I read her profile again. This went on for quite some time until I had her whole profile and picture etched in my memory.

What stood out from studying her profile was that she was indeed way above my league but a voice in my head kept telling me I had to send her a message. But in addition to her being out of my league there would be another major hurdle I would have to clear if I were to be successful in eliciting a response from her.

I didn't have a picture of myself posted on my profile. I knew from my own experiences that I would not respond or send messages to a profile that did not include a picture. Why would someone not post a picture? Either they were not confident in their appearance, they were not who they purported to be or they were hiding something. In my case, however, it was none of these. I would have to address this issue in my initial message if I wanted her to reply.

I worked the rest of the evening formulating my message, editing what I wrote, starting over, editing again, reading what I wrote, trying to express who I was, explaining the missing picture, and telling her why I was interested in striking up a conversation with her. By the time I finished, the second game of the doubleheader had finished and the post-game show was ending. I couldn't believe I spent the better part of five hours writing my message but it was finally ready and I clicked send.

Hello Theresa, please don't delete me. I know your initial thought will be to discard this message because I don't have a picture posted on my profile but I promise you I am not a stalker or axe murderer and I have a legitimate reason for not posting a picture, if you will give me a few minutes to explain. Truth be known, I am married and my wife would not appreciate me being on this dating site. Just kidding! Seriously, I'm joking. I'm not married. Really, I am not. I was married once but apparently my ex didn't think my jokes were funny either. Lol

I haven't posted a picture because I am a divorce attorney, meaning that I have found a lot of my clients on this site. I would find it very awkward if a client, or even worse their spouse or soon to be spouse, tried to connect with me on this dating site. By not posting a picture I have a better chance of screening contacts that would be awkward professionally. I would be glad, however, to send you pictures via email if you were interested in seeing who this mysterious person is sending you a message.

I have read your profile and believe we have a lot in common and would be interested in corresponding with you in hopes of getting to know each other better. I know my profile doesn't give you much information about myself (see reason stated above) but I will be glad to tell you more here. Again, please don't delete me yet because I hope you will agree we have a lot in common.

I live in Bloomington (well actually Ellettsville if you have ever heard of it). Ellettsville is a small town just outside of Bloomington that most people have never heard of so I say Bloomington to give you a point of reference and because my office and most of everything I do is in Bloomington.

I have two children (Brent, age 19, and Misty, age 14). They are the center of my life. Their mother and I divorced a few years back and after an adjustment period we seem to have an amicable relationship limited to matters pertaining to our children.

I am a sole practitioner, like I said with a primary practice in family law but also criminal law (you might be able to find more information about my practice online if you are interested in verifying anything I am telling you).

My mother and father live in Bloomington also. I have two siblings, an older sister who died shortly after my birth and a younger sister, Rae, with whom I am very close. Rae stole my best friend from childhood, Roger, and married him and they too live in Bloomington. They have three children, the youngest of which will be a senior in high school in the fall. My family is a big part of my life.

I like watching baseball, basketball and football games on television and in person. Of course, as an IU alum I like IU basketball and football. I also like the Pacers, Colts, Yankees and Cubs. I enjoy travelling, when possible. I like gardening and building things. I enjoy reading.

Although my professional life requires me to be serious, away from the office I like to laugh and joke. I can be very shy when first meeting someone but once getting to know the person I am outgoing. I love animals and have a dog named Buddy. I live by myself with the exception of sharing custody of Misty with her mother.

After my divorce I didn't really have a place to meet anyone. I don't go out socializing and I certainly don't meet anyone through work. I thought I would give these dating sites a chance. I have met people through these sites, I had some dates and found there are a lot of nice people out there and, quite frankly, some scary people who I couldn't get away from quick enough.

Getting to know people through these sites has allowed me to learn a lot about myself, what I value and what characteristics I find attractive in someone else. Most importantly, however, I have learned actively looking for a relationship doesn't work for me. Consequently, I stopped responding to messages and notifications of matches several months ago and just delete them as soon as they come in.

Today, I received a notification indicating I had a match for someone named "Theresa" (that's you by the way) and for some reason I opened the notification and read your profile (and maybe took a glance or two at your profile picture 😊) and was intrigued. So, I thought maybe a short message would be worth a shot ... and now after several hours of composing that short message, here we are.

I would be interested in exchanging messages with you (and pictures from me) if you are interested. I look forward to your response and if you choose not to respond I wish you the best and thank you for reading my message.

P.S. If you have made it to this part of my message you haven't deleted me yet which I hope means you are interested in corresponding. So, I have an initial question I would like to ask you about your profile. Your profile says you have a particular interest in celebrating Halloween? Did I read that correctly? I would be interested in knowing how you celebrate Halloween.

Interestingly, my mother shares that interest with you. We have a custom in our family where each of her grandchildren know that anywhere from October 1 to October 31 each year they can expect grandma to scare them at some point. They don't know when or where but they know it is coming and are on pins and needles until it happens. They call each other every day of the month to find out if grandma has started her scares yet and when they find out one has been scared their anxiety level rises a notch. Mom looks forward to the Halloween season every year. The grandchildren do not share her enthusiasm.

I honestly did not expect a response but couldn't keep "Theresa" out of my thoughts. Had she read my message yet? Of course not. I only sent it five minutes ago. Has she read it yet now? No, it's only been ten minutes. It eventually became apparent, sometime in the early morning hours that she either wasn't going to read it tonight, that she deleted it without reading it, or she had read it and decided not to respond. Time for bed.

I arose the next morning no different than any other morning, except before getting ready for work, the first order of business was to open my laptop to see if "Theresa" had replied. No such luck. My hope sunk just a little bit with the disappointment of no reply. But her profile did suggest a woman who was busy so I still held out some hope. That hope continued to dwindle with each passing hour throughout the day as I repeatedly opened my phone not finding an indication that she had replied. By late evening all hope was gone.

But just after I turned the lights off before going to sleep, there it was, that familiar ding from the dating app. Could it be? I reached for my phone and opened the app and there it was "Message from Theresa".

Hello. Thank you for the message. I admit, I don't respond to messages without a profile picture. I understand your reluctance to post a picture because of your profession.   I was reluctant to post a picture myself.

I haven't responded to any messages for quite some time because, like you, I had given up on online dating. But your message did spark my interest. It sounds like we might have a lot in common. I am not familiar with Ellettsville but have been to Bloomington many times for my daughter's games.

I am not from Indiana originally but moved here from the East Coast about fifteen years ago. I have four children, all over the age of nineteen. My father lives out of state and my mother passed away several years ago. My parents have six daughters of which I am the youngest. They all live on the East Coast. Although my family lives far away they are an important part of my life.

I can't say that I really follow college sports much but if I did, I'm sure I would also like the IU teams since that is my alma mater. I can't say I follow professional baseball and basketball much either but I am a huge NFL fan. I almost didn't respond to your message, however, because you mentioned you are a Colts fan. My two favorite teams are the Steelers and whoever is playing the Colts, as I find them repulsive. I was born in Baltimore and lived there part of my childhood. I will never forgive the Colts for how they left Baltimore.

You may have seen on my profile that I am a nurse practitioner. I work in the ER at Columbus Regional Hospital. I currently work night shift.

Yes, you read my profile correctly, I love Halloween. I go all out decorating for Halloween. I mean really all out. I even have a real coffin as one of my decorations. I host a large Halloween party every year. So, it sounds as though your mom and I definitely share a love for Halloween. I think that is great what she does with her grandchildren each year. They will always remember that.

Well, I guess I should be winding this message up as it is getting late and I need to get some sleep. I look forward to hearing from you again.

Wow! She responded, I thought. Not only that but she said she looked forward to hearing from me again. But she didn't ask to see a profile picture. I wonder what that means? Did she forget to ask? Was she not interested? Did that mean she only responded to be pen pals? She responded. Wow!

April 18, 2021

My reflection back to the first time I found Theresa brought tears to my eyes and made two things apparent. First, this drive to Jekyll Island wasn't going to be as easy as I hoped. If I couldn't even get to the interstate without memories of our past flooding my emotions, the next eleven and a half hours were sure to bring many more.

Second, it gave me trepidation about this journey. When I was actively participating in the online dating apps I searched and searched for a perfect match but didn't find one. The 'man look' had not been productive. It was only after I stopped searching that God brought Theresa and me together. It had to be God's intervention that caused me to look at the notification that I had a new match after all the previous unopened ones I had deleted. It had to be God's intervention that caused Theresa to respond to a message from someone without a picture. It had to be God's intervention that brought her from the East Coast to the Midwest to allow us to connect.

If I could not find Theresa before, when I was trying, could I expect anything different on this journey? Why did I believe I would find her on Jekyll Island? Even if she was on Jekyll Island, would I be able to find her? Would she want to be found?

Chapter 3: We Meet

Blessed is the man who perseveres in temptation,
for when he has been proved he will receive
the crown of life that he promised to those who love him.

James 1:12

April 18, 2021

The journey to Jekyll Island would take me from Columbus, Indiana down *I-65* to Nashville. In Nashville, I would connect with *I-24* to Chattanooga. I would take *I-75* from Chattanooga through Atlanta to Macon. In Macon, I would connect with *I-16* to Savannah. From Savannah I would take *I-95* to *US 17* and the *Jekyll Island Causeway*. In other words, there was going to be a lot of time to reflect during this journey.

Sometimes in life things happen to us and we wonder why. I don't believe God punishes us for our actions but sometimes it can be hard to understand why he doesn't stop bad things from happening. Other times, however, good things happen to us and we just know that those things could be nothing other than a blessing from God.

Meeting Theresa, the crown of my life, was one of those occasions. I still couldn't wrap my head around why she had left me almost three weeks ago. We had so many unfulfilled dreams. Having learned from prior relationships to fight for what I believe in and to never give up on my dreams, I knew I had to find Theresa. My heart was telling me I would find her on Jekyll Island but if I didn't find her there, I would keep searching until I found her.

As I merged onto *I-65* and set my car to cruise control I thought back to when Theresa and I first met. It was almost eleven years ago. More than a decade ago but it seemed like just yesterday. A lifetime of memories packed into eleven years, with so much more of life yet to live.

June 5, 2010

After those first messages in early May, Theresa and I exchanged messages daily, usually multiple messages per day, over the course of the next several weeks. We had become friends through our messaging. I eventually sent her some pictures, but only because I suggested I do so, not because she requested to see them. It was my hope that we would soon meet but I wanted her to have an idea of what I looked like before agreeing to meet me in person.

After I sent the pictures to her (and in case you are wondering, yes, they were current pictures) Theresa expressed her continued interest so I suppose she liked what she saw. She would later tell me, however, that it didn't matter what I looked like. She had already decided she wanted to meet me because of the connection we had made in our messages.

In the later part of May I summoned the courage to ask Theresa if she would like to speak over the phone and she readily agreed. I recall that first phone call vividly. We set a time earlier in the day for me to call her that evening. I couldn't think about anything the rest of the day but calling her that evening. I was a nervous wreck because I didn't know what we would talk about. All of the usual subjects when you first meet someone had been discussed in our text messages and emails. At the same time, I was excited that I would be connecting a voice to the pictures she had posted and the messages we had exchanged. I would be able to hear her laugh (I hoped). I would get to know her a little bit more.

The time for our call arrived. Should I call her a little before the designated time, exactly at the time agreed upon or a little past the designated time so as not to appear desperate? I chose the safe option and called at our agreed upon time. She answered after just a few rings. She had a fun cadence to her voice and she didn't sound like Minnie Mouse – which I found to be appealing.

All concerns of what to talk about immediately evaporated. We fell into a rhythm of joking and getting to know each other. It seemed to me she was enjoying our conversation as much as me. The conversation lasted several hours. I don't recall previously speaking with anyone on the phone for that long. There came a point however that we were both getting tired and even though I didn't want the call to end we were going to need to end it.

I knew I wanted more so I took the plunge: "So, what would you think about meeting in person?" She eagerly agreed. Unfortunately, because of our work schedules and prior commitments for the approaching Memorial Day weekend we would need to wait until June 5th for our meeting. We agreed to meet in Nashville (a small town about half way between our homes) and have a late lunch at one of the local restaurants. Our first date was set.

We continued to talk by telephone during the days leading up to our date with each conversation occurring effortlessly. June 5th finally arrived. We decided to meet at a gas station in Nashville and figure out from there where to have lunch. It was a Saturday and Nashville, a tourist destination known for being the home for southern Indiana artists, was bustling.

When I arrived, the gas station we were to meet at was busy with cars everywhere and people walking in and out of the convenience store. I sat in my car for a few minutes to see if I could spot Theresa, believing I could identify her from her pictures. I didn't see her anywhere.

Maybe I should call her. She answered quickly and after saying "hi" I asked if she was at the gas station yet. She said yes and that she was sitting in her car that she identified as a silver *Infiniti G37*. I surveyed the parking area and spotted her car on the other side of the parking lot from where I was parked. She asked if I was there.

OK, time for some fun, I thought. I again surveyed the gas station and saw a biker with long hair in a ponytail wearing a bandana, a leather jacket and chaps walking across the parking area with a banana and cigarette in one hand and talking on his phone with the other hand and a woman dressed similarly walking next to him. I confirmed I was indeed at the gas station and described the biker guy as myself. She went silent.

Maybe now wasn't the best time to joke with her I quickly surmised. After a few short moments I confessed I was not the biker guy and gave her a description of my car as I exited it to walk toward her. By the time I got to her car I noticed she was laughing so maybe the joke wasn't such a bad idea after all.

We briefly talked before realizing we were in the way of other people coming to the gas station so we looked around and spotted a public parking lot across the street where we could park our cars and walk from there. We drove over to the parking lot and parked. I exited my car first an began walking toward her vehicle, parked about twenty yards from where I had parked. As Theresa exited her car I gasped and stopped dead in my tracks and just stared.

The woman exiting the *G37* was astonishingly more beautiful than the person I had become so familiar with from studying her pictures for the last several weeks. I would guess she probably noticed I was staring. I couldn't help it because I could not believe I was about to have lunch with the most beautiful woman I had ever met.

The other thing I noticed when I reached her was that I was looking directly into her eyes rather than gazing down. I'm six foot three inches tall so throughout my life I had grown accustomed to being much taller than the women I am around. Theresa was almost as tall as me (I later learned she was five foot ten inches tall and with heels she was easily six foot or taller).

In the mental checklist of characteristics I found attractive I had been developing since my divorce from Tina I did not include a consideration for height. Tina was five foot two inches tall and after twenty-five years together the height of a partner was of no relevance to me. So, it came as a complete surprise to me how appealing I found it to be looking into Theresa's eyes without looking down.

After our initial greeting, we walked several blocks to the *Hobnob*, a cozy restaurant with a rustic charm in the center of Nashville. We were quickly seated, sitting in a booth across from each other. Our free flowing and easy conversation picked up right where we left off the night before in our phone call. During our many telephone conversations I had discovered Theresa has a good sense of humor which continued during our lunch. I had a sneaking suspicion she would soon be plotting a "payback" for my gas station escapade.

It was so easy to stare into her eyes as we conversed and she must have felt the same way because she was staring right back. The waitress came and took our orders. I expected she wouldn't have anything to eat but was pleasantly surprised when she ordered a full lunch. I was hungry, so knowing that she ordered lunch it was safe for me to do likewise. All too soon lunch was over and we noticed there were people waiting to be seated. The waitress was kind but we suspected she was wanting to seat new customers so I paid the bill and we went outside to the sidewalk.

I know I wasn't ready for our time together to end so I asked Theresa if she would be interested in going across the street and sitting in the town gazebo for a while. She readily accepted my invitation, seeming happy our date would continue. We crossed the street and sat in the gazebo. Little did I know at that point but our time in the gazebo would prove to be the time when we really connected. We stayed there for hours talking.

Even though Theresa came from an east coast background and I was a midwestern guy, we were discovering our souls, our identities, our likes and dislikes, our sense of humor, our priorities, our politics, our hobbies, our values, our families, and how we were raised were identical. Sure, we had our own unique stories in life and a few different customs within our families but strangely it seemed the more we talked the more I felt I had known her all my life. Not only that, it felt like we had somehow been connected our entire life. I felt as though my entire life had been preparing me for this one single day and the days that were to follow.

We shared some funny stories from our childhood. Pride and frustrations related to our children. Our fears and accomplishments. Some of the most intimate parts of our life. Small details that might seem meaningless. Like she found the first spoonful scoop of peanut butter from an unopened jar to taste better than the rest of the jar or that she could not stand a knife being put in the sink with peanut butter still on it or her first order of business in the morning was to brew a fresh pot of *Lipton* black tea and mix it with *Kroger* French vanilla coffee creamer (noting that it had to be *Kroger* brand and it could not be fat free). It seemed as though we had no inhibitions and felt safe to tell each other everything about ourselves, as one would do with their best friend.

Although it felt we had only been sitting in the gazebo a short time, we realized it had been hours when we noticed the sun disappearing behind the tree line and dusk settling upon us. Reluctantly, we decided it was time to bring our date to an end. We slowly sauntered back to our cars and as I leaned against the side of her *G37* while we said our goodbyes, I couldn't help but think, as crazy as it may sound after just one date, I was falling in love with the most amazing woman I had ever met.

I opened her door for her and as she moved to get in, she caught me by surprise when she leaned into me and gave me a long wonderful hug followed by a short but intimate kiss. When we parted ways on that memorable day, Theresa took my heart with her and to this day has never returned it.

We pulled out of the parking lot and went our separate ways. To say I was ecstatic over our date would be an understatement. I couldn't believe we had kissed. My mind was telling me Theresa was just being polite, not knowing how else to say goodbye, but my heart was telling me that it meant more. I had to see what she was thinking so I called her about five minutes after leaving the parking lot to tell her I enjoyed our date. She agreed she had also.

Anxious to see her again I asked if she would be interested in another date and she asked me what I had in mind. Trying to think of something quick I suggested that I come pick her up on Tuesday (knowing she had told me that was her next evening off) and take her to dinner and go to the horse races. She said she had never been to the horse races but would be interested in giving it a try. I told her I would figure out the details and let her know the particulars later. After telling her again I enjoyed our time together today, we hung up. I couldn't wait for Tuesday but was disappointed it would be three days before I could see her again.

We continued to talk on the phone and send messages to each other over the next three days but Tuesday could not come soon enough. The mere thought of spending more time with Theresa brought a ray of sunlight to my days and a smile to my face. I wanted to tell the world about her but didn't think anyone would understand how I could be feeling the way I was feeling after just one date.

I remember, however, expressing my feelings to my sister, Rae. I was sitting in Rae and Roger's living room having a discussion about the recent happenings in our lives and being giddy telling her about how I connected with Theresa on our first date. Rae expressed a sincere interest in what I was telling her and I could tell from the way she was smiling and looking at me she understood I felt Theresa was special. After I was finished telling Rae all I had to say I looked her in the eyes and in an emotional confession told her, "Rae, I found my Gabby".

Tuesday came and I drove to Columbus. Using the directions Theresa gave me I drove to her home through unfamiliar areas of town. It was located in a nice quiet residential neighborhood with shaded streets, freshly mowed lawns and kids playing in their yards. Her lawn was also well cared for and there was a basketball goal alongside the driveway.

To my surprise, there were two vehicles in her driveway, the *G37* that brought warmth to my heart as I pulled in and a *Ford Focus*. She had told me during our lunch that her son Jeff was home from college for the summer but for some reason I didn't anticipate he would be at her house when I came to pick her up. Well, I thought, maybe he's out with friends or maybe he will stay somewhere secluded in the house while I was there picking her up. I couldn't imagine she would want me meeting one of her children on our second date.

I walked apprehensively to the front door and rang the bell. The door opened and standing in front of me was a young man who appeared to be around Brent's age. So much for the thought of her son not being present. He greeted me and introduced himself as Jeff, Theresa's son. He explained that his mom was still getting ready and would be finished in a few minutes.

Jeff invited me into the living room to have a seat. He sat in a chair across the room from where I sat down and began exchanging pleasantries with me. Soon though those pleasantries began to feel like a father's inquisition when meeting his daughter's new boyfriend for the first time. Eventually, Theresa came out from the back rooms of her house and rescued me from the interrogation. I had a sneaking suspicion that she had intentionally stayed in the back room allowing Jeff to question me.

Much later in our relationship Jeff expressed to me that he indeed was questioning me to gain more information because he was skeptical of this new man in his mother's life. He confessed his skepticism hadn't been eased by the fact that I pulled up in a 2000 *Buick LeSabre* wearing a polo shirt and shorts. It was not his idea of what an attorney would be driving or wearing on a second date with his mother so he had his doubts as to whether I was actually who I said I was. He also told me that after Theresa and I left the house to go on our date he started doing searches online to see if he could find out more about me.

Relieved to be out from under the hot lights of the cross examination of my prosecutor, I walked Theresa to my car and opened the passenger door for her. I walked around the car to the driver's side, got in and glanced over at her. She had a smirk on her face that broke out into a smile and then a laugh followed by an apology for putting me in that situation. She explained that Jeff insisted on having an opportunity to speak to me before we left because of his concern about his mom going off with a stranger. Getting to know Jeff much better in the years to come I would have expected nothing less from him. Looking out for his mom has always been one of his endearing traits.

On our drive to the horse track, we continued our easy banter from our first date. The half hour drive passed quickly. We arrived early enough to have dinner with plenty of time to spare before the races commenced. Theresa ordered a full dinner showing again that she was comfortable eating with me. As we left the restaurant and walked to the horse track Theresa reached for my hand and we enjoyed a leisurely walk hand in hand. I remember thinking life could not get any better than this.

The first several races didn't prove lucrative for us as we seemed to be exceptionally talented at picking the last place horse each race. Unfortunately, there was no monetary reward for that incredible feat. About halfway through the racing program, however, our fortunes turned. As the horses were coming down the stretch in the sixth race, we were surprised to see our horse making a run for the lead. We were both yelling and screaming for our horse to run faster, as if it could hear us or understand us for that matter. Our horse must have heard us because it continued its charge and won by a nose. We won!

Theresa was elated and turned to me and gave me a big hug. As she began to pull away, I pulled her back to me and gave her a kiss, just as intimate as our first kiss but longer. As we separated, I continued to hold her and stared into her eyes and she returned the stare as we both reciprocated with smiles that spread across our whole face. If I thought I was falling in love before, I knew it now. We didn't win any more races but that was ok because I already felt like a winner.

We returned to Theresa's home late and Jeff's car was in the driveway and the lights were on in the living room. I walked Theresa to her door and we stood on her front porch saying our goodbyes rather than going inside to face questions from Jeff as to why I was bringing her home so late. We kissed again and parted ways. The hour drive back to Ellettsville was a blur as I reflected on the wonderful evening I had shared with my Gabby.

The next day I was at work when I received a text from Theresa. She indicated that she was taking Jeff, his friend and her step-grandson to the public pool in Nashville and wondered if I would be interested in joining them. Coincidently, my afternoon was free so I eagerly accepted the invitation. I rushed home and got my swim trunks and quickly made my way to Nashville, excited that Theresa had taken the initiative to invite me and, I would also have to admit, eager to see her in her swimming attire.

By the time I arrived at the pool Theresa and her entourage were already there. As I approached the group Theresa walked to me and gave me a hug and then introduced me to Mark, Jeff's friend, and Billy, her step-grandson. The afternoon was filled with me getting to know Jeff, Mark and Billy and competing with them to determine who had the best dives off the diving board, but more importantly in my eyes, showing off for Theresa. When it came time to part ways again Theresa gave me a hug and we kissed. The fact that she was willing to kiss me in front of Jeff told me that she must have been thinking the same about our budding relationship as I was.

June 10, 2010 – 7:14 a.m. text to Theresa

Good Morning,

I hope your morning is off to a great start and you had a pleasant evening last night.

53

I enjoyed our talk on the phone last night. I know I already told you this but I also enjoyed our day at the pool yesterday.

You expressed a concern last night during our call that my experience in my previous marriage may have jaded me in future relationships. I'm not sure I gave you an adequate response on how I view that so I want to make sure you know my true feelings.

What I experienced with my ex was the worst pain I have ever experienced. It was like the closest person in the world to you dying, but dying only to you and not to the rest of the world ... so you go through the grieving process alone. It was not until I finally began to understand that I too had not been happy in the relationship and allowed myself to forgive, that I began to be happy again. Now, looking back on it I can see how much happier I am today. Yes, I don't ever want to be hurt like that again but I am not consumed with that concern.

I believe what happened in my marriage was unique to our relationship and is not representative of all relationships. The reason for telling you all of this is to ask you to please not think my experience in my marriage has jaded me in any way toward future relationships. I still believe in the fairytale relationship.

I appreciate very much you being honest with me last night. That means more to me then you can imagine. It tells me that you think enough of the possibilities of a future that includes me that you didn't want to complicate matters by withholding something from me ... that tells me (and I hope I am correct) that you are thinking of the concept of an "us".

I hope this does not scare you off but I have an odd feeling about us. If I am completely open about my feelings, which is probably way too soon to do at this point, I have a feeling that we are meant to be together. I think the possibility is there for us to be very happy together and to be what we are each looking for in a partner. So, if given the chance, I believe we could develop a relationship in which neither of us would be intimidated by the other's past relationships.

Theresa, you are so refreshing to me. The thought of you is like a spring morning with the sun rising up from the horizon, the happiness of birds chirping in the air and a cool gentle breeze soothing one's skin, everything being so fresh and new. As you know, I have dated other women since my divorce. But with none have I ever believed there was a connection like I already feel with you.

Obviously, we are in a process of discovering each other and how we fit together so it is early to be confessing these feelings. But with you I see a difference from other women I have known. With you I can see a happiness in my life and growth as a person. With you I can see someone with whom I would want to build a partnership and relationship. With you I can see someone with whom I share an intellectual stimulation. With you I can see someone I would be proud to introduce to my children, my parents, my sister and the rest of my family and friends. With you I can see a deep physical attraction that goes well beyond outwardly beauty ... someone I would believe will always bring a sparkle to my eyes and a smile to my face.

Well, I should be getting ready for work. I hope I did not scare you with my frankness about my feelings. I just wanted to express my feelings that you are different. I am realistic though and understand that for us to build a relationship that can withstand any potential storm that may develop on the horizon, we have to build it the correct way. So, I am not trying to rush anything ... and I am prepared to let a relationship take on its own pace ... whatever that may be.

June 10, 2010 – 9:29 a.m. text to me

Good Morning,

WOW talk about a breath of fresh air...you amaze me with your letters. I cannot express how much I appreciate the amount of thought you put into a subject and your ability to articulate your feelings. This is so different than anything I have ever experienced.

Candid conversation increases our risk of being hurt, but is vital in the discovery process. I would rather know the ugly truth than to discover what I believed to be true is really just a false perception of reality. I respect you for your ability to be human and in-touch rather than an image or shield you use to protect yourself.

On to the honesty...

I have told you I am very honest. Sometimes it is brutal honesty. I take things very seriously and I live by the golden rule ... treat others as you would want them to treat you. So even though being brutally honest may hurt someone's feelings, they never have to guess where they stand with me. I am not phony and I am usually able to express myself pretty well.

I will do my best to keep everything open and honest between us. Sometimes we get stuck in the tunnel vision of our own lives, so please feel free to ask for clarification if things become murky or if I am not communicating very well.

So let me be very honest here and clarify the confusion...I HATE THE COLT'S not just a little...big bunches!!!! Just in case you were confused!

As far as an "us" I do see the potential, but as you said, we are in the discovery phase. I do respect that potential and will do everything in my power to give "us" every opportunity to grow. In the continuing spirit of honesty, I really like what I see, hear and feel. No red flags and that is a pretty good start. I hope when you said an "odd feeling about us" that was a good odd...the supporting paragraph led me to believe that is what you meant. I too want to take the time to make a solid relationship and I am willing to work and take the relationship at its own pace.

Ok enough of all the serious stuff ... onto to more fun subjects ... I would like to kiss your face...right now!

Hope you have a super awesome day!

T

June 10, 2010 – 9:52 a.m. text to Theresa

Good Morning (again),

Thank you for the compliment about my letters. I have no idea how well others articulate themselves but I know you do quite well yourself.

I find it so appealing that you and I can communicate our feelings to each other and that we seem to have similar feelings. And I will be honest about something else that I find very, very appealing ... referring to you and I as "us". I really like the sound of that

You are correct that candid conversation risks the chance of being hurt. But I guess the way I look at it is that if there is something you think is worth having, the risk of getting hurt is worth taking. And for "us" I am willing to take the risk of getting hurt because I know for there to be an "us" we need to know each other's hearts.

Now, one more piece of honesty ... my intentions are not pure ... it is my intention to steal your heart.

Also, in the spirit of openness and honesty, I have to tell you something that I should have told you from the beginning and it will probably change the whole way you think of me ... and to your relief ... no, it's not that Peyton Manning is my cousin -

although that would be cool. I didn't tell you about this before because it is hard to explain.

I have another identity you are not aware of ... literally ... lol I am the third Paul in the line of four generations of Paul's. Needless to say, it creates a lot of confusion in the family. So, when my dad was young, long before I was born, the family called him Junior. My grandfather passed away before I was born so that reference to my dad is only used by the old timers these days. But my birth re-created the dilemma. Junior was not an option for me (thankfully) because it was still being used for my dad so they came up with a nickname for me that all my friends and family call me to this day ... guess what it is .... unless you have paid very close attention to my emails you may not be able to guess ... it is P.D. I only use Paul in a professional setting. My son's name is Paul also but we use his middle name "Brent".

I know that kind of causes you to have to re-learn the whole concept of what to call me and I should have started off telling you that, but it is awkward explaining that whole thing when introducing yourself to someone.

Theresa, seeing the potential of an "us", I too intend to do everything within my control to give us that opportunity to grow. I also really like what I see, hear and feel with you. Yes, the odd feeling I was referring to is a good thing ... by odd feeling I meant I have this feeling that you and I are meant for each other ... and to be totally blunt, I could see myself growing old with you in my arms.

I know that sounds crazy not knowing you for any longer than I have but that is why I said I have an odd feeling ... odd being crazy ;) But, having said all those things, I still believe it is crucial we allow the relationship to proceed at its own pace so we can build a foundation upon which the relationship can be based. What that means ... I have no idea ... I just want to make sure we do this right so that it will last, if that is what we both want.

As for moving on to more fun stuff ... you brought a giant smile to my face saying you want to kiss my face right now:) What a coincidence because I was thinking the very same thing!!! Well, I need to get back to work. What would you think about the possibility of coming over to Bloomington tomorrow? I hope you have a great day!!! I look forward to hearing that sweet voice of yours soon.

P.D.

June 10, 2010 – 10:31 a.m. text to me

P.D.

I too have an admission to make ... an identity problem I too am afflicted with ... my family calls me Terri. I have corrected them over and over ... but they still use that name. Another alias is T ... or T squared (TT) as the doctors in the ER refer to me ... so like you, I answer to many names. Just thank God neither of us has Colt's lineage!

I have read your last email 4-5 times ... you make me smile!

As for "US" I will give you a little insight into me. I have a tendency to get a little frightened/confused when things move too fast. My natural instinct is to stop talking and distance myself. That has been my history ... things between us have progressed kind of quickly ... and I have to tell you ... I have not felt the need to pull back or feel frightened or confused.

I look forward to seeing, talking/texting or emailing you. You make me smile and feel good inside. I look forward to getting to know more about you and your family and what makes you tick! My mom and dad have always told me you will know when it is right ... I have learned from hindsight that I really knew when things were not right (even though I may have proceeded!) I want you to know my heart is here to be stolen! :)

I would love to come to Bloomington tomorrow but could I ask one favor? Would it be OK if I brought Jeff and Mark with me? I haven't seen much of Jeff since he returned home from college.

Talk to you soon

T

April 18, 2021

Passing through Louisville I was deep in thought about those first few times Theresa and I shared time together and my initial feelings for her that were the beginning of the deepest love I will ever share with anyone. My sight was again clouded with tears for that love we have shared together. With my thoughts distracted I missed the directions from my *Waze* app resulting in me making a wrong turn. It took me several miles before I was able to find a place to turn around and retrace my path to get back on my journey to find Theresa.

As I merged back onto *I-65* to get back on the correct path, Rascal Flatts' *Bless the Broken Road* began playing through my *Bluetooth*:

I set out on a narrow way many years ago
Hoping I would find true love along the broken road
But I got lost a time or two
Wiped by brow and kept pushing through
I couldn't see how every sign pointed straight to you
That every long lost dream led me to where you are
Others who broke my heart, they were like Northern Stars
Pointing me on my way into your loving arms
This much I know is true
That God blessed the broken road
That led me straight to you

I couldn't help but think the song was written about my own journey or about Theresa's. Our roads were also broken and we were lost a time or two ourselves before we met. We pushed through not realizing all of our heartaches were pointing us toward each other. Every lost dream we had over the years, every wrong turn we made, every tear shed, every mistake made along the way led us to each other.

Reflecting on the road my life had taken me, I realized it led me to Theresa. It taught me how to love her. It taught me how to cherish her. It taught me to appreciate her. As the song reminded me, each lost dream I experienced in my life acted as a Northern Star pointing me into Theresa's loving arms, all part of a grander plan blessed by

God. I would do it all again if I knew Theresa was my life destination. The crown of my life.

Chapter 4: Meeting the Family

Look at how good and pleasing it is
when families live together as one.

Psalm 133:1

April 18, 2021

Continuing toward Nashville my mind drifted toward thoughts of our family. My family, especially my children, my mom and dad, and my sister have always been the center of my life. They have always supported me in everything I do and have been there for me during all the good times and bad times in my life. They were there offering whatever support they could give after my breakup with Kathy and during my separation and divorce from Tina. I am not sure how I could have ever gotten through the dark times without them. They have always been the light in the darkness that guided me through those difficult times.

Theresa's family, her children, her father, and her sisters and their families, have also been part of that light since we met. They took me in as one of their own and have been there for me when I needed them most and I have come to love them as part of my own family. Now, since Theresa left me, both of our families have rallied around me, again offering whatever support they could.

But they all were worried about the journey I was taking to find Theresa. They were concerned I was taking this journey alone. It had been less than three weeks since Theresa left me.

I am sure they thought the timing wasn't right. They did not believe now was a time for me to be alone. They had to be troubled by the real possibility I would not find Theresa on this journey and how I would handle such a possibility.

In my heart, I knew that if I could just find her, I might be able to explain to her I understood why she left me. I could tell her that I still loved her no matter what has come between us. I would make her realize that no matter what, she will always be the spark that makes my heart beat. But I had to find her first and my family was worried for me if I didn't.

As I continued on I-65 toward Nashville, my thoughts turned to when we introduced each other to our families.

June 11, 2010

I was elated Theresa would be coming to Bloomington to see me and I was happy to be spending time with Jeff and Mark again. I told Theresa I thought it would be great having Jeff and Mark join us, knowing also I still needed to ease some of Jeff's concerns about who I was and my intentions. I had a great time with them at the pool and anticipated they would be fun to spend time with again.

I suggested that we go to laser light tag. They made the hour drive from Columbus and we met at the laser light tag facility and had a great time playing several games (which I had never done before). After we finished, I suggested another idea. The facility was only a half-mile or so from my parents' home. I knew my dad was at work but suspected my mom would be home. I asked if they would be interested in playing a prank on my mom. Jeff and Mark, always being game for a good prank, were all in. Theresa, on the other hand, never having met my mom, was reluctant to have my mom's first impression of her to be associated with a prank but after some cajoling reluctantly agreed.

The plan was to have Jeff and Mark knock on mom's door, while Theresa and I were hiding. Jeff and Mark would pose as travelling salesmen with foreign accents trying to convince her to invest in a timeshare in San Diego. Mom is known to be gullible so I figured this might be entertaining.

After several knocks mom finally appeared at her front door and Jeff and Mark transformed into character. It was hilarious to watch and listen while mom tried to understand their thick accents and what they were trying to sell her. Jeff and Mark were persistent in their sales pitch but mom kept trying to explain to them that she had no use for a time-share in California and was becoming frustrated with their inability to understand her midwestern accent.

Theresa and I appeared from our hiding spot when we thought the prank had gone far enough, which only seemed to confuse mom further. Eventually, we were able to explain the prank to her and she got a good laugh out of it. Theresa and mom hit it off splendidly from the beginning, no doubt aided by the fact that they shared a similar sense of humor accentuated by our prank on her.

It was around this time Theresa began telling me about her family's annual gathering in Myrtle Beach. She, her father and her sisters each owned a one-week per year time-share at a condo in Myrtle Beach. They would schedule their weeks for the same week as each other in the summer to allow them and their families to have a week-long reunion. This year's week would begin on Friday, June 25 and she wouldn't return home until Saturday, July 3.

Theresa had been telling me she was close to her father and sisters and this was an example of how they remained close even while living so far apart. I was impressed with her dedication to family but, to be honest, was saddened that in the very near future I would not be seeing her for more than a week.

We made the most of our time seeing each other at every available opportunity before Theresa was scheduled to leave for Myrtle Beach. We fell into a rhythm where I would usually go to her home in Columbus but when her work schedule permitted, she would come to Ellettsville. During that time, we introduced each other to our children. I had introduced Brent and Misty to one other person after my separation from Tina but they didn't seem overly impressed with her. Their reaction to Theresa was completely different. I could tell from their first meeting with Theresa, Brent and Misty hit it off well with her.

I had already met Jeff, the youngest of Theresa's children. I met Jeff when I was least expecting it so I didn't have time to give it much thought beforehand. Meeting Scott, Ben and Stephanie was different. Theresa and I planned a cook-out at a local park which would be attended by Scott, Ben and Stephanie. I had several days to think about meeting them. I was more than twenty years older than them so I was surprised by how nervous I was to meet them. I knew they were the center of Theresa's life so I figured their acceptance of me was imperative if Theresa and I were to have a long-term relationship. Thankfully, they accepted me with open arms.

Soon after the cook-out in the park I scheduled a dinner at *Outback* to introduce Theresa to my sister Rae and her family. I suspected Rae and Theresa would hit it off but until seeing them actually interact I was a bit apprehensive. I valued my family's opinions and lean on them heavily when it comes to the people I bring into my life. So, I was anxious to see how they interacted and to hear what Rae thought of Theresa.

In my opinion, the dinner could not have gone better. Rae and one of her daughters are registered nurses which gave them and Theresa a lot to talk about. There was no shortage of conversation as the dinner went on. Rae was quick to tell Theresa a lot of embarrassing stories about me from our childhood such as when mom told her to wake me up for breakfast on a lazy Saturday morning. When her attempts proved to be unsuccessful, she went to the kitchen and retrieved a bottle of syrup and came back into my room and poured it on me. Everyone was laughing and having fun during the dinner, mostly at my expense. I didn't mind because it was obvious Rae and Theresa were enjoying their time with each other.

After we all parted ways at the end of dinner, I was quick to call Rae to hear her thoughts. Rae said that from the way Theresa and I were looking at each other, talking with each other, joking with each other and unconsciously leaning into each other it seemed as though we had always been together. At the end of the debriefing Rae told me that she had a feeling I indeed had found my Gabby.

June 20, 2010 – 9:38 a.m. text to Theresa

Good Morning Theresa, Terri, T, TT, or whatever you are going by this morning (lol),

Sorry I didn't call last night but we didn't get home until about 12:45 this morning. I hope you had a great day yesterday and that the cookout was fun.

Back to the "US" discussion from last week. Certainly, you know I don't want you to stop talking and distance yourself from me because you are frightened / confused by moving faster than you are comfortable. I am a bit confused by what you are telling me about things between us progressing kind of quickly though ... are you saying we need to slow down? I don't think you are but I just want to make sure I am understanding what you are telling me.

As I have said, I am willing to allow things to go at its own pace to make sure we do this right ... we just need to make sure we keep communicating our feelings to each other so we know what the right pace is. I have really enjoyed the time I have spent with you and find myself wanting to spend as much time as possible with you. But that may be more than you are comfortable with? That's one of those matters where the communication is important.

I am very glad you haven't felt the need to pull back, feel frightened or confused. Theresa, you said I make you smile and feel good inside ... that comment makes me smile and feel good inside ... but everything about you makes me feel that way. I look forward to every contact I have with you. When I open my emails, I am hoping to see a message from you and when I hear my phone signal a call / message I am hoping it is from you.

I will be honest with you about something. When I meet someone, I have a litmus test I use to help me determine whether I want to explore the relationship any further. And almost without exception, I have not found the need to use the litmus test with anyone because I know beforehand they can't pass it. The litmus test and what I believe tells me more than anything about how comfortable I would feel in a relationship is how my children, my parents (mom specifically) and my sister and her family react and interact to the person I introduce to them.

I had no hesitation introducing you to my mom, my children and my sister and her family. Without exception each of them enjoyed meeting you and were genuinely impressed with you ... I know the rest of my family would love to meet you also. You have passed the test with glowing reviews!!!

I want you to know everything about me, my family and what makes me tick ... and it makes me very happy knowing you want to know all of that. And I want to know the same about you. I am very glad your heart is available to be stolen. Like I said, it is my intention to steal it. And when / if I do, it is my intention to never give it back and to work as hard as I can to make you as happy as possible with "US".

I will call you later this morning.

PD

June 20, 2010 – 10:27 a.m. text to me

Hello PD

I hope you got some much needed rest. I figured you would be exhausted when you got home. All day in the sun and then a long drive, tends to be a tough combination. I am glad you all had fun and the weather cooperated!

So, the nicknames ... my family always called me Terri and I did not like it as a child and still do not, but somethings you can't change. Most of the time people refer to me as T or Theresa ... you can choose whatever you want to call me ... as long as it is sweet! LOL

As for the "us" ... I was only telling you that so you could be aware/know me. I do not feel the need to do any of that with you.

Do you realize we only met face-to-face less than a month ago? I feel like I have known you for a long time. Do you believe in old souls? I do. I know I have one and believe you do as well. Things are very different with you and "us". Different in a good way and a way I can't honestly say I have ever experienced.

I too check my phone and hope there is a message from you. Someone commented at work the other day, that something must be going on because they noticed a big smile on my face after I checked my phone ... of course it was a message from you!

I like you way more than a smidge and a tick over a tad ... in case you hadn't noticed! :)

WOW I passed the litmus test? That is pretty big! I am glad you believe your family would like me. I like your mom, children and sister and her family already ... with the whole October tradition and all and how well she enjoyed our prank and how easy it was to speak to your children and sister and her family.

I like how much you love your family and how much you respect their opinions. It would be very important for people that mean that much to you, to like the person you are choosing to spend time with. If they're anything like you, I think I will like them very much!

I am looking forward to seeing you today!

T

Later that afternoon I made what was becoming the familiar drive to Columbus, frustrated that the traffic on the windy road was not allowing me to arrive at Theresa's home faster. When I arrived, my heart swelled with love when Theresa answered her door looking more beautiful than any of the previous times we had been together. Theresa asked me what I would like to do. To me it didn't matter what we did as long as we were able to be together.

Theresa had previously worked as a private nurse for a prominent family in the Columbus community who played an integral part in revitalizing the downtown area. She was proud of the work and success of the family in their efforts and suggested we drive downtown and walk around to view it. It was a beautiful June evening with the heat of the warm day giving way to a pleasant cloudless evening so I eagerly agreed.

After the short drive to the downtown area, we exited my car and strolled along the sidewalks while Theresa pointed out all the improvements in the city she felt were noteworthy. Eventually, we made our way over to a city park near the downtown area that was bordered by the convergence of the Driftwood and Flatrock Rivers forming the east fork of the White River. There were benches near this convergence which we sat on giving us a great view of these two rivers joining together as one. We leaned into each other and I put my arm around her as we watched the water of the rivers lazily drift by.

I will never forget how Theresa gazed into my eyes this evening and I'm sure she felt me returning the same gaze. The intimacy we shared on this evening sitting on the bench was made more intimate as we held hands and lightly traced each other's finger tips with our own finger tips. I had never felt such an intimacy through just the touching of hands. It felt as though we were each giving the other our very souls as they passed through our finger tips. We sat there for probably an hour or more engaging in small talk as our hearts and souls experimented with the idea of becoming one, just as the two rivers a few yards in front of us were becoming one.

The days leading up to Theresa's departure for Myrtle Beach were passing by way too fast. We were still building our relationship and I was afraid the time apart would somehow change that. The Monday before she was scheduled to leave, we were talking and she said she had a crazy idea and asked if I was willing to listen to it. I said sure. She asked me what I would think about going to Myrtle Beach with her and her kids.

I was elated by her invitation but wasn't sure if I could arrange the time off with my work schedule. I pulled my phone out to look at my schedule and determined there would be some appointments at the end of that week I couldn't reschedule but I could go the first part of the week. I asked her if that would be OK and she agreed. It would require us to take two cars to allow me to leave early but Jeff agreed to drive her car and follow us. The opportunity to spend time at the beach was a nice perk but for me the main attraction was all of the time I would be spending with Theresa.

As I was packing to leave, reality hit me. I wouldn't only be spending time with Theresa. Her children, daughter-in-law and granddaughter would be there also. That was OK, I had already met them and enjoyed their company. But I would be meeting her father, Jim, for the first time. Jim served in the *Navy* in the Pacific fleet at the end of World War II and was a retired Baltimore police officer so I anticipated he would be a hardline, no-nonsense kind of man. Theresa's sisters would also be there, Tammy, Beth, Karen, Julie and Nancy (although Nancy wasn't sure she would be able to make the trip) and their families (Theresa's nieces and nephews and their families). Theresa told me to expect around forty to fifty people from her family in total. Oh my! What had I gotten myself into?

I was sure to be the center of attention being the new person in the group. What would happen if they didn't like me? Would they convince Theresa I wasn't the man for her? Was it too early to meet all of them at once? It didn't matter at this point because I had already committed to go. Besides, all I had to do to steady my nerves was think about all of the time I would have with Theresa.

We left early Friday morning. The week in the time-share condo didn't actually begin until Saturday afternoon but it was the practice of a couple of the sisters and Theresa's father to arrive in Myrtle Beach the night before and stay in a hotel so they could get to the condo early on Saturday and spend an extra day at the beach. The drive would take eleven hours and we left early enough that we would arrive before Theresa's sisters and father, giving me time to settle in at the hotel and relax a little from the drive before I met them.

Those plans, however, didn't account for the accident that occurred on *I-75* in Tennessee that shut the interstate down in both directions for hours. While parked on an interstate in rural Tennessee it became obvious as the minutes ticked away, we would be arriving after Theresa's family.

Sure enough, we arrived in Myrtle Beach much later than planned. Theresa had apparently texted her sisters, Karen and Julie, and her father as we were coming into town because as we pulled into the parking lot of the hotel, she pointed to a crowd of people standing in the parking lot and excitedly announced to me they were her family. Talk about being thrown into the fire.

After we parked our cars and were getting out stretching, I noticed the crowd walking toward us. I thought I knew then what General Custer must have felt like during his last stand at the *Battle of the Little Bighorn*. Leading the charge was no other than Crazy Horse himself, in this case also known as Jim, Theresa's father.

Jim walked straight up to me with a stern face, introduced himself and then proceeded to ask me if I heard about the police officer who arrived at an accident scene. Confident I was about to receive a stern lecture about how much Theresa means to him and that in some way he was going to tell me I would be that accident scene if I hurt her, I hesitantly replied I had not heard about that police officer.

Jim then said: "A police officer arrived at the scene of an accident where a car had smashed into a tree. The cop rushed over to the vehicle and asked the driver, "Are you seriously hurt?' 'How should I know?' the driver answered, 'I'm not a lawyer!'. My first experience of Jim's keen sense of humor but more importantly an understanding of his welcoming demeanor. He knew I would be nervous meeting the family so he wanted to set me at ease with a joke (one that combined his and my professions, no less).

Theresa seemed to enjoy this exchange a little too much and I later learned it was something she and her father had conspired to do as a "payback" for my biker guy joke at the gas station. Damn, although I suspected it would be coming, I had forgotten about the inevitable payback.

Jim welcomed me as one of the family. He went out of his way the entire time I was in Myrtle Beach to spend time with me to assure that I was feeling comfortable. I particularly enjoyed everyone checking in at his room each morning and sitting around talking while 'the sisters cooked breakfast. I got to know Tammy, Beth, Karen, and Julie during these talks (Nancy was unable to make the trip) and all did everything they could to make me feel welcome. I met Tammy's husband, Frank, and Julie's husband, John, and started a lifetime friendship with each of them.

We would set up tents on the beach during the day and spend time going back and forth from the beach to the condo pool. We made several visits to the ice cream trucks that would being playing their carnival music to alert the kids as they approached the condo. We all would gather again as a group for lunches and dinners (usually homemade at the condo with an occasional night out at their favorite local restaurants, *Giant Crab* and *Drunken Jack's*). A group of about twelve of us went jet skiing through the mangroves of the intercoastal waterway making memories that will last a lifetime.

Mostly though I enjoyed spending a lot of time with Theresa. We were together almost the entire time, taking long walks on the beach, laying out on the beach, swimming in the pool and sitting around in the evenings with her family playing card games. Our one bedroom condo was packed with the two of us, her four children, Mark (who drove down a day later than us), Theresa's daughter-in-law and granddaughter. To say we were crowded in the condo would be an understatement. But that was OK because it required Theresa and me to share the bedroom together. Consequently, for all intents and purposes we were together twenty-four hours a day during this period, each day being better than the previous.

I remember thinking that Theresa was becoming part of my soul. She had invaded every crevice of my identity, and I couldn't be happier. But in an odd way, it also felt as though she had always been there. We thought alike, we had the same sense of humor, and her family felt so familiar. I could also see myself in Theresa. I would look at her and see a better version of myself staring back. The version I wanted to become.

All too soon, Tuesday evening arrived, the night before I was to return to Indiana. Tammy's birthday was approaching and the family decided since I would be leaving the following morning, they would hold an early birthday celebration for Tammy before I left. Some of the adult kids concocted a tasty tropical adult beverage that seemed to be well received, evident by the need to make several batches throughout the night. The inhibitions began to fade as the night proceeded and many in attendance took turns at karaoke. Seeing Theresa singing karaoke with her sisters without a care in the world, laughing, and having fun continues to be right up there in my favorite memories of our time together.

The celebration began to wind down around midnight and thoughts of having to leave in the morning were creeping into my mind. Seeking to squeeze in a little more alone time with Theresa, I asked her if she would be interested in taking a walk on the beach and she agreed. It was a warm but breezy night, perfect for a walk.

Walking north toward a deserted part of the beach with no hotels or condos we came to a darker area where the stars were more visible. We walked hand in hand snuggled up next to each other while looking out over the ocean and up to the stars. Only an occasional couple or late-night jogger would pass by. It seemed, however, we had this part of the beach all to ourselves.

We walked for about fifteen minutes engaged in small talk recapping how our week had gone since arriving in Myrtle Beach and how much I enjoyed meeting each of her family members. When we reached a point where I knew there wasn't anyone around, I stopped her and turned to face her. I stared into her eyes and my heart melted as the wind kept blowing her hair in front of her face and she kept pulling it back to return a stare into my eyes.

I pulled her close and gave her a long kiss holding her tightly. When we stopped kissing, I pulled back just enough to look into her eyes while still holding her close. I tucked a loose strand of hair blowing across her face behind her ear to have a better view of her eyes and after a short pause said "I love you" for the first time. She pulled me tight again, rested her head on my shoulder and after a few awkward moments whispered in my ear that she had enjoyed our time together and was glad I had come.

Her noncommittal reaction felt like an arrow piercing my heart. What was that, I thought? She didn't express her feelings for me. She just responded with a simple "glad you came" acknowledgement. Had I been reading our relationship wrong? Was she not thinking of our relationship in the terms of love? Had I not passed the litmus test with her family and as a result her feelings for me had changed? Would our relationship be over once I left in the morning? Why did I have to leave so early? If only I could stay the whole week, I would have more time to rekindle whatever we had apparently lost since arriving.

My mind was whirling. I was confused. I had been sure she had fallen in love with me. But I had misread love once before in my life so what did I know. We walked back to the condo in an awkward silence. We both knew our relationship had changed on this walk. I, unfortunately, didn't know how it had changed or even why for that matter.

April 18, 2021

Continuing the drive on my journey to find Theresa again, I was approaching Nashville. I couldn't help but think of the irony that almost eleven years earlier I was leaving the East Coast in solitude leaving her behind, thinking I had lost her forever. Now, here I was, returning to the East Coast in solitude, once again hoping I had not lost her forever.

The love we had shared transcended any love I knew existed. Theresa was my blessing from God. That blessing extended to her family. She had become a part of me. She was my soul. When I left Myrtle Beach eleven years ago it felt as though I had lost part of myself. Since Theresa left me three weeks ago, that familiar feeling of having lost part of myself had returned again. I was determined to find her on this journey. I just didn't know if that would be possible since she had eluded me for the past three weeks.

Perhaps my family was right thinking it was not a good idea for me to take this journey. Perhaps it was too soon. If I was unsuccessful finding her, how would I go on? Even if I did find her, would it even make a difference?

There was no going back to what we once had. The events of the last several months assured we would never have that again. What I knew with certainty however is I had to try. I once told Theresa I would always fight for our love and would do anything I could to make sure we wouldn't lose it. In my mind, I had no option but to take this journey.

Chapter 5: Reformation

Do not conform yourselves to this age
but be transformed by the renewal of your mind,
that you may discern what is the will of God,
what is good and pleasing and perfect.

Romans 12:2

April 18, 2021

As I came into Nashville, I knew I would be changing course to take *I-24* toward Chattanooga. But as I approached the interchange a construction detour had traffic backed up. I didn't want to make the same mistake I had made in Louisville by going the wrong direction so I remained alert for the signs that would point me in the right direction.

All too often in my life I had not been vigilant in looking for those signs, causing me to steer off course. It happened in my first love with Kathy. It happened in my marriage with Tina. It seemed to have happened with Theresa at some point leading up to that fateful night in Myrtle Beach.

Sometimes in life we get caught up in the fast-paced world around us and fail to see what is directly in front of us. The road map of life is often times clear but we still don't follow it. We think we know a better direction and elect to take our own detour. The problem is all too often we don't know the better direction. Other times, we just get too busy and fail to recognize the correct turns, as I did in Louisville and in my relationships with Kathy and Tina. Yet other times we don't have faith in the detour life is taking us and rather than trusting the signs we forge straight ahead, causing more troubles than had we followed the map laid out for us.

June 30, 2010

We arose early on June 30 and I packed for the return trip to Indiana. The tension between Theresa and me from the night before was still thick in the air. We went to Jim's condo where all the sisters were gathered and I said my goodbyes to those who were there, which was an impressive number given the early hour and the festivities from the night before. After our goodbyes were exchanged, Theresa, Jeff, Jim and the sisters came down to the parking lot to see me off. Theresa and I hugged and said goodbye and I drove off.

As I left, tears were forming in my eyes with thoughts of the possibility of this being the end of my relationship with Theresa playing havoc in my mind. I took *Veterans Highway* to *501*. By the time I reached *I-95* my emotions had overtaken me. Theresa and I texted a few times during this first hour of my drive but her responses were generic, not giving me any true indication of what she was thinking and, more importantly, feeling. On my end, I was already missing her and wanting to turn around but knew my work schedule would not allow me to stay.

Trying not to interfere with Theresa's time with her family I tried to keep my texting with her to a minimum. Ashville, North Carolina is about the half-way point home. When I reached Ashville, I texted her that I was beyond the point of no return, meaning that I was now closer to home than I was to her. It was an hour or so before she replied with a response that only amplified the pain I was feeling: "Lol. My point of no return would have been Florence" (a point about an hour from Myrtle Beach).

Wow. What did that mean, I thought? I was hurt. I decided I wouldn't initiate any more texts until I arrived home to see if she took the initiative. She did not. I arrived home late in the evening and sent a text to Theresa: "I made it home. I hope the remaining part of your week with your family is great. Miss you." She replied after a few minutes: "I am glad you made it home safe. Thank you. Spending time with family is good."

Wow, again. Thoughts of what had happened continued to swirl in my head. Our relationship seemed to hit a wall with three small worlds, "I love you." Not only did it hit a wall but Theresa seemed to put our relationship in reverse and was speeding away at full throttle.

Clearly, she was wanting space so I decided to give it to her and not text her again unless she initiated it. I didn't hear from her again until late Saturday evening. I knew from speaking to her at the beginning of the week she would be home early Saturday evening so I assumed she was home when she finally texted.

"I would like to talk. I have to work tomorrow night but would you be willing to come over at noon tomorrow to talk?" Well, that is interesting I thought. Finally, maybe I will have some answers. "Sure, I was hoping to have an opportunity to talk. I will be there at noon."

I was happy that she reached out but the fact that she did created even more confusion. If our relationship was over, why would she want to talk? Maybe she felt an obligation to end our relationship in person. Maybe, on second thought, she wanted to continue the relationship but didn't want it to progress where I was clearly trying to take it. I wasn't sure I could have a relationship with her like that at this point. I was all in on our relationship and didn't know if I could pull back from that. But Theresa meant way too much to me to walk away without hearing her out to see what she was thinking.

When I arrived at her house the following day, I was pleasantly surprised to see a driveway with only the *G37* parked on it. It had been my experience that Jeff slept in late on the weekends, even under the best of conditions. Their return drive home the day before made for a long day so I had anticipated Jeff would be at her house resting. I wondered what it could mean that he was not home. Had she asked him to leave for our "talk" and if so was that a good thing or a bad thing?

I went to her door and rang the bell. When Theresa appeared at the door, I had to catch my breath because she looked amazing. The week in the sun radiated from her skin and she had definitely taken the time to look exceptionally beautiful today. I hoped her appearance was for my benefit.

She asked me in and asked me to have a seat. I sat on her couch and she came over and sat next to me. There was definitely tenseness in the air (on both of our parts), a significant departure from our usual carefree, free flowing and natural cadence. Not knowing how to begin our conversation I asked her how the week had gone in Myrtle Beach after I left. She politely answered my question but it was obvious she was not interested in small talk. She had something on her mind and was trying to figure out how to tell me.

"There is something I need to explain to you and I need you to just listen and not respond because this is difficult for me to talk about". I responded OK and with trepidation leaned back into the couch.

She took my hands and said, "I am scared. I am not scared of you but I am scared of a relationship with you. I've told you I was divorced from my ex about fourteen years ago. But what I haven't told you is that talking about my marriage causes me too much pain and anxiety so it's not something I can talk to you about right now. But I can tell you it has caused me to have a lot of issues in relationships since my divorce. So much so that I've not been able to have a relationship since my divorce that has lasted more than eighteen months. Something clicks in me when I have a relationship that gets serious and I have to end it. When you told me that you love me on the beach it scared me. Not because I don't want to be with you but because I want more than anything for us to be together. So much so that I'm scared that if I make that commitment, I will eventually fall back into those same habits and lose you. You are different

P.D. I don't want to lose you. I know I hurt you on the beach but I didn't know what to say. I didn't know how to express these feelings to you. I didn't even know if I could express these feelings to you. But I know if I don't, I may lose you and I don't want to risk that chance. I am asking you to please understand, well you can't understand, but I am asking you to accept what I am telling you and to please be patient with me as I work through my feelings and insecurities."

I was speechless. A week's worth of worrying began evaporating as quickly as freshly fallen rain on a hot blacktop road in the middle of summer. She didn't tell me directly that she loved me but her message did. She was facing some of her deepest fears and insecurities to keep from losing me ... to keep from losing us. She was telling me she felt as much about our relationship as I did. Her words confirmed that I had not been wrong about her feelings for me.

How should I respond to her revelation? Clearly, it was something that has caused her considerable consternation not just in our relationship but also in prior relationships. My initial response was to tell her "Of course I will be patient with you." I told her about being confused in Myrtle Beach by her reaction to me telling her I love her and how I had been worrying all week about what it meant and that I thought she wanted to end our relationship.

She apologized and said she was concerned also that I wanted to end our relationship since I hadn't called her since leaving Myrtle Beach. She told me she had talked to her sisters about me and her concern that I had not called. I reassured her I would be as patient as she needed me to be and told her again that I loved her.

This time she smiled and we embraced and kissed as all of my sadness and concerns from the past five days rushed out of me. Theresa pulled back from me and looked down into her lap for a few moments and then looked back up at me and stared into my eyes as she said "PD you have stolen my heart and I couldn't be happier than how I feel when we are together, when I am in your arms. I've known how I feel about you way before Myrtle Beach but didn't understand how I could be having those feelings so quickly. I love you with all my heart like I've never loved anyone before."

July 5, 2010 – 8:42 a.m. text to me

Good morning PD

I know you probably think I am a neurotic flake, but I'm really not. I love you and these feelings scare me. I have imagined finding someone like you all my life. Now that you are here, I get so confused by all the feelings and experiences of the past. I would love to let go and just let it happen, but seem to struggle with that concept. I love you like I have never loved anyone before, I would be soooo very devastated if the "we" part of us fell apart.

I am not perfect and I know you don't expect me to be. There are a lot of things about the way I deal with issues that you don't know, most based on learned behavior, but that is a face-to-face conversation for another time. The process of discovery will take both of us time. We are both still discovering things about ourselves we may not even be aware of yet.

So, to put this in the simplest of terms ... I LOVE YOU and I thank God for sending you to me!

Please be patient with me...

Your NGF (neurotic girlfriend)

July 5, 2010 – 9:16 a.m. text to Theresa

Good Morning Theresa,

I am hoping you have a chance to read this before going to work today because I want you to be reminded of how very very very special you are to me. I want to strive to make sure you never have to wonder how much I love you. The depth of my love for you is like an abyss the extent of which cannot be accurately measured by words.

You have become the essence and charm of my life. The simple mention of your name is music to my ears. Your concerns are my concerns. You are my best friend. I cherish you and your love like I have never cherished anything before. Your presence brings a beautiful fragrance to my life.

With the thought of us together I love life as never before. You have added meaning to my life. Everyone sees your physical beauty but I am privileged to know the beauty within you. Without a doubt those two combine to make you the most beautiful woman on Earth. And that, my dear, makes me the luckiest man on the face of this planet.

Theresa, if there is anything I know for certain it is that I want to live the rest of my days on this Earth by your side. When the day comes when you are ready, I want you to be my wife - that I have no doubt. I will not push you to take that step before you are ready but likewise, I will not hesitate to take that step when you are ready.

Together we will have the fairytale marriage we each have dreamed we would have some day and we will be an example of an unmatched love to all who witness what we share together. The intimacy we share together is like nothing I have ever experienced before. "We" and "Us" is defined by our love and friendship. Our understanding of each other, our partnership and companionship, our fun together, the sharing of our emotions with each other - joy, sorrow, happiness, sadness, excitement.

You are the light in my day, the wind in my sail, and the spark that lights my fire. It seems as though I have lived my entire life for the sole purpose of preparing for our life together. Now that the time has arrived for us to commence our life together, I couldn't be happier. Having you in my life is an answer to my prayers.

I love you so very much!!!!! I hope you have a great day. I cannot wait to see you tonight.

PD

Coming off vacation our work schedules would not allow us to see each other again for several days after that evening but we texted and spoke on the phone several times a day. Multiple hour phone calls became the norm when we couldn't see each other. Eventually, however, we were able to set an evening to see each other again. We decided we would go out to eat and then come back to her house and watch TV.

I arrived at her house a little early and she was still getting ready in her bedroom. She asked me to join her as she was finishing up. I went into her bedroom and sat down on her bed as she was fixing her hair. I asked her to stop for a moment and to have a seat next to me on the bed. She looked perplexed but took a seat next to me and noticed I was hiding something behind my back. She asked me what I was hiding.

I pulled it from behind my back and handed it to her. She asked what it was. I told her it was a book written by Nicholas Sparks called *The Choice*. I asked her if she would read it and she asked me why. I told her it was about a love between two persons named Travis and Gabby. I described the love that Travis and Gabby shared, the depths of that love and the lengths to which Travis went to preserve that love. I then told her she was my Gabby.

I could tell from the tear forming in the corner of her eye that she was genuinely touched by this gesture. She jokingly scolded me for making her cry while she was getting ready. She agreed to read the book but from that moment on she always knew I considered her to be my Gabby.

We went to dinner as planned and then returned to her house to watch TV. We sat on the couch with her leaning into me while we basked in each other's company. I'm not sure what we were watching nor do I think either of us cared because all that mattered to both of us was being together in each other's arms. The evening grew late and when I announced it was time for me to leave Theresa proposed that I spend the night at her house.

Although I was not prepared to spend the night having not brought any clothes with me for work the following day, I readily agreed rationalizing that I could get up early and run by my house in the morning to get dressed before work. It would be the first night either of us spent at the other's home but from that night forward I would always spend the night in her home if it was a night Misty was with

Tina and Theresa would spend the night in my home if she was not working and Misty was with me.

The summer flew by but with each successive day our love grew deeper. Way too soon the most memorable summer of my life unofficially came to a close with the arrival of Labor Day Weekend. Theresa's birthday was on the Wednesday following Labor Day. As her special day was approaching, I knew I wanted to do something extraordinary for her to express how much I loved her. So, I planned a surprise birthday party for her at her house.

I wanted to go above and beyond it just being a surprise party. With the three-day Labor Day Weekend allowing for an opportunity for some of her family to travel to Indiana, I made arrangements for Jim to fly to Indiana from Virginia Beach and invited her sisters to come in from their homes on the East Coast (Julie and John were able to make arrangements to attend). To this day a smile comes to my face when I recall the pure joy I saw on Theresa's face as we walked around the side of her house and she came through the privacy fence into her backyard and saw Julie and John and everyone else that was there for her party. Jim was hiding inside as an extra surprise once her initial shock was over.

After Theresa took a few minutes greeting everyone, Jim came out of the house. It took a couple seconds for Theresa to register and believe who she was seeing walking out of her house but when she did she went running straight to him with a loud squeal and gave him a giant hug. She looked over his shoulder to me as she was hugging him and mouthed the words 'thank you' to me with tears of joy on her cheeks.

If I didn't think before my love for her could grow deeper, I realized in that moment it most certainly could. Even though I knew before this party that someday I wanted to marry her, seeing her happiness and the fun she was having at her surprise party convinced me that I wanted to spend the rest of my days on Earth making her happy.

After the party, when we had a few moments of alone time, I announced to Theresa an additional surprise I had arranged for her. I had booked a one-week cruise in the Caribbean for us in March of the following year.

Theresa was excited by the thought of going on a cruise together but as the initial excitement waned in the following days it reignited some of the fears and anxieties she had discussed with me upon her return from Myrtle Beach ... the same fears and anxieties that ended other past relationships she had after her divorce. Although she had experienced these feelings when we were in Myrtle Beach in response to me telling her I love her, the scheduling of the cruise as a birthday present brought a new element into the equation. With the cruise being six months away, it introduced the concept of long-term planning of our future together. Up to this point we were living day to day. Now a long-term element had entered the picture. Theresa decided it was time to address her fears and anxieties head on. Thankfully, however, she continued to express her love to me.

September 15 – 2:17 a.m. text to Theresa

As I write this, I am sure you are asleep by now. I know that we don't spend nights apart much these days but when we do I miss you so much. I was laying in bed and couldn't fall asleep because thoughts of holding you in my arms and kissing your soft lips are filling all of my thoughts. So, I thought I would send you a note to let you know I am thinking of you.

We have said many times that it feels as though we have known each other for a long time and that we are old souls but it feels like it is so much more than that ... like we are soulmates ... like our souls are one and the same. I will be honest, when I was first divorced my biggest fear was never loving anyone again. Even though I have been divorced for some time now, I would have to admit that has always been something I wondered about. But because of you I no longer have that fear or wonder if that is a possibility.

In fact, knowing how our love feels, I wonder if I have ever actually loved before. When we touch, I feel like I can fly. When we kiss, I know true happiness. When I look into your eyes, I see my soul reflecting back at me. Most people have to sleep to have dreams but since meeting you I have been living a dream.

Before meeting you, I had thoughts and ideas of what I thought the perfect woman for me would be like. And now having met you I realize my thoughts of my perfect mate were wrong because you are so much more than anything I knew existed. God has truly blessed me.

There is one bad thing when we spend time together and that is there is always a time when we must part ways. I want to spend as much time with you as possible. I am sooooo looking forward to the next time we are together. I should be going to try to get some sleep. Sweet dreams.

I love you!!!

PD

September 15, 2010 – 7:53 a.m. text to me

Good Morning,

I must tell you I read your note at about 3:30 am (puppies had a rough night). It was a very pleasant surprise when I got up and my phone was flashing. I slept very well when I went back to bed ... thanks to your sweet thoughts.

I wish I could express my thoughts as well as you do. What you wrote is exactly how I feel also. Even though summer is winding down and fall is approaching, I wake up each morning feeling like it is a spring day when everything feels so new and fresh. I so look forward to being able to spend time with you. I love the way it feels just to hold your hand when we are walking, not to mention when you hold me in your arms! Spending time with you just seems so natural.

I am starting to feel a peace within me I am not sure I have ever felt before.

I love you!!!

T

September 15, 2010 – 8:32 a.m. text to Theresa

Theresa, it is my wish to share many new experiences with you. Simple things, extravagant things, fun things, serious things, everything. Things you have done but I haven't, things I have done and you haven't and things neither of us have done and we experience them together for the first time.

I look ahead with the idea of us experiencing life together ... the joys, the sorrows, the laughter, the sadness, the silliness, the seriousness. I envision a time when we join our families and become one. I can envision a time when we develop our own family traditions, some taken from your family, some from mine and some that we develop together. I want us to help each other grow but most importantly grow together as "us".

Your Madly in Love Boyfriend

PD

Theresa and I also made another decision during these early months of our relationship that would eventually lead to fundamental changes in our lives and relationship. Theresa is a cradle Catholic (her parents are Catholic and brought her up Catholic). She had been baptized Catholic and received First Communion. She had not, however, received the Sacrament of Confirmation. Theresa brought her own children up in the Catholic faith. Each of them was baptized Catholic and received First Communion. The older three were also Confirmed. Each of her children attended Catholic school up to a certain point. When they lived in Virginia Beach Theresa assisted with fundraisers at *Star of the Sea Catholic School* and worked in their afterschool child care. Later, when they moved to Indiana, the older three children were altar servers at *St. Bartholomew Catholic Church*.

As her children were approaching their late teens, they began protesting regular mass attendance and, working three jobs while going to school, it became harder and harder for Theresa to find the energy to fight the children's protestations and find the time to attend mass on a consistent basis without missing much needed sleep. Eventually, she and the children stopped attending mass on a regular basis.

When it became apparent that we were both looking at our relationship long term Theresa asked me if I would be interested in attending mass with her at *St. Bartholomew*. With my faith journey slowly moving toward a desire for a closer relationship with God, I found her invitation appealing but, I will have to admit, I was somewhat intimidated with the prospect of attending a Catholic church.

I had always considered the Catholic faith to be the cornerstone of Christianity but didn't understand the mass and sacraments of the Church and, quite frankly, was uncertain as to whether I would feel as though I belonged. One thing I believed I had learned from my past, however, was that God was leading me somewhere and that His absence in my marriage with Tina was a mistake I didn't want to make again. So, when Theresa asked me to attend mass with her, I apprehensively agreed.

We attended sporadically at first and found the priest (Father Steve), Deacon (Deacon Mark) and staff went out of their way to be welcoming. I slowly began to build a rapport with them. I also discovered that with God as the cornerstone of the relationship Theresa and I were forming we were falling deeper in love with each other, fostered by the stronger trust and understanding of each other we were developing through our faith. This invitation for God to be at the center of our relationship would later prove to be a blessing neither of us could have expected as our relationship progressed.

April 18, 2021

As I came into Chattanooga, and was preparing to change course by taking *I-75* south toward Atlanta my app warned that there were additional construction zones ahead which would cause considerable delays in my journey. We all are aware of those familiar road signs warning of construction ahead. The construction is an inconvenience for those travelling on the roadways, causing unwanted delays.

We have become accustomed in our society to having what we want, when we want it, to be able to move about freely and to have instant gratification. When those expectations are met with unforeseen roadblocks, we can become frustrated, not wanting what we deem to be unwarranted obstacles being put in our way. In the end, however, those irritating construction projects are undertaken for our benefit to allow for a better journey when they are completed.

Ironically, as I reflected on those early days of my relationship with Theresa, I was reminded of our budding relationship being filled with our own construction projects. Theresa and I were both in need of some "construction" of our own. Theresa had her past she had to confront to make our journey together smoother as our relationship developed. I too was in need of construction. My relationship with God needed development and would be a source of strength that I would be able to lean upon during difficult times in the years to come. It was also necessary for me to have a better understanding and compassion for where Theresa had been in her past to allow me to be strong for her and a source of comfort during her difficult days.

Chapter 6: Traditions

And progressed in Judaism beyond many of my contemporaries among my race, since I was even more a zealot for my ancestral traditions.

Galatians 1:14

April 18, 2021

In due time, my journey was able to pass through the construction in Chattanooga but only after an exercise of considerable patience and an acceptance that the delay was a necessary impediment to the possibility of finding Theresa again. After what was probably an hour in stop and go traffic, I was able to merge onto *I-75*. After leaving the metropolitan area of Chattanooga, the traffic thinned as I continued toward Atlanta.

With a clearer road ahead, I was able to return to thoughts of my life with Theresa. My thoughts went back to the first fall and holiday season we shared together and how we began intermixing traditions within our respective families and building new traditions unique to us. Traditions, that if all went well, might become part of our identity and help define who we were to become as a couple. It also might help bringing our two families together as one.

October, 2010

As October arrived, Theresa's excitement for "her season" amplified. She had been telling me since we first met about the annual Halloween party she hosted each year. Her friends, who were quickly becoming my friends, began asking us about when this year's party would occur. We scheduled the party for October 30.

I quickly learned Theresa took her season even more serious than I anticipated. As soon as October 1st arrived she insisted we begin decorating for Halloween. I questioned why it was necessary to begin decorating so early. We had thirty days, after all, to decorate for the party. I knew she had a lot of Halloween decorations, having seen the room in her house where they were stored, but as we starting pulling them out of the storage room, I was amazed by how many decorations were actually in there.

It took a full day to just pull them all out of the storage room. There was the coffin that required both of us to awkwardly carry it as we maneuvered it through some very difficult angles and up a set of stairs from the basement. But the coffin was just one of the many Halloween props she had acquired over the years. What I was discovering over those first few weeks of October was this woman I loved with all my heart was a freak when it came to Halloween. She was truly obsessed with it.

Theresa explained she bought a large prop each year for Halloween. Over the years she developed theme rooms for the decorations (such as a psychic room, a surgery room, a clown room and even a scary baby room as examples).

This particular year we added a graveyard outside and borrowed a hearse to park in the yard.

Theresa's house had become legendary in the neighborhood for the kids and their parents during trick or treating. It was the house in the neighborhood known for giving out good treats but many of the kids were reluctant to knock on the door because of the scary decorations. The parents, however, always encouraged the kids to come to the door because they were interested in seeing the decorations themselves.

True to her word, decorating did in fact take up the whole month of October. Theresa proved to be an artist when it came to Halloween decorating. We would decorate and place props where she thought they should go only to change the setup many times until it was what she considered perfect. One would think decorating would be made easier in succeeding years by referring to the previous year's setup but Theresa made it a point to have a 'fresh' look each year to avoid two years being identical. We had a blast decorating and it became something we looked forward to each day when we came home from work.

Another staple I discovered Theresa had in her October itinerary was "Halloweening." Although not an official word in the *Merriam-Webster Dictionary*, "Halloweening" in Theresaism is the act of visiting the seasonal haunted house attractions that pop-up during the month throughout central Indiana. She had her usual attractions. *Nightmare on Edgewood Haunted House. Hanna Haunted Acres. Fear Fair. The Haunting.* She was also always looking for others to add to the list. Our weekend nights in October were filled with Halloweening at these various attractions, joining many of our friends who would participate in the festivities with us.

Theresa's parties were legendary. They always had a theme. She decided the theme of our first party together would be "celebrities". Theresa and I decided to dress up as Sonny and Cher, going full 70's retro. The party was well attended and was a smashing success. There were representations of celebrities of all forms. The entire Kardashian family made an appearance. The Mario Brothers were present. Colonel Sanders was there. Mr. Clean made an appearance. Darth Vader brought the dark side of the force to the party. Everywhere you looked it was clear everyone had done their best to come in costume and it was entertaining to see the ingenuity that had gone into their preparations for attending the party.

The highlight of the evening for me was karaoke. I had never participated in karaoke previously, even during the party in Myrtle Beach, understanding I was not blessed with any singing talent. But with the appropriate amount of liquid courage and the encouragement from the woman of my dreams, Theresa and I sang a duet together. Appropriate for the costumes we were wearing but made even more so because of who I was singing it with, it was a special time I will never forget as we faced each other, stared into each other's eyes and sang "I got you to hold my hand. I got you to understand. I got you to walk with me. I got you to talk with me. I got you to kiss goodnight. I got you to hold me tight. I got you, I won't let go. I got you to love me so. I got you babe." From that point forward Theresa and I have always used "Babe" or "Baby" as a pet name for each other.

The first "vacation" we would take together, other than Myrtle Beach, also occurred that October. I say "vacation" loosely in this instance because it was anything but a vacation for Theresa. We were traveling to her childhood home in Virginia Beach to visit her dad, Jim, and her sister Nancy. It had been a while since Theresa had gone "home" and if we didn't go in October it would be a while longer with all the holidays and work commitments in the coming months.

Theresa always missed her dad and sister dearly but returning home caused her a lot of mixed emotions because of the difficult memories it brought back of her marriage. Theresa expressed to me how happy she was to have me coming with her to divert her thoughts away from those bad memories. I, on the other hand, had never been to the East Coast north of Myrtle Beach and looked forward to seeing this part of the country. I also looked forward to spending more time with Jim and meeting Nancy for the first time.

We would be staying at Jim's house. He had a large house with six bedrooms so he had more than enough room to host us. We unpacked our car upon arrival at Jim's house and started taking our suitcases inside. I followed Theresa with our suitcases down a hallway into a bedroom. I had assumed Theresa and I would be sleeping together in the same room, just as we did at our homes, so I followed her into the bedroom. Before I could put my suitcase down, she shook her finger at me with a coy smile. I asked her why she was doing that and she said we were under her dad's roof and not married so out of respect for him I would be sleeping in the bedroom across the hall. I respected Theresa unconditionally but the thoughtfulness she exhibited for her father's feelings in that moment made that respect grow exponentially.

Nancy was very welcoming during our visit and it was a pleasure to meet her. I particularly enjoyed getting to know Jim better. I had spent some time with him in Myrtle Beach but often it was in the accompaniment of other members of the family making it hard to have candid conversations with him there. In his home, however, there were many more opportunities for those candid conversations, especially when Theresa and Nancy would be off somewhere having their "sister time".

A few things I quickly learned about Jim was that he had a rigid television schedule in the evening. He would religiously watch *Judge Judy* followed by *Blue Bloods*. Every evening. Something else I learned from those candid conversations was he loved Theresa's mother, Elizabeth ("Beth"), beyond words. He spoke of her often, even though she had passed away eleven years earlier.

He also loved his girls with all his heart and would do anything for them. He told me of countless memories of the good times he had with the girls as they were growing up. I heard a story of a family camping trip where he asked a very young Theresa to climb on top of the camper to brush the locusts off the top (to know Theresa is to know her biggest fear in life is bugs so that had to be a sight to behold).

He told me of taking the girls to get ice cream and always ordering small scoops for the five older sisters while ordering a large scoop for Theresa. He would then tell Theresa he had to "clean it up" when her ice cream showed signs of melting. Theresa thought she was extra special because she got a large scoop, not realizing Jim was eating most of her ice cream.

He told me of a time when he and Beth went out for the evening and told Theresa she was in charge of the older five girls (the oldest being some fifteen years her senior). Upon Jim and Beth's departure Theresa immediately announced it was bed time and instructed her sisters they had to go to bed. The sisters were in no way amused by Theresa's authoritative form of rule.

He told me of an occasion when a bad thunderstorm was approaching their home and tornado warnings sounded. He and Beth sat a chair in the kitchen and instructed a very young Theresa to sit in it and to not move. He, Beth and Theresa's five sisters exited the kitchen leaving Theresa there alone. Eventually they came back and took Theresa with them to the basement. Jim explained that he didn't realize Theresa had always assumed the family had intentionally left her in the kitchen to face the tornado by herself. When she confronted him and Beth about this in her teens it was only then that Theresa discovered she was instructed to sit in the chair while her mom, dad and the older sisters went outside to find the family dog before going to the basement.

He told me of the time when Theresa was working at *Hardees* when she was a teenager. She asked before work one day if she could go out with her friends after her night shift ended. He told her no and she begrudgingly complied with his order. The next time she worked night shift, however, she went out with her friends after work without asking for permission first. When she arrived home late Jim was up waiting for her. When Jim asked her why she had gone out with her friends, Theresa replied she wasn't told she couldn't (figuring if she didn't ask, Jim couldn't say no). Jim assured me that was Theresa's last shift working at *Hardees*.

While we were visiting Jim a problem developed. A leak under his kitchen sink developed. Since my divorce I had been expanding my handyman skills so I told Jim I would be able to fix the leak easily. This was my opportunity, so I thought, to impress Jim with my abilities and be a hero by saving him the expense of having to hire a plumber to come in to fix the leak.

Jim reluctantly agreed upon my repeated assurances I knew what I was doing and could fix the leak. He gave me his debit card and off I went to *Lowes* to buy the necessary supplies that would be needed. About half a day later I found myself pulling myself out from underneath Jim's kitchen sink, walking into his living room with my tail between my legs and awkwardly announcing my failure in fixing the leak and the need for Jim to hire a plumber … as soon as possible because the leak had worsened while I was working on it. If Jim was upset, he did a good job of hiding it as he laughed about my exploits, which would forevermore be an ongoing joke between us.

November, 2010

October came and went all too quick. With the arrival of November thoughts shifted to taking all of the Halloween decorations down to begin preparing for Thanksgiving. Just as setting up the decorations was no small feat, taking them down was equally as challenging because we were on a tighter schedule. We had volunteered to host Thanksgiving this year for both of our families as well as a few friends, meaning we would be hosting about thirty people at Theresa's house. Not only would the Halloween decorations need to be stored away for the year but the house would need a thorough cleaning. With Thanksgiving being on November 26 we had less than four weeks to complete these tasks.

One thing I didn't calculate into this short turnaround was *Pie Weekend*. Early in November Theresa announced to me the weekend of November 14-15 would be *Pie Weekend*. "What exactly is *Pie Weekend*", I asked. Theresa explained each year she selected a weekend in November before Thanksgiving to bake pumpkin pies for friends and family and deliver them as a show of love and thanks for them being in her life. She explained that because we would also be baking pies for my family and friends, this year's production would be on a much grander scale than she had ever done before.

What a wonderful idea, I thought. Why had I never thought of such a thoughtful and kind expression of gratitude. Why? I knew why. Because I wasn't Theresa. Only Theresa would be so caring and thoughtful to take the time out of her busy schedule to spend an entire weekend baking pumpkin pies for family and friends. One, two, three … even five pumpkin pies maybe. But I'm talking forty-five pies.

I looked at her when she gave me the final tally of pies we would be baking and asked, "Are you serious?" She looked at me with that beautiful mischievous smile, causing my heart to melt, letting me know that she was indeed serious. She replied, "Why do you think we are doing it on a weekend I have the whole weekend off. I wouldn't want you being left to do this by yourself. I want people to be able to eat them without getting sick", giving me a wink.

On the evening of November 13, we visited *Kroger* to purchase the ingredients that would be necessary to bake forty-five pumpkin pies. Thankfully, our baking was two weekends before Thanksgiving because we depleted *Kroger's* stock of pumpkin pie mix and pie shells. I would have hated to think we depleted the stock the weekend before Thanksgiving.

It was late by the time we returned home from *Kroger* and placed all of our supplies in an orderly fashion on the counter and in the refrigerator. Theresa suggested we go to bed early warning the following two days would be long days of baking. I found myself having trouble falling asleep when we laid down for the evening with my excitement for the day to come running through my mind. I would have never imagined I would be excited about baking but the prospect of baking all day with Theresa for so many of our family and friends was a new experience I anticipated would be enjoyable.

The next morning arrived like any other Saturday morning with me waking up before Theresa and eating breakfast. Soon enough, Theresa awoke and had her morning *Lipton* tea mixed with *Kroger* French vanilla coffee cream, *Ritz* crackers and cream cheese (her weekend morning ritual). I was eager to start our day of baking but Theresa seemed to be in no particular hurry for our task to begin and she assured me before the end of the day I would appreciate the relaxing start to the day.

Within the family I had learned that Theresa's cooking skills were, at times, the subject of some loving jokes, having had more than one holiday turkey come out of the oven surrounded by smoke or charred black or dropped on the floor. The saying in the family when Theresa was cooking was you knew dinner was ready when the fire alarm went off. I have to say, however, there were certain entrees even a master chef at *Crown Shy* in New York City couldn't match. Her spaghetti was legendary. Her meatloaf was loved by all who tried it. When she cooked biscuits and gravy all who were invited to breakfast were sure to come.

I quickly discovered her limited but refined repertoire in the kitchen also extended to baking pumpkin pies. Like the great maestro Carlos Kleiber conducting one of his famous concerts, Theresa was at her best in the kitchen on *Pie Weekend*. She set up two mixing stations, a pouring station (pouring the mix into the pie crust), and cooling stations with cooling racks. She assigned us each specific duties (I was not permitted near the mixing stations as she deemed that task way too important for the quality of the finished product to assign to a rookie such as myself). I did volunteer, however, to be the official "taster" of the mix before it was poured into the pie crust and I must say I excelled in that position.

True to her word it became obvious by mid-afternoon that Theresa didn't exaggerate her estimation that our pie baking operation would be a two-day affair. Although Theresa had designed an efficient production line that allowed for us to have four pies baking in the oven at all times, there was not enough time in one day to bake all forty-five pies. That was fine by me because it meant Theresa and I would again spend Sunday together side by side in the kitchen. I had come to realize that any day with Theresa by my side was a great day, and it was even better when we were working together to bring a smile to others' faces.

Nevertheless, I was relieved on Sunday afternoon when we pulled the last pie out of the oven. The whole pie baking event had been a success. Seeing the care and compassion in her heart during this weekend caused my love for her to grow deeper. Although the process was long and tiresome, Theresa's undertaking of this act of kindness knowing what it would entail was a perfect example of who Theresa is and the kind of love she has for those in her life. That love and kindness is the core of Theresa.

After *Pie Weekend* our attention quickly returned to thoughts of hosting Thanksgiving dinner together. The immediate concern was how we would seat thirty people for dinner. There wasn't sufficient seating or table space in her dining room for thirty people. Of course, with Thanksgiving being on November 26, sitting outdoors in Indiana wouldn't be an option. We would have no other option but to rent some tables and chairs, clear out her living room and set up a second dining room in that area.

The next order of business after determining how we would accommodate so many people was planning a menu and confirming who would be responsible for preparing what dishes. If we thought seating thirty people would be difficult, establishing the menu and the responsibility for preparing it proved to be more challenging. We discovered that each side of our families were accustomed to having certain dishes prepared in particular ways the other side didn't customarily prepare them and there were pre-established expectations of who would prepare each dish.

Theresa's children loved how she baked the turkey and how Scott prepared the dressing but Rae and her family loved my mom's preparation of the turkey. Mom would also customarily cook a ham while Theresa did not. Theresa's family loved her deviled eggs and my family loved Rae's. Of course, no one would be baking pumpkin pies as Theresa and I had that covered and, if I can say so myself, they were quite delicious. What we eventually decided was that because of the number of people who would be attending, everyone would maintain their traditional roles for preparing the dinner and we would sort it out in the future. This proved to be an effective strategy in that it allowed all of us to have our traditional dinners but to also experiment with the additional dishes from the other family.

Bringing our two families together for Thanksgiving, more than anything, taught us our families were more similar than not in our holiday traditions. We cooked similar meals, albeit the preparation of those meals was a bit different between families with Theresa's being more of an East Coast variation and my family's being from our Midwest upbringing. But we took special pride in everyone contributing to the meal preparation. Our families enjoyed getting to know each other better. Of course, there were several of us who watched some football on television and a few who took carb overload induced naps. Our families seemed to enjoy each other's company and comingled with each other with ease.

Several of us played cards after our meal. My family taught Theresa's how to play euchre – which is apparently more of a Midwest game. Theresa's family taught my family how to play canasta – which we surmised was more of an East Coast game. We heard how Theresa's Nanna was particularly adept at gaining unfair advantages while playing canasta ... to use a more politically correct terminology than how it was described to us. We also learned that both of our families were particularly skilled in consuming more food than they probably should, leaving several of our loved ones in self-induced misery.

December, 2010

As much as Theresa enjoys decorating for Halloween, I equally enjoy decorating for Christmas. It's not that Theresa doesn't enjoy decorating for Christmas but definitely not with the same gusto as she does for Halloween.

As soon as Thanksgiving was behind us our thoughts turned to setting up our Christmas decorations. We had decided during our Thanksgiving dinner that Rae would host dinner on Christmas Day and Theresa and I would host a Christmas Eve party at her house. We wanted Theresa's house to reflect the festive atmosphere of the holiday for the Christmas Eve party we would be hosting. The decorating didn't take quite as long as it did for Halloween but it was time consuming.

Theresa had previously been a civilian member of the *Columbus Firemen's Cheer Fund. Cheer Fund* was a local organization run by the *Columbus Firefighter's* that raised money and sought donations to provide Christmas gifts for local children and Christmas food baskets for their families. *Cheer Fund* conducts fundraisers throughout the year to allow them to meet these goals. It is a monumental task undertaken each year by the firefighters. One of those many charitable activities undertaken by public servants that too often don't receive the recognition it deserves. Knowing Theresa's kind heart, it was no surprise to me she was involved in this organization.

In recent years, however, due to her busy schedule, she had not been able to be as involved in the organizational aspect of *Cheer Fund* as she once was. Nevertheless, she took every opportunity she could to assist them when needed.

My first experience with *Cheer Fund* was on December 4, 2010 – "delivery day." Hundreds of people throughout the community lined up in their cars before sunrise for the opportunity to deliver *Cheer Fund* presents and baskets throughout the community. The effort and organization of the *Cheer Fund Board* and the participation of the community to provide a better Christmas for thousands of youth was unlike anything I had ever experienced. We spent the entire morning of December 4 delivering presents with our friends George, John and Kerry.

By the end of the morning, we all had received a greater gift than any of the presents we had delivered knowing that we played a small part in helping ensure Christmas was just a little bit better for so many children. After our deliveries were completed, we met George, John and Kerry at *Bob Evans* for a well-deserved breakfast reveling in each other's company.

Not to be outdone by *Pie Weekend*, Theresa announced the following weekend would be *Cookie Weekend*. *Cookie Weekend* would entail us baking a variety of cookies for the same friends and family that received our pumpkin pies. The goal was to provide a platter of assorted home-baked Christmas cookies for our family and friends. Of course, there would be the staples of chocolate chip, sugar and peanut butter cookies. But Theresa was also one to try novelty cookies. In all, I would guess we baked well over a thousand cookies for delivery, and of course it would be necessary to keep several for ourselves.

Just as she was with the pumpkin pies, Theresa was a magician in the kitchen baking cookies with several different stations set up to increase efficiency. I, once again, took on the title of official taster and found again I excelled in that position. It became a game between Theresa and me for me to try to sneak tastes of the batter without her knowing. She pretended to get mad at me for doing so but secretly I think she got a laugh out of all the ingenious ways I came up with to sneak tastes "without her knowing".

Theresa's heart was on full display during the holidays. Of course, there was *Cheer Fund* delivery and *Cookie Weekend*. She also insisted we spend a day volunteering at the food pantry during December. Likewise, a day serving at a hot meal site in December was scheduled. Not that volunteering at these locations didn't occur at other times during the year but she found doing so in December to be particularly important. She picked two names off the giving tree at church. We made sure the children whose names we picked received presents in excess of what we gave our own children. She also organized a caroling group to go sing at local nursing homes.

Explaining her reasoning for her emphasis on volunteering Theresa quoted to me Wendell Berry's words that we have to be able to imagine lives that are not ours to be able to allow us to not only understand what others need but to also do whatever we can to assure they have it. I was learning Berry's words were not just a motto for Theresa but rather a way of life and that was never more apparent than during Thanksgiving and Christmas.

Theresa, always one to come up with ways to make a party lively, as I discovered during the Halloween party, asked me if I thought it would be okay for her to put together some Christmas games for us to play at our Christmas Eve party. I thought that would be a wonderful idea and her wheels started turning. After researching options online, she settled on four games, each which would provide a special prize to the winner.

The first contest was "The Christmas Cookie Cook-Off". Simple enough. Each person attending the party was invited to bake their own unique cookie and bring two dozen of them to the party. A set of three "neutral" judges would determine the best tasting cookie. The winner would win a special traveling trophy in the form of a silver spatula engraved with "Cookie Cook-Off Champion" that they could proudly display in their home. The second game was an ugly Christmas sweater competition with the winner receiving a gift certificate to a restaurant. The third game was what we called the cellophane ball game in which candy, small presents, and gift cards were wrapped in cellophane creating a ball about as large as a beach ball. The object was to try to unwrap as much of the ball (and presents) as possible before the person to your left rolls doubles with dice, at which point the ball is passed to that person. The game became very aggressive as the ball was being unwrapped as quickly as possible. The fourth game was the typical "Dirty Santa" present exchange. I have to say my family had never played Christmas games at our Christmas gatherings in the past and the addition of these games brought a whole new excitement to Christmas, all courtesy of my beautiful Theresa.

My Birthday

My birthday is close to Independence Day which historically throughout my life has resulted in its celebration being lost in July 4th celebrations. I always found my birthday being close to July 4th was neat because there are some good celebrations that occur during that time … cookouts, parades, pool parties, fireworks just to name a few.

I guess at some point I must have mentioned to Theresa, however, that most of my memories of my birthday were more of July 4th celebrations than celebrations of my actual birthday. On December 26 she woke me up early in the morning and told me to get ready and to pack a suitcase for four days. I protested because it was a Sunday and I had things on my schedule at work for the next several days and couldn't just go away on the spur of the moment.

Theresa said she had it all covered and for me not to worry about it (not knowing she had been secretly scheming with my office to make sure my schedule was clear … not withstanding what they put on my schedule to throw me off). I asked her what we were doing. She replied it was my "X" birthday present. "What is an X birthday?", I replied. She indicated I would be receiving X birthdays for now on with the date and present being a surprise each year. "And why will I be having an X birthday?" I asked. "Because" she answered "your real birthday is overshadowed by July 4th so you need a day that is all about you."

I learned later in the morning Theresa had booked us four nights in Chicago which would be highlighted by a *Bulls / Bucks* game the final night (knowing I had been a long time *Bulls* fanatic even after Michael Jordan's departure from the team). The four days in Chicago were a perfect X birthday surprise topped off by a *Bulls* victory. I have to admit I enjoyed the idea of a X birthday immensely.

April 18, 2021

As my journey continued, I came into the metropolitan area of Atlanta. I had traveled through Atlanta on many occasions before on my way to vacations in Florida. I had even spent a week in Atlanta back in 1987 when the *IU* football team played *Tennessee* in the *Peach Bowl*. But it had been quite some time since I was last in downtown Atlanta so I elected to take *I-75* straight through rather than take the bypass.

As I entered downtown, I was amazed by how much the skyline had grown. Its enormity was much more spectacular than any of the previous times I had been there. It was beautiful and nothing like I expected. Sure, the traffic created some difficulties in the downtown area but the effort was well worth the experience.

I couldn't help but reflect on the correlation between the unexpected beauty of the skyline to the unexpected beauty I found in my relationship with Theresa. Our relationship, our love, the way our souls had connected, everything about "us" proved to have an enormity all its own amplified by the "traditions" we were creating during the holidays we celebrated together. Halloween, Thanksgiving, Christmas and my X birthday were beyond my wildest imagination. Never before had I experienced a more meaningful "holiday season". As much as I knew I loved Theresa before, that love grew deeper and deeper as we continued to form that special bond that was "us".

Life could not have been any better. But creeping in the back of my mind was the thought of the time in my relationship with Tina when I felt life couldn't get any better only to have it all taken away from me in an instant. Would my relationship with Theresa produce a similar result? I couldn't imagine it would but if I had learned anything in life, it was that sometimes we don't have control of where life takes us.

Chapter 7: Confronting the Past

There is no fear in love, but perfect love drives out fear
because fear has to do with punishment, and so
one who fears is not yet perfect in love.

1 John 4:18

April 18, 2021

It seemed as though my journey had already brought me a long way after reaching the other side of Atlanta. Even so, according to the *Waze* app it was still almost five hours and three hundred and twenty miles before I would reach Jekyll Island, under ideal circumstances. I was soon to learn, however, that I would not be encountering ideal circumstances as I came to a major construction project just south of Atlanta. *I-75* had been transformed into the longest parking lot I had ever seen. I was anxious to begin my search for Theresa but as fate would have it my journey was turning into an ongoing practice in patience.

Just like my drive to Jekyll Island, after spending the holidays together I was anxious for our relationship to move forward. Much to my chagrin, I was soon to learn my desire for our relationship to move forward would also require patience.

Sometimes there are things in life we can't avoid or rush, just like never ending construction projects. Attempts to take our own detours will only make matters worse. With the coming of the new year our relationship ushered in the apex of one of those projects that had been in the works for several months, if not years.

January 1, 2011

The arrival of a new year is a time when we reflect on the year that has just come to an end and the dreams, goals and possibilities of the year ahead. As Theresa and I entered 2011, reflecting on those first seven months of our relationship in 2010 felt as though our love for each other had brought us so far and had already given us so many wonderful memories. We had shared a magical summer getting to know each other, a fall filled with countless activities and a holiday season merging our families into one. Even in this short amount of time our love had grown to be deeper than anything I had ever experienced.

Theresa and I clicked from the moment we first started corresponding through social media and our connection only grew stronger after we met in person. Our souls were united as if they had always been joined as one. We shared similar beliefs about the importance of God in our life, dedication to family, morals, interests, political views, dislikes and what brought us joy. We had also begun establishing those special traditions for the holiday seasons that draw families closer together. Most importantly, we enjoyed each other's company and were committed to the happiness of each other. Theresa had quickly become my best friend and was always eager to promote my best interests and I believe I did likewise for her. I always wanted to be in her company and when I was unable to be with her, she was all I thought about.

Shortly after I told Theresa on her birthday that I had planned a cruise for us in March, she began seeing a counselor to address the fears and anxieties she had from her previous marriage. She saw her counselor on a consistent basis, usually about once a week, as her schedule permitted. These counseling sessions proved to be challenging for her. They required her to relive the most difficult times of her previous marriage, bringing back memories that she had tried to suppress for over a decade.

She and I began having some strained moments in our relationship following her counseling sessions as she processed what was covered during the session. It also didn't help that I was struggling understanding the emotions the counseling was causing her to feel and failed to properly respond to those emotions. What I learned is that there are no detours or shortcuts in sorting through our thoughts, fears and anxieties.

Even though I tried my best to exercise patience, the further she went in counseling, the more it appeared she was struggling with her past. Those struggles manifested themselves in our relationship, mostly because of my failures to understand what was occurring. At times it felt as though the counseling was causing more harm to our relationship than helping. Unbeknownst to me, as Theresa began to trust her counselor and the process of therapy, she started opening up to him addressing the deepest parts of her fear and anxiety. Issues she had not allowed herself to process since her previous marriage ended. It was an emotional process for her and it changed our relationship forever.

January 3, 2011 – 7:11 p.m. text to me

Hello Baby,

I thought this may be a good way for me to talk to you about some of the things running through my head. Don't panic everything is ok! We are ok!!!

We spent a good bit of the counseling session today talking about last week and the reactions you and I had to that session. The counselor asks very direct questions and sometimes I find answers to my own behaviors that I did not even realize.....so here goes.

I understand you want me to get this stuff out in the open. You want that so that I can move past my fears and anxiety. I want that same thing, but the reality of the situation is that talking to you about this stuff is excruciating. When the counselor and I discussed this, he asked what specifically would happen if I told you everything. I responded that I thought your opinion of me would change. I told him you had assured me that it would not...but in my head I can't believe if I have such little respect for the person I was, hating what I was and where I was ... I can't believe that you would be any different.

He pushed further and asked what would happen if your opinion changed. I told him that I would fear that we would not get back what we have now. He asked if I was protecting you from my past. I told him I am afraid you would no longer view me as a strong independent person. Continuing to look at this, I realize that my ex was not born evil ... everything is action/reaction. Meaning his action evoked a response from me that led him further and further in his actions. NO, I am not excusing his behavior, but if I take the easy way out and blame him solely, then I set myself up to have that happen again.

I fear that if you hear some of this stuff and subconsciously you lose some respect for me that with human nature you will push me on things, expecting me to cave. I know you think that sounds crazy and I know you are not that type of person but think about it. If someone lets you do something to them and you did not expect that they would let you get away with it, you will continue in that path. That does not make you a bad person, it is simply human nature.

I have such a distaste for confrontation (learned behavior) many times I will retreat rather than fight. Granted that is not all the time and not who I believe I am today. But I am afraid of myself. I know that you cannot even fathom what I am talking about.

I told him my analogy of the house and how it looks ok and stable from the outside, but is not so ok on the inside. His response was that certain people have access to your home. The mailman for example would have only access to the mailbox and maybe the front porch. Friends may be welcomed into the dining room and living room but their access is limited in the bedrooms.

You are requesting access to all the private areas in my home/head...the "closet". Unfortunately, there are things in the closet that I have not even looked at in years. I need time to sort through these things and take them out and deal with the shock of the emotion. Then at that time I hope I can start sharing them with you.

I asked if the ripples that occur after our sessions and my inability to put them away after a few days was normal or ok. He felt that if there were no ripples or emotions after our sessions, then we were not working hard enough. Sorting through the boxes and taking this stuff out week after week helps me get to the bottom of the closet and will hopefully allow me to share some of the stuff with you and eventually give all the boxes to Goodwill. I am anxious for that day! I hate feeling this way...

I love you and I love how I feel with you when I am not pressed to deal with this stuff, but then I hate the urge to run/escape when we discuss marriage and commitment. Not because that thought is not appealing ... it is!!!

I will conquer this stuff. Please be patient with me. Please don't see this as a reflection of you...

I hope this will answer some questions you may have. Someday I hope I will be able to answer any questions you want to ask. I hope this letter does not make you feel bad. That is not my intention. I am just trying to make sense of this.

I love you!!!

T

Theresa had told me from early in our relationship that there were issues from her previous marriage that she still needed to address, even fourteen years later. She even explained early on that those issues had caused her to be overly cautious. She had explained those issues had caused her problems in other relationships since her divorce, contributing to those relationships ending when she felt someone was getting too close to her.

Nevertheless, from what she told me about those other relationships, I felt that she and I shared something more than she had ever experienced before and was hopeful we would be able to work through those issues. We connected on all levels. I believed that we could conquer her fears and anxiety by working together.

But Theresa was not prepared to discuss those fears and anxieties with me or the history in her prior marriage from which they arose. How could I help her if she didn't discuss those issues with me? If she wouldn't discuss those issues with me, I couldn't help make her understand her past was not the person she is today and that she is so much stronger than she gives herself credit for. If she wouldn't discuss those issues with me, how could I make her understand that I loved her for who she is today, not who she was in her previous marriage.

Her refusal to discuss those issues with me made me feel as though she didn't trust me with her emotions. If she didn't trust me with her emotions, in my mind she didn't understand the depth of my love for her. If only she would discuss those issues with me, she would know from my reactions she had nothing to fear in our relationship and that she could trust me. In my impatience and failure to understand the process of her counseling, I was becoming frustrated not being able to help her.

I am sure my responses and frustrations exacerbated Theresa's fears and anxieties. I wanted to forge ahead in our relationship, thinking that if she would just share her thoughts with me everything would be better. I was, in a sense, wanting to take a detour around them because of impatience on my part. For the life of me I couldn't understand she had to address them on her own terms first before sharing them with me.

My impatience only worked to cause further issues in our relationship. Even though I knew she was trying to conquer her fears and anxieties through the counseling, I was becoming frustrated with the process. It seemed each session caused her to regress further rather than become more comfortable in our relationship. Things were about to take a more dire turn in our relationship.

January 24, 2011 – 12:54 p.m. text to me

PD

I first want to tell you I love you. I appreciate your patience with me and for trying to understand me. I am trying to make this as

134

uneventful for you as possible, but I realize that I am failing miserably.

This next statement, you will scold me about, but think about it before you do. There is a lot of crap under the surface and it is gut wrenching to discuss and I am finding it very difficult to discuss it with you. You don't need this in your life, and I would understand if you felt like you were not able or didn't want to deal with this, but please tell me now. With that said, I already know what your answer will be and you're very sweet! Just know there are options!

Driving to the counseling session today, I felt like I was standing on a cliff over an abyss of blackness and I was getting ready to jump. I was scared (to say the least), my heart was racing and I was sick to my stomach, but there was a part of me that wanted to jump. I wanted to take the chance and see what happened. I wanted to actually say the words to someone else to see if I spontaneously combusted ... guess what, I didn't. It hurt and I cried and felt like I could not breath. But I have finally said it to another living being.

We discussed time frames and the emotions. I told him that it is almost like being there again. I can feel my skin crawl and the fear, anger, disgust, when I think back to those events. Because I have never disclosed these events or dealt with them, they are fresh in my mind.

The other night, when we were holding each other, you took me to a place where my guard was down. I was not able to block the flood of emotions that are welled up inside. I have spent fourteen years running from these emotions/events. When I spoke that night, it was not to you to whom I spoke, it was to him. I was in a very different place momentarily. Please don't interpret that to mean that I think about him when you hold me, it just releases an emotional vulnerability in me.

I have kept my mind busy over the years to avoid dealing with my emotions. I am sorry that you have to see any of this. I am sorry that you feel like you are bringing these emotions back. Nothing about you reminds me of him. It is truly situational.

I feel bad that I am having trouble trying to see things from your perspective. I am not usually a selfish person, but I feel like I am in this situation on my own. I am so wrapped up in my crap I am not taking very good care of you and us. I apologize for that as well.

We talked about the idea that if I don't work through this that our relationship would suffer or possibly end, and the concept of me telling you and you walking away or me running because I feel embarrassed/or that you look at me differently. Then the third option is that you and I talk about these things and we work them out.

His concern is my hyper vigilance. My experience has been that even when things appear good, they can become very unstable in just the blink of an eye. So, I am very alert to subtle changes in mood, body language, anything. He is worried that I will read into your actions and create problems. I too am afraid of this. He suggests disclosing small bits of information and then slowly building a trust between us.

I can't help feel like you are getting a very raw deal with this. I feel like I have misled you, appeared to be emotionally very healthy and really I am just a fruitcake! I am sorry!

I love you

T

As Theresa advanced in her counseling, I noticed she seemed to be under a greater stress in all parts of her life but most notably in her interactions with me. She was not herself. Often times, her mind seemed to be pre-occupied. Her emotions were all over the place. She was not as attentive to "us" as she had been. Something was going on and I had a growing fear that she was starting to distance herself as she had done in prior relationships before ending them.

She started the email off by addressing me with PD. Since Halloween we had been calling each other Baby. Why did she start the email out with PD? I knew the fears and anxieties Theresa had from her prior marriage were something that had caused her difficulties in other relationships but I felt that somehow our love for each other was strong enough to withstand those difficulties. I knew in the past she would begin to distance herself from a relationship when it was feeling like it was requiring a deeper commitment.

But I knew, or I thought I knew, our souls were connected and we would be able to withstand any fears and anxieties that may arise. Here we were though, Theresa reverting back to calling me PD. She told me I didn't need her "crap" in my life, that I had options, that I got a raw deal, that she felt as though she had misled me and that she would understand if I didn't want to deal with it. It seemed as though she was rationalizing an exit plan and how to distance herself from me.

Our seven-day cruise to the Caribbean was quickly approaching. At the rate we were going I wasn't sure our relationship would last that long and, even if it did, whether she would be in a frame of mind that she would want to go. These emotions had been bottled up in her for over a decade. She had been in counseling for just over four months and it seemed her ability to deal with these issues had significantly deteriorated. As each successive day passed, I became more and more convinced Theresa was internally convincing herself to end our relationship before the cruise. Until ...

One evening around the beginning of February we were reclining on the couch in her living room watching television (most likely *Big Bang Theory* as we were known for binging on the show). Out of the blue, Theresa reached for the remote and turned off the television with an announcement that we need to talk. Uh oh, I thought, here it comes. She had had a counseling session earlier in the day and had seemed apprehensive the entire evening. I told her OK and she asked me not to say anything and to just listen to what she had to say. I agreed.

Theresa, to my complete surprise, then proceeded to give me a detailed narrative of the deepest secrets of her previous marriage she had been keeping bottled up in her mind for over a decade. I was shocked. Not by the details because by this time I had surmised most of what she had to tell me. Rather, I was shocked by the fact that she had finally opened up to me and was able to give me the details. I'm not a counselor but in my thoughts, this had to be a major breakthrough. It had to mean she was working through those emotions and doing her best to set up our relationship for

139

long term success. We both cried when she was finished, although probably for different reasons, or possibly similar reasons I suppose.

There was a remarkable change in our interactions in the days following this revelation. The emotions stirred up from Theresa's counseling over the past several months seemed to be evaporating just as an early morning fog gives way to a wonderful cloudless blue sky. The Theresa I had fallen in love with was re-emerging in all her beauty. If there was any doubt as to whether we had reached a breakthrough, the text I received from Theresa in mid-February left no room for doubt.

February 12, 2011 – 9:55 a.m. text to me

Baby,

Wow, I can't believe how fast the last nine months have passed and we are now more than a month into 2011! What a fantastic nine months it has been ... I bet you cannot guess why? You are smart and I am sure you have already guessed. So, I just thought I would let you know in writing just how much I love you and how thankful I am you are in my life!

Before we met, I just existed. I wasn't unhappy, I just lived. Nothing was very special, days turned to weeks and months to years. I looked forward to vacations with no real luster or excitement. The holidays came and went and I muddled through, all the while never knowing what it could be like with someone you love. Truly love!

The last nine months have been the most blissful, exciting, emotion-filled (good emotions) in my entire life. Yes, I have had some difficult times with my emotions during these nine months but that is because I refused to address those issues in my past.

Because of my love for you and my wish not to lose you, I was forced to finally look at those issues. I've probably not conquered those issues entirely, but after I told you about my past and understanding your response was genuine, I can see a light at the end of a dark tunnel knowing that my past will no longer have the grip on me that it once did.

I have woken up every day since the day I met you ... thinking about you. Excited to see, talk to or just think about you.

I admit at first I was skeptical about things between us, and there will probably be times when I still question things (but that is my past) it is not us or you. You have made a believer out of me!

I was surprised when you told me yesterday you were just a man, nothing special ... I adamantly disagree! You are so very special to me. I think you really are just who you are, you have just found someone who appreciates you for being you! You are so different from any man I have met, so much more thoughtful, caring, loving, interesting, sensual, respectful, even patient! I could go on and on.

I want you to know as 2011 moves on, that I think I am the luckiest person on this earth! I hope that my children and your children too, find someone in their lives who love them the way that we love each other. It is incredible to love, trust and be respected by the one you love. Just an incredible feeling. I hope none of them settle for less!

My wish for the remaining part of 2011 and beyond is to continue our relationship as strongly as we have this first nine months. I hope that nothing comes between us to change our feelings toward each other (I know I can hear you saying nothing can). I hope that I can somehow make you as happy as you make me every day.

I love you Baby!!!!!!!!!!!!

April 18, 2021

The construction traffic on *I-75* seemed to have appeared out of nowhere. Sitting in the traffic for approximately an hour and twenty minutes or more there appeared at times to be no end to the traffic jam. As time passed, I felt I was only driving deeper and deeper into the problem. I was beginning to think there had to be a better route to my destination. I began looking on my phone for possible routes that would provide a quicker detour but found nothing. Thinking I could find a better route on my own I even considered taking a few exits that looked promising only to find as I inched closer the exits were themselves parking lots that showed no signs of being better alternatives.

My journey taught me the only option was patience and, whether I liked it or not, it would prove to be the one sure way of reaching my final destination with the least disruption. Sure enough, with considerable patience the traffic jam seemed to end without notice. One second, I was at a dead stop and the next second it was as if the green flag was waved at the *Indianapolis 500* and the cars were accelerating as fast as possible. It was smooth sailing from there and the 'great Atlanta traffic jam of 2021' soon became a distant memory.

Tears of joy appeared again as I re-read Theresa's February 12th email. For several months our relationship journey felt as though it was stuck in its own traffic jam as we attempted to sort through past emotions that had been put away without being dealt with. Try as I might I repeatedly made suggestions on how to detour the issues.

Thankfully, because of her wish to give our relationship the best chance, Theresa knew the issues would require patience and a commitment to address them head on, regardless of how painful that might become. Much to my dismay, the detour and quick fix to the delay in our relationship was not going to work. Just as with the traffic jam, the further we traveled in the counseling, the deeper Theresa's fears and anxieties grew. But just when it seemed there would be no end, Theresa unexpectedly opened up to me causing that green flag to wave on our relationship. Finally, we were racing toward a deeper relationship than we had enjoyed previously.

What we both learned in the process is that true love does in fact drive out fear as John's Gospel tells us. More importantly, however, we discovered to be in love requires more than the good times. Its not just about the traditions, parties and holiday gatherings with family and friends.

Love is perfected in those times when a relationship is struggling. When it is easier to walk away then to work together to solve problems. A deeper love is the product of figuring out together how to navigate the difficult times in a relationship. Refusing to walk away when we are scared. Learning to be patient, especially when the relationship is not going in the direction we would have it go. Withstanding the trials and tribulations of the relationship with a hope and steadfast belief love will conquer all obstacles encountered.

I was soon to discover just how far and how fast our love would extend.

Chapter 8: A New Relationship

*Entreat me not to leave you, or to turn back from following
after you; For wherever you go, I will go; And wherever
you lodge, I will lodge; Your people shall be my people,
And your God, my God. Where you die, I will die, And
there will I be buried. The Lord do so to me, and more
also, if anything but death parts you and me.*

Ruth 1:16-17

April 18, 2021

Having finally broken through the obstacles in
Atlanta that were delaying the journey toward my
destination to Jekyll Island, the travel was quick and smooth.
I was making good time toward the next city on the map,
Macon, Georgia. The *Waze* app was telling me the
remaining portion of my journey should be relatively free of
any further delays. A welcomed thought with what seemed
to be the endless construction I had encountered on the
journey up to that point.

As I was cruising down *I-75* I couldn't help but think
how much this journey had resembled my life. As I reflected
on the similarities it struck me that I am not alone in that
respect. In life we often plan on a destination and a path to
get us to our destination. Experience teaches us, however, it
is not uncommon to hit roadblocks, traffic jams and detours
along the way, changing our course and sometimes requiring
us to accept that detours are necessary.

We often begin our adult life with a goal of where we want it to take us and a plan on how to get there. For example, in high school, as I approached graduation, I was certain I would one day marry my high school sweetheart, go to college, become a CPA, live in my hometown my entire life and have two children.

Just like my trip to Jekyll Island, however, fate would have different plans for my life or, as I prefer to see it, God had His own plan for my life. I would not marry my high school sweetheart. I would not become a CPA. I would not live in my hometown my entire life. But the change, God's plan, was better than I could have ever imagined myself.

Shortly after Theresa left me almost three weeks ago, my sister and I were having a conversation about life. More specifically, a conversation about my life. I mentioned to her that I had always felt like I lived a charmed life. Rae looked at me oddly and replied that she was surprised I felt that way because she had always thought I had a difficult life. I asked her why she felt that way. She rattled off a litany of reasons: When I was a child I was critically injured and almost died when I was run over by a semi-truck; I was not able to marry my high school sweetheart; I had to have a hip replacement when I was forty; My marriage to Tina had ended in a divorce; I've had multiple surgeries over the course of my adult life (I believe eight at last count); and, of course, Theresa left me.

I explained to Rae I had never focused on those things. They were just bumps in the road. Each of the reasons Rae listed were obviously difficult stretches in my life journey but they were not how I identified my life.

Rather, I viewed them, in many instances, as detours, changes of course or delays in my life journey. To me they all were in one way or another the broken road that led me straight into Theresa's loving arms. There were many other things I did identify my life with which caused me to believe my life was charmed. At the top of that list were my children and Theresa. But Theresa had left me. I had to find her again.

February 26, 2011

The time had finally arrived for the long-anticipated cruise to the Caribbean. The cruise that sent shock waves through Theresa when I announced it back in September of the previous year. The cruise had been the catalyst for Theresa's decision to seek counseling and the months of working through issues that had haunted her for way too many years. Although every day since she sent me her beautiful email in mid-February suggested we were moving further away from those difficult issues being a hindrance in our relationship, I wasn't sure how far or how fast she was prepared to allow our relationship to advance. One thing I did know, however, was we would find out during the cruise.

Our friends, John and Kerry, joined us on the cruise. We flew down to Miami the day before the cruise was to set sail. The cruise would be a seven-day adventure taking us to the Bahamas, St. Maarten, and Saint Thomas. I had been on cruises before and Theresa and I had been on a couple short vacations together prior to this cruise. Normally, I would be excited as the days before a vacation were ticking away. This vacation was different. I was nervous. Very nervous. I knew, in one way or another, this cruise would change the course of our relationship forever and I was uncomfortable not knowing in advance what direction our relationship would go once we arrived back in Miami at the end of the cruise.

Our overnight stay in Miami was relaxing and it gave us a little time to unwind before boarding the ship the following day. We had dinner with John and Kerry and then retired to our rooms for a good night's sleep. The following day we made our way over to the Port of Miami as soon as boarding commenced and initiated the boarding process onto the ship. Once we boarded, we found our cabins and shortly thereafter met John and Kerry on the Lido Deck where we treated ourselves to a round of tropical adult beverages to celebrate the beginning of our vacation.

Alcohol is not my normal beverage of choice but on this occasion I think I had two or three knowing I needed some liquid courage for what I was about to do. I had a very important telephone call to make before the ship left port (not knowing whether I would have cell service once leaving port). The problem I encountered was the call needed to be in private, outside of earshot of Theresa, John and Kerry. I didn't want them hearing who I was talking to or the topic of the conversation.

After a few drinks I announced I needed to visit the restroom. I'm not sure if they noticed but when I excused myself, I went in the opposite direction of the Lido Deck restrooms, intending rather to make a quick trip to our cabin to have privacy for my call.

Upon entering our cabin, I locked the door behind me and went out onto the balcony and shut the balcony door behind me to help create an additional layer of privacy. Pulling my cell phone out of my pocket I was about as nervous as I had ever been in my life. I opened my contact list. I scrolled through my friend list until I came to the correct contact number and pushed call on the number. I couldn't leave port without making this call first. My plans for the cruise wouldn't have the same meaning without first taking care of this detail.

I prayed there would be an answer on the other end. The phone rang, and then rang again, and then once more before finally, an answer. "Hello", I heard from the other end. "I thought you were on vacation, what are you doing calling me?" "Hello Jim", I responded. "We are on vacation. We boarded the ship an hour or so ago and are waiting to set sail. Theresa, John and Kerry are up on the Lido Deck for the pre-cruise festivities. I snuck away to come down to our cabin for some privacy to call you."

A short silence and then he responded, "Is everything OK?" "Everything is OK Jim", I responded. "Actually", I continued, "everything is more than OK. Everything is wonderful and that is the reason I'm calling you. I have fallen so deeply in love with your daughter. I think I knew from the moment we first met that she was the love of my life. Each day since then I have loved her more than the day before. She is my soulmate. With her by my side I feel like

I am becoming the man God meant for me to become. She is the best friend I have ever had, she comforts me, she encourages me, she makes me laugh, she makes me feel loved, she makes me feel needed, she is my cheerleader and she doesn't hesitate to tell me I'm wrong. Over these past ten months I've come to realize I don't want to live another day of my life without her in it and I want her to be my wife. I've known for a while I want to ask her to marry me but, as you know, she has been working through some things related to her previous marriage and I knew she needed to get through that before I asked her. I believe she is ready now and I would like to ask her to be my wife during this cruise. But I will only do that with your blessing so I wanted to call before leaving port to ask you for your blessing to marry your daughter."

I thought I was prepared for an array of responses. Jim and I had developed a good friendship since first meeting back in Myrtle Beach the previous June. I knew Jim was a jokester so I half expected him to tease me by jokingly declining his blessing. I also knew Jim's girls were the most important thing in his life so the other half of me thought he would take this moment seriously and ask me a series of questions to determine whether he was prepared to give his blessing. I have to admit, though, I was not prepared for the response he gave me.

He was silent for a moment and then I heard a distinct chuckle before he responded, "Well of course you have my blessing". And then another chuckle before continuing, "good luck and make sure to let me know what her answer is as soon as you find out".

Jim knew Theresa's history in her previous marriage as well as the relationships she had after her marriage so I am sure he was questioning in his mind whether Theresa would be prepared to accept a proposal. Regardless, I had received his blessing which was what I needed to continue with my plan. I assured Jim I would let him know as soon as I could and said my goodbye. Jim said his goodbye and then followed that up with "take care of my baby girl" before hanging up.

Prior to leaving Indiana for the cruise, I went to a local pawn shop and purchased a nice, but relatively cheap, engagement ring to give to Theresa when I proposed to her. I hoped my belief that we shared the same thought about our relationship's readiness to proceed to the next level was correct, but I wasn't sure. The purpose of purchasing the ring at the pawn shop was not, however, because of this uncertainty.

Even if now was not the right time I had a good feeling it would be someday. The purpose of the pawn shop engagement ring was to have a temporary ring to give to Theresa when I proposed to prove to her I was sincere about the proposal. But I wanted to give her the opportunity to pick out her own engagement ring. We were travelling to the Caribbean which is known for quality duty-free deals on nice diamonds. If all went according to plan it was my thought we would be able to find a "real" engagement ring for her while we were in the Caribbean.

Soon enough, I was making my way back to the Lido Deck with a new set of nerves churning in my stomach knowing I now had the approval from Jim to proceed with my plans. The Lido Deck was in full blown party mode by this time with loud music, dancing, swimming, free flowing alcoholic beverages, camaraderie and good cheer. I found Theresa, John and Kerry and joined them in the celebration. The ship set sail at the designated departure time as we stood along the rails of the Lido Deck holding Bahama Mamas in one hand and waving to the onlookers on the dock below with the other hand.

Later that evening we shared dinner with John and Kerry before retiring fairly early to our cabin after an exciting beginning to our cruise. Our first destination would be Princess Cays, a tropical beach in the Bahamas owned by the cruise line. We were told we would be in dock in Princess Cays at sunrise so we decided to go to bed relatively early to allow us to get up early in the morning to be prepared to debark the ship as soon as we were allowed.

I awoke first the following morning, as the ship was docking at Princess Cays. I took a shower and finished getting ready as Theresa woke up. We chatted for a few minutes, gave each other a nice embrace and quick kiss and then she went into the bathroom to get ready. I'm known for being meticulous in preparing vacation itineraries. Not necessarily an OCD type of meticulous, but certainly detailed enough to know exactly when and where I wanted to propose during the cruise. The plan was to propose to her on the cliffs overlooking Magens Bay Beach on Saint Thomas, ranked as one of the top ten beaches in the world.

What I failed to consider in my preparations was that Saint Thomas was the final destination of our seven-day cruise. Here we were, the first morning after our departure, and I was already bursting with anticipation to pop the question. My original thought was I didn't want to ruin the vacation by proposing at the beginning of the cruise in the event Theresa declined my proposal. Obviously, I had failed to consider how nervous I would be all week waiting to propose.

As I sat on the bed while Theresa was in the bathroom getting ready, I began rationalizing why I should ask her now, in our room, at the beginning of the cruise. Asking her in private would give her the freedom to give me an honest response, I reasoned. Also, asking her now, if she accepted my proposal, would give us additional ports of call to shop for an engagement ring. Also, it would allow us to celebrate our engagement the entire cruise. My mind was set. I would ask her now. I pulled the engagement ring from deep in its hiding spot in my suitcase and put it in my pocket as I waited for the sound of the shower to stop.

A few minutes after I heard the water stop, I asked Theresa to come out of the bathroom for a moment. She replied she didn't have any clothes on and was only wrapped in a towel. I replied that was OK because I only needed her for a minute. She came out of the bathroom looking as beautiful as I had ever seen her even though she was only wrapped in a towel, as was her hair. I asked her to sit at the edge of the bed. With a quizzical look she complied. I kneeled down in front of her and, being more nervous than anticipated, fumbled through a speech that was not nearly as eloquent as my speech to her father the day before.

"Baby, I thought I loved you the day I met you. I still believe I loved you then but my love for you has grown every day since that first day we had our long conversation in the gazebo in Nashville. I can't imagine how deep our love will be in the future knowing how much it has grown since we met. But what I can imagine is you being in my life for as long as I live. I don't ever want to experience life again without you by my side. Theresa … my love … would you please marry me and make me the happiest man on earth?"

Silence. And then a smile. And then a playful punch to my shoulder causing me to lose my balance and fall backwards. "Stop joking around!", she responded as she started to get up off the bed. I guess I am partially to blame for her disbelief because in my nervousness I forgot to pull the ring out of my pocket and present it to her during my proposal. I replied, "No, I'm not joking. Please sit back down. I'm serious. Here is the ring I have picked out for you" as I took it out of its box and slid it onto her finger.

With that, our eyes locked and I saw in her eyes that it was only then she understood I was indeed serious and my proposal was genuine. Theresa looked down at the ring on her finger and, as I began to explain about this only being a temporary ring, she interrupted me and said, "Baby, I love you too and want to spend the rest of my life with you also. Yes, I will marry you". She leaned in and gave me a long embrace followed by an intimate kiss.

Theresa finished getting ready with me standing by her in the bathroom as we excitedly talked about our new status as an engaged couple. We were both beaming with giant smiles on our faces as we kept giving each other quick kisses. My heart was exploding from my love for Theresa. With her four words "I will marry you" she made me as happy as I had ever been (matched only by the births of Brent and Misty). I couldn't wait to shout to the world Theresa was my fiancée.

We joined John and Kerry for breakfast in one of the ship's restaurants. As soon as we met up with them in the restaurant, they could tell something was up and asked us what was going on. Theresa held up her ring finger for them to see her new bling and Kerry let out a squeal as she asked if that meant what she thought it meant. In response, we announced publicly for the first time our exciting news.

After breakfast we disembarked the ship and enjoyed a day of sun and fun on the beach of Princess Cays, meeting new friends from the ship as we proudly referred to each other as "my fiancé." The day passed in a blur of new found intimacy with us holding each other's hands, hugging each other and stealing kisses for no reason throughout the day.

Our next port of call was St. Maarten. As we disembarked the ship the first thing we came upon was a shopping area dedicated to fine jewelry. Of course, I suggested to Theresa that we do some engagement ring shopping for her. She insisted she didn't need another ring because she thought the one I gave her on the ship was beautiful. I persisted, however, and she reluctantly agreed we could just browse.

After perusing through several stores, we found a diamond we both agreed was beautiful and I was able to convince her to let me buy it for her. We also found a ring on which to set the diamond. The salesperson assured us they would be able to have the diamond set on the ring and ready for us to pick up at the end of the day when we were ready to get back on the ship.

Theresa then turned her attention to me insisting we also search for my wedding ring. I hadn't expected this possibility. For some reason still unknown to me the act of searching for my wedding ring was surreal. I guess because I had been completely focused on Theresa and kind of forgot I was also part of the equation. After a careful search we also settled on a ring for me and Theresa purchased it. Much to my dismay, however, she wouldn't let me wear it, insisting I would have to wait until we were married.

We had a wonderful day on St. Maarten highlighted by sightseeing and a visit to Orient Beach where we discovered we had ventured upon a clothing-optional beach. I would be remiss if I failed to mention two things about this discovery. First, we did not participate in the non-clothing option. Second, those who did participate in that option probably should have thought twice about their decision. I have to admit, John and I were a bit disappointed by the sightseeing at Orient Beach and I'm guessing Theresa and Kerry probably felt likewise.

We returned to the ship about a half an hour early to assure we had time to stop at the jewelry store to pick up Theresa's engagement ring. We were shocked to learn upon entering the store that the diamond and ring were not at the store. They had been sent off to a jeweler for the setting. The store's "runner" had not yet returned to the store with the ring from the jeweler. We were told the jeweler was located up in the mountain regions of St. Maarten. Anxiety and fear of missing the boat or having to leave the ring behind immediately fell upon us. The store called the jeweler and was informed the runner had just left on his bicycle to bring the ring to the store. The clerk told us the bike ride would take about twenty minutes, further increasing our anxiety and fear.

The ship's horn blasted signifying final boarding before the ship left. Just when we decided we couldn't wait any longer, the runner literally came running through the door of the store with Theresa's ring. We quickly opened the box only to discover the diamond had been set incorrectly. It was so crooked even the salesperson had to agree it was unacceptable. Suddenly we were presented with the dilemma of whether to leave the ring behind for the store to fix and trust it would be sent to us or take the ring with us and drop it off at the store's Saint Thomas branch and hope they could fix it. We chose the latter option thinking it would be better to keep the ring in our possession rather than trusting it would catch up with us across the Caribbean.

Our last port of call was Saint Thomas. We were able to find the Saint Thomas branch of the jewelry store as soon as we disembarked the ship. When we initially arrived at the store the clerk asserted she had no knowledge of our problem and did not appear as though she wanted to assist us. After repeated requests for her to call their St. Maarten branch, she complied and was able to receive a briefing on our issue. The clerk's demeanor quickly changed after her call and she became accommodating and acknowledged the poor workmanship of the setting on the ring. She assured us the ring would be fixed while we enjoyed our remaining time on Saint Thomas.

Spending in excess of an hour trying to explain the issue to the clerk, we were eager to get out of the store and do just that. Our remaining time on Saint Thomas was highlighted by a photo op recreation of my proposal to Theresa with me down on one knee on the cliffs overlooking Magens Bay, just as I had originally planned to propose. Highlighting how everyone seems to enjoy a good love story, after I kneeled on one knee and proposed to Theresa for the second time in two days, we discovered we had a sizeable audience watching when they began cheering and clapping as I slide the pawn shop engagement ring onto her finger.

At the conclusion of the day, we returned to the jewelry store before boarding the ship, giving ourselves more time to spare than in St. Maarten ... just in case. When we arrived, we were pleasantly surprised when the clerk informed us the ring had been repaired. The clerk pulled the ring out of its box and to our utter disbelief the setting was no better. We were convinced the ring had not been touched since we dropped it off. The clerk was unable to explain to us why the setting on the ring was still crooked but at least acknowledged there was something terribly wrong with the setting.

With no time remaining to repair the setting before the ship left, the clerk called the international headquarters of the company for directions on what to do in the situation. After the call, the clerk informed us a return and refund wasn't possible because the ring was purchased at a different branch in a different country and the diamond had been set on a ring. We were told the only remaining option was to take the ring with us and deal with the company's New York headquarters when we returned home.

I will spare the details here but having no other option we took the ring home with us and after an appraisal from our local jeweler, many emails and calls to the New York office, sending the ring off to New York, the ring being out of our hands for far longer than it should have been, involving the cruise company with assistance to get our ring back, and another appraisal upon its eventual return, we finally received the ring back, with diamond set correctly. The appraisal for the ring after its return came in at an amount more than five times what we purchased it for. Its beauty is only surpassed by that of the person who wears it.

October 15, 2011

After resolving the engagement ring debacle our attention turned to thoughts of a wedding. Theresa didn't have a wedding in her first marriage and I wanted her to have the experience of being the center of attention for a day just as she would be the center of my attention for the rest of my life. At first, we agreed on a wedding date in the spring of 2012 to give ourselves plenty of time to plan our special day. We knew the wedding would occur in Indiana because all of our children lived there at the time, an overwhelming majority of our friends and co-workers lived there, all of my family lived there and with Theresa's family spread out from Jacksonville to Baltimore there was no central location on the East Coast that would be any more convenient for all of them than Indiana.

As the spring of 2011 arrived, we began having concerns for Jim's declining health. He had traveled to Indiana for Theresa's birthday the previous September, as he had done many times before, but it became apparent the trip hadn't been as easy for him as it had been in the past. Since his September visit his mobility had declined and we were concerned a delay of a wedding date to the spring of 2012 would see a further decline of mobility that would prevent Jim from returning to Indiana. We agreed we should move the wedding date up and settled on October 15, 2011.

By the time we settled on the October wedding date we only had about six months to find an available venue, find the needed vendors and make the preparations for the wedding. Being a naïve groom-to-be, I found no issue with the time frame we had remaining to make the arrangements. Theresa assured me we didn't have as much time as I thought we did.

I quickly learned she was correct. We were blessed, however, that many of our friends and family were willing to pitch in to help with our preparations. My sister Rae and her two daughters (my nieces Nicole and Brooke) took charge helping us with many of the details. We put them in charge of the flower arrangements, decorations, and table arrangements and they turned our venue into a magical setting worthy of a celebration for the love Theresa and I shared.

For the most part, Theresa and I had no trouble agreeing on the details of our wedding. The venue, the officiant, our vows, the colors, the decorations, the DJ for the reception, the menu for the dinner at the reception, the wedding cake, and our first dance song.

There was one detail, however, that I had to put my foot down and adamantly say no to her request. With the wedding being in October she felt it would be a nice touch to the ceremony if we sat her coffin front and center with me laying in it with the lid shut. She suggested after she walked down the aisle I would open the coffin and rise out of it. I loved all of her Halloween traditions but there was no way I was going to lay in a coffin on my wedding day.

As our wedding day approached the time finally arrived for Theresa and me to send out invitations for the wedding. We would be inviting approximately three hundred guests but as a fun little gesture we each agreed to invite one special guest for the other (not really expecting to receive a response to the invitation from either of these special guests).

Theresa knew my favorite author was Nicholas Sparks and that he held a special place in my heart by creating "Gabby" who inspired my hope that my own special Gabby was waiting for me. Theresa chose, therefore, to send her special invitation to Nicholas Sparks.

Theresa was a big fan of Indiana's governor at the time, Mitch Daniels. Governor Daniels had previously served on the staff of President Reagan as assistant to the President and on President George W. Bush's cabinet as the

Director of the Office of Management and Budget. There was considerable speculation at the time that he would be seeking the Republican nomination in the 2012 presidential primary election. I chose, therefore, to send my special invitation to Governor Daniels.

A few weeks before our wedding we received the following handwritten note, written on the back of an invitation we had sent out:

Dear Paul & Theresa,

Thank you for the invitation and I wish you all the happiness in the world. Unfortunately, I will not be able to attend on October 15. I'll be in the midst of my book tour for *The Best of Me*, my latest novel.

Thank you for thinking of me –

Peace,

Nicholas Sparks

The very next day we received the following type-written message on *State of Indiana Office of the Governor* letterhead, dated October 15, the day of our wedding.

Dear Paul and Theresa,

Thank you for the invitation to your wedding. I am sorry that I am unable to join you on this special day and want to offer my sincerest best wishes as you begin your life together.

I hope you have many years of good times, good health and happiness. Thank you for the opportunity to share in this joyous occasion.

Sincerely,

And then in handwriting,

Mitch Daniels

I'll pray for a life of joy for you both

Theresa and I never expected Nicholas Sparks or Governor Daniels to attend our wedding or really to even respond to our invitations. So, we were quite touched that they both took the time out of their schedules to respond to what for them was an invitation to a wedding of complete strangers. It would have been easy for them to dismiss the invitations without a second thought but they took the time to send a response obviously understanding their response would make our wedding just a little bit more special. So, for that I would like to thank both Nicholas Sparks and Mitch Daniels for their thoughtfulness.

To say Theresa had completely gotten past her anxiety and fears from her first marriage during this time would not be accurate. She continued to see her counselor as the wedding date approached. She even told me that her counselor had agreed to be on call the day of our wedding just in case she needed to call him for reassurance.

From my perspective, I didn't feel her anxieties and fears ever returned to the level they had been previously. In fact, she seemed extraordinarily calm as the wedding day approached, notwithstanding the many planning and preparation obstacles that came up. I, on the other hand, would not say the same about myself. I definitely exhibited signs of stress as the wedding day drew near and in an ironic twist found Theresa being the one consoling me many times to help keep me calm.

My daughter Misty decided to become a dog owner about four weeks prior to our wedding. I was not happy with this decision as the dog would be living at my house on the nights Misty was in my custody and I already had a dog. Misty's dog was a Pomapoo she named "Sam". Despite my protestations, the dog quickly captured my heart and he and I became good friends in a matter of days.

About two weeks before our wedding, Misty discovered Sam had gotten into a one-pound *Hershey* chocolate bar she had in her room. Sam was clearly not feeling well so we had to rush him to an emergency veterinarian clinic in the middle of the night. I learned from the vet that chocolate is very dangerous for dogs, especially small dogs like Sam and especially in the quantity that Sam had consumed. The vet explained that it was possible Sam would not make it, that his stomach would need to be pumped and he would have to be kept for observation. We left the vet's office that night not knowing if this little dog we both had fallen in love with would make it through the night. Thankfully, after a two-night stay at the vet clinic Sam was cleared to come home but the uncertainty about his health during that forty-eight-hour period added to my stress that was building as our wedding day approached.

We would be having a large number of guests coming in from out of town for the wedding because Theresa's father, sisters, brothers-in-law, nephews and nieces were coming from the East Coast. Many would be staying in hotels but several would also be staying in Theresa's home. We also decided to host a rehearsal dinner for about forty-five people at Theresa's house the night before the wedding. Consequently, the week of our wedding became a stressful time of preparing the house for guests, making arrangements for hosting the rehearsal dinner and the usual pre-wedding stressors.

Theresa not only held up well with all the stress, she flourished. She made sure we stayed on track to prepare the house for guests. She prepared the shopping list for the rehearsal dinner making sure we had everything that would be needed. She came up with the solution for hosting forty-five people in her home with limited space. She confirmed that everything was set for the day of the wedding (such as hair and make-up appointments for herself and the bridesmaids). She was a calm and gracious hostess the evening of the rehearsal dinner. She was everything I loved about her.

I, on the other hand, felt like a bundle of nerves. My nerves caught me by surprise. I wanted nothing more than to be married to Theresa. I knew I wanted to be with her the rest of my life. She was everything, and more, I could ever want. I had no idea why I was nervous.

After the rehearsal dinner the plan was for me to stay in a local hotel near the wedding venue to make more room for Theresa's family but, more importantly, to follow the tradition of not seeing or speaking to your fiancé the day of your wedding. My daughter, Misty, would stay in a room at the hotel I was staying in and brought Sam with her.

I got up early the day of the wedding to go to the wedding venue to help with setting up all the decorations. Misty took Sam over to Theresa's home to let Jim and Theresa's sisters watch him while she participated in all the activities Theresa had scheduled for the bridesmaids (with Misty being one of them).

About midday on the day of the wedding I received a call from Jim. He told me that Sam had become very lethargic and was having bloody stools and indicated he was worried about Sam. I was able to reach Misty by telephone to let her know about Sam's condition but neither of us had any options at the time to tend to Sam because our wedding obligations were in full swing.

Misty was at the beauty salon with Theresa and the other bridesmaids having her hair done. Brent, who had arrived early in the morning and was assisting with wedding decorations, suggested that he run over to the hair salon to pick Misty up after she was finished and take her over to Theresa's house for a quick visit with Sam to see how he was doing. I readily agreed thinking it would be good for Misty to see for herself how Sam was doing (and admittedly I too was wanting a firsthand account of how the little guy was doing). Brent took off for the beauty salon. I was deep in decorating mode and forgot that he had left.

Probably about an hour after Brent left, Rae approached me and asked if I had talked to Brent since he left. I replied no. She then told me that Misty had called her to say Brent's car had caught on fire. After questioning her about the details Rae apologized and said that is all she knew about it at this point. If I thought I was stressed before, this news took it to another level. I immediately tried calling Brent but there was no answer … elevating my concern and stress even further. I tried calling Misty and again no answer. Finally, I called Theresa (disregarding any tradition about not speaking to her before the wedding).

Theresa answered on the first ring. Just the sound of her voice was soothing. She knew exactly why I was calling. Before I had a chance to say a word Theresa said "He's OK". I asked what happened and she replied, "His car was parked outside the beauty salon. He wasn't in the car. He was inside waiting on Misty when someone came in and said there was a car in the parking lot on fire. Brent went outside to take a look and discovered it was his car on fire." I asked her how bad the fire was and she said it was bad.

A fire truck had to be called to put the fire out and the car was totally destroyed. This was not shaping up to be how I hoped our wedding day would begin. Brent was able to make arrangements for a rental car but there was some initial concern the delay in getting the rental would make him late for the wedding, which was not an option because he was serving as my best man. Fortunately, that didn't happen.

After a stressful and eventful week leading up to our wedding, the wedding itself turned out to be a beautiful outdoor lakeside ceremony with a breathtaking backdrop of fall colors along the hillsides beyond the lake. The reception that followed was a fun filled giant party as we enjoyed the beginning of our new life together with family and friends.

Theresa, being just as much a jokester as I, had made special plans for a surprise for my mother during the reception. With the wedding being in the middle of October she was determined to have something related to Halloween associated with our special day. Since I had vetoed the coffin idea she came up with another idea ... one that I agreed would be a fun way to incorporate the Halloween spirit.

With the history my mom had of scaring the grandchildren, Theresa schemed with the grandkids for a little payback. She had each of them, several of our nephews and nieces, Rae, Roger, Theresa's sisters and a few friends bring scary Halloween masks to the reception and hide them. At one point during the reception the DJ announced a car was parked in the parking lot with its lights on giving a description of mom's car and her license plate number.

Mom left the reception hall to check on her car and while she was gone, we all put our masks on and positioned ourselves near the entrance of the reception hall to scare her when she came back in. The lights to the reception hall were turned off and as mom walked back in she was met with the sound of the DJ playing Michael Jackson's *Thriller* followed by all of us jumping out at her. The prank may have been a little over the top to play on an "elderly" lady and maybe I should have considered the possibility it would cause mom to have a heart attack. After the initial shock, however, mom started laughing and appreciated Theresa's "thoughtfulness". My mom had grown to love Theresa as her own daughter and it was things like this that connected mom and Theresa so closely.

Following the reception Theresa and I retired to the hotel room I stayed in the evening before. In the morning we awoke to a whole new set of problems. Theresa and I were scheduled to depart for the airport around noon to begin our honeymoon in Cancun. But as soon as I got up, I was greeted with a text message from Misty asking me to call her as soon as I woke up.

I called Misty and she informed me Sam had been having bloody stools throughout the night and was just laying around not moving. I also had a text from Brent asking me to call him. When I did Brent informed me that his rental car was still at the wedding venue because he couldn't find the keys to the car. He was able to get a ride back to his home in Bloomington after the reception and was wanting to know if I could go to the wedding venue to search for his keys.

Not the way I had hoped to start the first day of our honeymoon. With help of family and friends we were able to get Sam rushed back up to the emergency veterinarian clinic and were told Sam must have contracted Parvovirus ("Parvo") during his stay at the clinic two weeks before. We were also told Parvo could have a mortality rate of up to ninety percent in untreated cases. A hospital stay would be required and again, within a two-week period, we were being told Misty's little bundle of love might die.

This was hard news to receive as Theresa and I were heading off to another country, not knowing how much contact we would be able to have with Misty for updates on Sam's condition over the next week (thankfully Sam made a full recovery while we were gone but we did not learn that until we returned home from our honeymoon). The problem with Brent resolved fairly easily once calls were made to several family members and we eventually learned Brent had given his keys to his cousin to assure he would not be driving the car later in the evening after consuming alcohol during the reception.

With the exception of our concern about Sam, Theresa and I were looking forward to beginning our honeymoon and unwinding. I will admit it took me a couple days to unwind after arriving in Cancun. It was my first time being out of the United States and I was uncomfortable seeing armed soldiers in the airport and standing in the beds of pick-up trucks patrolling the streets of Cancun with mounted machine guns. A definite culture shock for a guy from southern Indiana.

At one point during the week Theresa and I took a bus excursion to Chichén Itzá, which is about a three-hour drive from Cancun. About half way there we were stopped by a military road block and soldiers boarded the bus to search for 'unusual activity'. Thankfully, none was found. The Mayan ruins were quite fascinating and well worth the time to visit. But again, once we arrived at the ruins, a heavy military presence was in full view, most notably military helicopters circling overhead during our visit. I suppose seeing the heavy military presence should have been reassuring but the fact that it was necessary in the first place was concerning in itself.

On our way to and from Chichén Itzá we passed through a Mayan town and were sad to see the conditions in which the occupants lived. Many of the homes they occupied had no windows or doors. There was no sign of electricity or running water. We didn't see any operable modes of transportation (but there were numerous abandoned vehicles). The occupants of the town were barefooted and it appeared as though no one in the town worked in what we would consider a 'traditional job'. There were a lot of men sitting on what would be considered porches of their homes consuming what were clearly alcoholic beverages.

We had heard stories of the plight of people living in third world countries but had never really understood what they experience on a daily basis. Although Mexico would probably be best described as a developing country rather than a third world country, I have no doubt what we witnessed in the Mayan town we travelled through is what one would see in a third world country. I had never seen poverty like this before. It was hard to comprehend we were passing through such dire conditions when the resort we were staying in not too far away provided world-class luxuries. A saddening testimony to the inequities our world has created.

Toward the end of our honeymoon Theresa and I took a walk on the strip to find a place to eat. We were surprised to find several "American" restaurants on the strip. With all the American tourists and American restaurants it almost felt like we were back in the United States, a stark contrast to all of the military presence we had experienced up to that point. We came to a nice little area for tourist shopping and decided to stay there until sunset as the area presented a good opportunity to take some nice pictures of the setting sun.

We were carrying a camera bag in which we placed my wallet with my identification, some spending money and a spare camera lens. After we took our pictures, we placed the camera back in the carrying case and had a seat on a nearby bench, basking in the joy of each other's company and the relaxing atmosphere. It may have taken the bigger part of our honeymoon but we were feeling as though we were finally relaxing.

We noticed a young couple trying to take a selfie with the backdrop of the fading remnants of a beautiful sky. Theresa and I walked over to them and asked if they wanted us to take a picture of them together. They readily accepted our invitation. After a few pictures we were able to show them the pictures we had taken and they were thankful for our assistance. We engaged in a short conversation with them and learned they were fellow *Hoosiers*, also on their honeymoon. They lived in Lafayette, a city about one hundred miles from where we lived. After our short conversation we walked back over to the bench where we had been sitting only to realize we had forgotten to grab our camera bag when we got up to assist the young couple.

A sickening feeling overcame us upon the realization the camera bag was not where we left it. Remembering my identification was in the camera bag an overwhelming fear replaced the sickening feeling as we considered the possible consequences that may occur from losing my identification in a foreign country. We looked frantically everywhere we could for signs of the camera bag or my wallet but there was no trace of either to be found. The only option that remained was to report the incident to local police. We got directions to the police station and made our way there to make the report.

What we experienced next seemed to be straight out of a scene from a bad spaghetti western. When we entered the police station there was no one at the front desk. An overhead fan creaking and wobbling as it slowly turned provided the only form of air conditioning in the humid and sticky foyer. There was a small bell at the front desk we rang to no avail. After a minute or so we rang it again and heard a deep male voice grumbling something in Spanish from the back rooms. When we responded hello in English we believe the voice responded in broken English something to the effect, "I am busy at the moment and will be out in a few minutes."

After about five minutes, a young lady, probably in her early twenties, sheepishly came out from the back rooms with a faint smile on her face tugging her very short mini-dress down in an attempt to make it appear more appropriate for the 'official' setting of the police station. The young lady spoke very little English, much less than the male voice we heard earlier. Communicating with her was difficult but we finally understood there was a form she was asking us to complete. When she handed it to us it was written in Spanish which led to another long exchange with her trying to find a form written in English. Finally, we received the appropriate form in English and completed it. We knew it was unlikely we would see our camera bag or my wallet again but knew completing this form was necessary to assist with any identity theft issues we might encounter upon our return home.

We arose before sunrise on our last morning in Cancun. We went out to the beach and spread our beach towels on the cool sand and sat while waiting for the sun to rise. We brought a blanket with us because the temperature had been unseasonably cool overnight. We cuddled together in the blanket and stared out over the Caribbean as the first hints of daylight were appearing on the distant horizon.

Although there had been some stressful moments during our honeymoon, it went by far too quick. After a whirlwind six months preparing for our wedding, spending a week alone with Theresa was paradise in itself but it was accentuated by the beauty of Cancun and its surrounding area. Theresa and I had been dating for sixteen months but somehow it felt like we had known each other all of our lives. Everything that occurred in my life before Theresa made sense now. It was all leading me to her. During our wedding ceremony I vowed to always cherish us in everything I do. As she slipped my wedding ring on my finger, I gave her a big grin knowing it had found its permanent home.

With shades of red, orange and yellow beginning to stretch across the horizon signifying the sun was soon to follow, I turned toward Theresa and stared into her eyes. Returning my stare, I could actually see love in her eyes. Its hard to explain but in that moment, all of her feelings for me, all of my feelings for her, our two souls joined together as one, my identity, everything that completed me … it was all there in her eyes. A love so pure and consuming.

She leaned deeper into my embrace and breaking away from our loving stare rested her head on my chest. After a few moments, I slowly and ever so gently traced my finger across her eyebrow allowing my light touch to continue to the top of her ear and around its circumference and then down the length of her jaw to her chin. With my finger under her chin, I ever so gently lifted her head until we were looking into each other's eyes again. My lips inched closer to hers. I felt her breath on my lips. Our lips drew closer until they were barely touching, like a feather. Exchanging each other's breaths as our lips ever so slightly touched, I continued to stare into her eyes and whispered "I do" as we joined together for a much more intimate kiss.

As we finished our kiss, Theresa pulled back a few inches and with a whimsical look asked, "You do what"? In the preparations for our wedding, we put considerable thought into what our 'first dance' song would be at the reception. We agreed our perfect song would be "*I Do*" by Mark Wills. I listened to the song so many times leading up to the wedding I had memorized the lyrics. So, when Theresa asked me "You do what?" I responded:

All I am, all I'll be
Everything in this world
All that I'll ever need
Is in your eyes
Shining at me
When you smile I can feel
All my passion unfolding
Your hand brushes mine
And a thousand sensations
Seduce me
'Cause I
I do cherish you
For the rest of my life
You don't have to think twice
I will love you still
From the depths of my soul
It's beyond my control
I've waited so long to say this to you
If you're asking do I love you this much
I do
In my world, before you
I lived outside my emotions
Didn't know where I was going
'Til that day I found you
How you opened my life
To a new paradise
In a world torn by change
Still with all my heart
"Til my dying day
If you're asking do I love you this much
I do
Oh, I do

April 18, 2021

After navigating through the traffic in Atlanta, the drive to Macon seemed to pass quickly, although it actually took another hour. In Macon I would be connecting with *I-16* to continue toward Savannah. It seemed as though my journey was starting to smooth out a little and I was finally moving along as expected.

The time from my proposal on the cruise all the way through to our honeymoon went by in a flash. Although it covered a period of about seven or eight months, it seemed as though it was only a month or so. From a nervous proposal, dealing with the fiasco of the engagement ring purchase, planning the wedding and anxious anticipation of marrying the woman of my dreams, Sam's illnesses, wedding week preparations, Brent's car, our wedding and reception, and our honeymoon, we had experienced a lot in a short period of time.

Even though everything didn't go as planned, by the end of our honeymoon we could look back and proudly say we had a beautiful wedding, a wonderful honeymoon and were right where we wanted to be in life. Our hope from there was to live happily ever after in each other's arms until we grew old. As we had already learned, however, things don't always go as planned.

Chapter 9: Upon this Rock

And so I say to you, you are Peter, and upon this rock I will build my church, and the gates of the netherworld shall not prevail against it. I will give you the keys to the kingdom of heaven. Whatever you bind on earth shall be bound in heaven; and whatever you loose on earth shall be loosed in heaven.

Matthew 16:18-19

April 18, 2021

I-16 from Macon to Savannah was clear sailing. It was nice to have a long stretch of the road to relax without having to devote all of my attention to other vehicles and the dangerous construction hazards that had plagued most of the drive up to this point. This was only possible though because I had weathered the storm of the difficult parts of the journey I had already travelled.

During the calm of this part of the trip my mind could not help but reflect upon the life Theresa and I continued to build together after our marriage and the calm that settled upon both of us as we grew in our marital love. We had both been through unsuccessful marriages and we were committed to making our marriage work. Not only because neither of us wanted to have a second failed marriage but more importantly because we loved each other more than we had ever loved anyone else and we didn't want to ever lose that feeling.

179

One thing that was missing in our prior marriages was an invitation to a third person to join our marriages. We were committed to not making the same mistake again.

October 30, 2011

We awoke early on the first full Sunday after our return from our honeymoon. It had been almost a full week since returning and after a few days of re-acclimating to the real world, we for the most part fell back into our normal routine. To be honest, not a lot had changed from our pre-marital life except now I was the proud recipient of a wedding ring I vowed to never take off my finger.

Often times during my marriage to Tina I didn't wear my wedding ring. I reasoned Tina knew my love for her and I was certain others did likewise because of the life we shared together. After our separation and divorce I realized not cherishing that ring was a mistake because it represented my devotion to our marriage. I came to understand my wedding ring should have been my attestation to Tina, as well to all with whom I came in contact, of my love and commitment to Tina. I vowed to never take my wedding ring for granted in my marriage with Theresa.

One of the most important things I learned through my divorce from Tina was the importance of always showing your significant other she is the priority in your life. When I stopped to think about it I realized there were so many small things I could have done every day to show her my commitment to her and our marriage. Letting her enter doors first. Letting her order first at dinner. Random "I love you" texts throughout the day. Sending flowers to her work. Making it a point to occasionally arrive home from work before her to do the laundry and dishes and sweep and mop the floors before she arrived home. Taking her on regular dates to allow my attention to be focused solely on her. I was determined to do those small acts of love with Theresa.

When we first started seeing each other I vowed to Theresa to always open her car door for her and I asked her that if I ever forgot to do it, please don't open the door herself, even if I went ahead and got in the car on my side. I have honored this vow throughout our marriage, rain or shine, notwithstanding our moods. I kept this promise all the way up until the day she left me. Yes, there have been a handful of times when I have forgotten to open the door for her, and as asked, there have been an equal number of times when Theresa has stood outside of the car door waiting for me to come around the car to open her door. It always brings a smile to my face knowing she remembers my vow and is holding me to it.

The reason for our early morning on this first full Sunday after our return from our honeymoon was to begin another pledge we made to each other, to bring that third person into our marriage. God was not present in either of our prior marriages and we both felt his absence left us without valuable tools to deal with the issues that caused their failures. This was the day for us to begin in earnest laying the foundation upon which our marriage would be built.

As the days leading up to our wedding approached, Theresa and I spoke not only of our commitment to attending church on a regular basis but also of a desire to become active members of the church. Knowing that I had not had a lot of experience with organized religion, Theresa suggested that maybe we should attend other churches in the Columbus community to determine what we felt as a couple would fit us best. I suspect in her mind she already knew what my answer to her suggestion would be and was not surprised when I declined the offer and told her I would prefer to continue attending *St. Bartholomew*, if she was agreeable.

We had attended mass at *St. Bartholomew* several times over the past year and a half since we met but not with a committed regularity. I had developed a general familiarity with the Catholic mass but didn't really understand what was occurring and it continued to be a bit intimidating to me. Theresa had previously introduced me to Father Steve, Deacon Mark and many of the staff and parishioners. I always found the parish to have a welcoming atmosphere.

So, on October 30, 2011 Theresa and I began attending *St. Bartholomew* on a regular basis as a married couple. I can't say we have attended every Sunday mass from that point forward but we certainly attend an overwhelming majority of them. Over time *St. Bartholomew* started to feel like our home away from home as I began to get to know Father Steve, Deacon Mark, staff and parishioners better. The mass itself stopped being intimidating as I learned more about it and understand the beauty of the service and its deep connection to Jesus Christ and scripture.

In approximately May of 2014 Theresa asked me if I would be interested in attending *RCIA* classes (*Rite of Christian Initiation of Adults*). My first reaction was, "Huh???" I was not aware of anything called *RCIA* or its purpose. Theresa explained *RCIA* is the process non-Catholics go through to become converts to Catholicism.

I suppose I was a bit surprised because we had been attending *St. Bartholomew* regularly for two and a half years by that time and I guess I just assumed by attending I was Catholic. Eager to learn more about the Catholic faith I agreed to attend the initial *RCIA* class scheduled for the first Thursday of September.

The summer of 2014 seemed to come and go faster than a shooting star. Before we knew it September had arrived and it was the first Thursday of September. Theresa reminded me of the *RCIA* meeting the night before.

I will confess, throughout the day of that first meeting I was apprehensive about attending. I didn't feel prepared. I was concerned the other attendees would have a much deeper understanding of Catholicism and scripture. I wasn't even baptized. Although I had learned more about the mass I still had yet to develop a strong understanding of it. I didn't understand the true meaning of the sacraments of the Church. I kept hearing of the Church's social justice platforms which I didn't fully understand but knew some of them were not what I believed. I knew the Church placed a lot of importance on charitable work but didn't feel as though I measured up in that respect.

I simply didn't belong, I reasoned. Nevertheless, I re-affirmed with Theresa my agreement to attend the initial *RCIA* class confident that once the powers that be learned where I was in my personal faith journey we would agree I was not 'official' Catholic material.

Thursday evening arrived and Theresa and I made our way to *St. Bartholomew*. As soon as we entered the building we were greeted by a bubbly, energetic and charismatic lady who introduced herself as Barb. Barb could not have been more welcoming, somehow making us feel as though we had been her best friends for years. I learned that among her other roles in the parish Barb was the director for *RCIA*.

As we began to mingle with other persons in attendance, we discovered many of them were *RCIA* "team members" who assisted Barb with the *RCIA* program. They each were just as friendly and welcoming as Barb. Among the team members was Deacon Mark. We had gotten to know him fairly well over the time we had been attending mass. Deacon Mark had always been a shining example of God's love toward all mankind with his genuine interest in all with whom he came in contact.

I quickly discovered that my concern for not having the credentials for entering the *RCIA* program was shared by many of the other attendees. This first night was set up to allow us to begin getting to know each other and the team members and for us to anonymously express our thoughts about the Catholic faith and any concerns we may have about it. Barb made it perfectly clear that going through the *RCIA* program didn't obligate us to become Catholics and that the program is designed to allow us to learn about the faith to discern if we wanted to become Catholic.

Barb told the attendees that if we chose to become Catholic we would have the opportunity to be initiated into the faith at the next Easter Vigil. She explained the *RCIA* program would continue over the next nine months or so (meeting each Thursday evening) and would provide a detailed description and explanation of mass, in depth lectures regarding each of the seven sacraments of the Church, an overview of the social justice platforms of the Church, and many other topics central to Catholicism. In other words, those very subjects I did not truly understand that caused me to feel inadequate to be in the *RCIA* program in the first place.

Looking around at my fellow attendees and hearing some of the anonymous concerns that were shared by the group, I realized we were all having the same questions and concerns. When I left the meeting that Thursday night, I recall expressing to Theresa that I was looking forward to learning more in the following weeks.

As the weeks passed by, Theresa and I began developing what would be lifelong friendships with members of the team, especially Barb and Deacon Mark and his wife Jane. I was also building the strong faith foundation I had been desiring for as long as I could remember. As we entered the new year of 2015 and were moving closer to

Holy Week and the Easter Vigil, the *RCIA* program shifted focus to the sacraments of the Church.

Of course, I was particularly interested in the Sacraments of Initiation (baptism, confirmation and first communion) as these would be the sacraments I received at the Vigil. Surprisingly, however, I found myself mesmerized by the talk Deacon Mark gave during one of the *RCIA* meetings regarding the sacrament of Holy Orders (ordination in the Church as a priest or deacon).

Deacon Mark began his talk with a discussion of the meaning of ordination and its significance within the Church. He then proceeded to discuss the responsibilities and vows of a priest and the process of becoming one. Next, he then spoke of the responsibilities and vows of a deacon such as himself and the process he went through to become a deacon. This talk remains vividly clear in my mind to this day because as he was speaking it felt as though God was standing behind me, tapping me on the shoulder and whispering in my ear: "Listen closely because this is how I want you to assist me."

I left the meeting that evening confused by the voice I had heard in my mind and the message it conveyed. Could that voice have really been God speaking to me and, if so, why was God suggesting something that would clearly be a big mistake. God knew my history and the limited knowledge I had at the time with Christianity in general and Catholicism in particular. I most certainly was not qualified to be an ordained clergy in the Catholic Church.

I kept the voice I heard to myself for a week or so but it kept coming back to me, each time seemingly louder than the time before. Finally, I knew the voice would not go away until I told someone about it and received reassurances I was crazy for having such a thought. Knowing she would set me straight, I told Theresa about this foolish idea. She is my cheerleader and my biggest fan. She often times has more confidence in me than I do myself. That is one of the reasons I love her. She is able to bring the best out in me. She encourages me to do so many things I would not have done otherwise.

As a surprise, she scheduled flight lessons for me to obtain a private pilot license allowing me to fulfill a lifelong dream of flying a plane solo. She encouraged me to enter into politics to run for judge even though the thought of campaigning was terrifying to me. She convinced me to change my antiquated method of advertising for my office to a more modern approach. She encouraged me to become involved in activities within our parish that were outside my comfort zone.

But she is just as willing to let me know when ideas I have are not in my best interests. She has convinced me not to make investments I thought were good ideas, only to find out later the investments would have been failures. She has advised me not to pursue certain hiring decisions at my office that upon reflection would have been mistakes.

Regardless of whether it is encouraging me to take action or discouraging me from pursuing a certain direction in my life, I always know Theresa has my best interests in mind, she is not hesitant to tell me her honest thoughts and almost without exception she is correct in her opinion.

So, when I took the idea to her that I thought God was calling me to serve him as a deacon, I fully expected her to laugh and tell me God may be calling me to do something but being a deacon would be the last thing He would want me to do. Instead, when I told her this absurd belief I thought God was calling me to be a deacon she smiled and said she had a feeling I would eventually be having this discussion with her. That is another one of the multitude of things I love about Theresa. She always has a way of knowing what is in my heart and on my mind. To my complete surprise she told me she thought it was a great idea and that she believed I would be an excellent deacon.

Becoming a deacon in our archdiocese is a five-year process and the next group of deacon candidates would not be selected for about another two years. We kept the idea of applying to the deacon formation program to ourselves for about a year to determine how strong that calling was in me. The calling did not wane over that year and, if anything, grew stronger. Even so, there were many occasions during that time when it seemed God had stopped talking to me about becoming a deacon which would lead me to believe that perhaps He no longer was calling me to the diaconate. God does indeed work in mysterious ways. Each time I allowed myself to believe God had changed His mind, a friend would suggest I should apply for the deacon formation program, I would read an article online about the Church's need for deacons, a homily during mass would recharge my thoughts of becoming a deacon, or something else would happen to assure me God had not changed His mind about my calling.

About six months prior to the beginning of the next deacon formation program the time finally arrived to discuss my interest in the program with someone other than Theresa. Having become good friends with Deacon Mark by that time we chose him as our sounding board. Not only was he a deacon himself and a perfect example of what a deacon is, he was also on the archdiocese board responsible for the deacon formation program. I knew he would not only have valuable information about what the archdiocese was looking for in deacon candidates, he would also be honest with us about whether or not I should apply. When Theresa and I asked him and his wife Jane to have dinner with us I told him there was something we needed to speak to him about during the dinner.

I'm not sure what he may have been thinking we wanted to talk to him about but during dinner when I announced I felt like I was being called to the diaconate he didn't look surprised. Slowly, a smile spread across his face, he glanced at Jane and then looked at Theresa with a wide grin on his face and then turned his attention to me. He told us more details about what the program entailed and his own ministry as a deacon. When he was finished, he expressed his sincere enthusiasm about my calling and assured me he thought it would be a good idea for me to apply to the deacon formation program.

I told Deacon Mark I was not sure his enthusiasm was deserved. When he asked why with a concerned face, I reminded him that I had only been a confirmed Catholic for a short period of time and there was no way I was qualified to be a deacon. I told him there was no way I could be the deacon he was.

Apparently, I wasn't very convincing because that smile returned to his face. He explained God wasn't looking for someone who emulates a current deacon. He said God wants deacons to be their own individual version of a deacon. He then told me God is not looking for deacon candidates that are qualified. He is looking to qualify those that are called. I was speechless. Recalling how God transformed Moses from one who himself felt unqualified into a powerful and effective servant able to lead the Israelites out of Egypt, how could I argue with God's ability to qualify the called to be a deacon?

With the urging from Deacon Mark and the unwavering support from Theresa, we applied and were accepted into the formation program. I say 'we' because Theresa and I are a team. Although a deacon in the Church is an ordained position only men are permitted to hold, Theresa had expressed she wished to be heavily involved in Church ministries also and I was grateful for her involvement.

Within the Church she was a communion minister, a member of the welcoming committee, a member of the peace and justice committee, a team member of *RCIA*, the organizer for campaigns within the Church for donations to the local food pantry, she was on the board of the *Ecumenical Assembly of Churches* within our community, she took charge in the Church recruiting participants for local *Feed My Starving Children* events, she volunteered to assist preparing food and serving it at the local soup kitchen and she volunteered at the local food pantry. Just as Deacon Mark is an excellent role model for aspiring deacons, Theresa is a shining example of how an aspiring deacon's wife could also serve the Church.

The five-year Deacon formation program began with a year of monthly discernment meetings in August of 2017. Anyone interested in joining the formation program was expected to attend each of these meetings. We were told that of the sixty to seventy men that were attending these meetings, twenty-five at most would be invited at the conclusion of the first year to continue on with the formation program.

The first year was essentially informational meetings held at various parishes throughout the archdiocese. During these meetings we were instructed on the basic requirements for being a deacon, the role of a deacon and the details of the formation process. Theresa attended each of these meetings with me encouraging and helping me to break out of my comfort zone to meet as many of the other men and their wives as possible.

We were blessed at the end of that first year to be invited to continue on with the formation program. The remaining years of the program would entail once a month weekend retreats for the next four years at either *Our Lady-Fatima Retreat House* in Indianapolis or *Saint Meinrad Seminary and School of Theology* in southern Indiana. Our archdiocese encouraged the men's wives to attend these retreats with their husbands (although it was not mandatory for them to do so). I was overjoyed that Theresa was eager to join me at these retreats.

The first of these weekend retreats occurred in August of 2018. The idea of a weekend retreat with a lot of people I didn't know and sitting in a classroom the majority of the weekend for master level theology classes was a very intimidating thought for me. I was a recent convert to Catholicism and I had learned that the other twenty-one men who had been selected for the program were "cradle Catholics" (Catholic since birth). Who did I think I was believing I could be on the same level as them in high level theology classes? As always, however, Theresa's reassuring support and confidence in me brought a soothing calm to the nervous anticipation that had been building as that first weekend retreat approached, as did the thought she would be by my side every step of the way. There are many things I love about Theresa, her ability to bring calm to my soul being one of them.

Another was her outgoing, friendly and compassionate attitude. At the conclusion of the first class of the weekend, she stood up and asked for everyone's attention (to my complete surprise because she professed to not being able to speak in front of large groups and there were about fifty people in the room at the time). I had no idea what she was about to say. She went on to explain that she was going to put a directory together of the deacon candidates and their wives and the program directors and had a form she was asking everyone to complete to assist in making the directory.

From that point on Theresa and one or two other wives seemed to take the lead as "unofficial" activity directors for our diaconate group. She also took it upon herself to prepare birthday and anniversary cards to handout during the weekend if the candidates and their wives had a birthday or anniversary in the coming month. At the beginning of each new academic year during the formation process she purchased gifts to give to the deacon candidates as a form of encouragement (such as matching ties or plaques with an inspirational quote inscribed on them). She encouraged the candidates and wives to unofficially adopt as our own the young daughter of one of the candidates and made sure to buy her birthday and Christmas presents each year. When the COVID pandemic arrived and our classes transitioned to online meetings for a period of time our class was unable to have the usual camaraderie we had enjoyed during the in-person retreat weekends. To combat this Theresa organized a daily evening zoom meeting for all who wished to participate to pray the liturgy of the hours together and catch up on the happenings in our lives.

Another example of her compassionate side occurred at the end of that first retreat weekend. Unfortunately, just before the weekend was to start, one on the deacon candidates suffered a major medical issue that required emergency surgery and a prolonged hospital stay and recovery that required him to miss the weekend and eventually withdraw from the formation program. As Theresa and I were leaving at the end of the weekend of that first retreat she suggested we go visit him in the hospital on our way home.

In all honesty, I was hesitant because he had just had major surgery and I suspected he was not feeling up to having visitors, especially ones who were distant acquaintances at best. But with Theresa's insistence we visited him for a few minutes. Many years later he told me that visit meant more to him and lifted his spirits higher than I would ever know. That is Theresa, always thinking about others and how she can make their day better.

Over the course of the deacon formation period Theresa and I became very good friends with the other deacon candidates and their wives. In time they became family. Theresa and I looked forward to our retreat weekend each month. It was a time to learn more about our faith but also a time to unwind, leave the troubles of the rest of the world behind and spend time with our deacon family.

I also learned that I excelled in the theology classes. Certainly not because I was an expert on the subjects but rather because I was very interested in learning as much as I could about what we were studying and found myself spending an exorbitant amount of time in my studies during the rest of the month when we weren't on the retreats. With our program beginning in 2017 we were scheduled to be completed in 2022 with ordination as deacons in June of that year.

Every relationship goes through difficult times and our relationship is no different. For the overwhelming majority of our relationship, I would describe it as a fairytale beyond anything I could have ever dreamed. But we have had a few moments.

There was the "Driveway Test of Wills." One evening after work Theresa suggested we go out to eat for dinner. I, on the other hand, was wanting to stay in and have dinner at home. A twenty-minute 'debate' ensued to determine whose plans would prevail. Finally, I announced we would have it her way and go out to eat. By this time, however, Theresa was done debating and said we were not going out to eat and she was going to prepare dinner. I insisted we were going out to eat as she wanted and said I was going out to the car and would wait there while she got ready. Five minutes passed, and then ten and then thirty. After an hour of sitting in the car I gave up and returned inside to find Theresa in the living room watching television, having already prepared and ate dinner and finished washing the dishes. That was the day I learned her will is stronger than mine.

There was the twelve-month period when her eldest son Scott separated from his wife and he and his daughter moved in with us. I was more than willing to agree to them living with us while his divorce was pending and as he looked for a new place to live. But having a three year old child living in the home who was adjusting to her parents' separation and two additional people joining us for all of our activities did create a strain on our relationship.

There was the failing health of her father requiring us to put everything on hold until his ultimate death. There was the unexpected death of my father just eight weeks before Theresa left me. There were times when Theresa became frustrated with me for being forgetful or being unable to multitask. There were times when we disagreed on finances, with me being much more liberal with spending than she felt was reasonable.

There were her frustrations with me being what she called an 'eighty percenter'. I always seemed to have multiple projects going at the same time. She pointed out to me numerous times that I always seemed to get a project about eighty percent completed and then move on to another project without completing the first one (I had never recognized this was occurring but when she expressed her frustration I realized she was absolutely correct and I had no explanation for it other than I guess I was getting bored with the original project so I moved on to the next one).

Some of the greatest love stories ever told were written by Shakespeare, Tolstoy, Bronte, Austen, and Mitchell. But God's love for us, as told through the Bible, is the greatest love story ever told. The life-long journey Theresa and I embarked on by bringing God into our marriage is our own personal chapter in this love story.

Scripture tells us that God is the perfection of love. Our marriage opened a door for us to be able to participate in that perfected love. A perfected love we are called upon to practice each and every day. A perfected love that has allowed us to weather the storms. I have no doubt, the faith Theresa and I have formed together by bringing God into our marriage is what assists us in weathering our storms. It has helped us to develop the tools to work through any issues that might arise in our marriage.

Our faith teaches us that our love for each other is not measured by the love we experienced at the beginning of our relationship or on our wedding day. True love is measured in the moments when we have disagreements with each other or difficult periods in our marriage. How we respond to those disagreements and difficulties is the true measure of our love for each other. It is measured by our ability to continue to say I do to our wedding vows in the midst of challenges. In the midst of our sacrifices.

Marriage can be hard at times but it is ok for it to be hard. God wants us to stretch. He wants us to grow out of our selfishness and grow in love. Our faith allows us to understand the only way we can do that is through the cross, through the suffering, through the hard times where we have no option but to figure it out through love, even when we don't feel like loving each other. It is during those times our faith teaches us to call upon God's grace to allow us to continue aiming for that perfected love God asks us to share with each other. It is through His grace our marriage is a beautiful chapter in the greatest love story ever told.

April 18, 2021

My attention shifted back to the present as the road signs indicated I was approaching Savannah. When Theresa left me on April 1, among the many life altering decisions I was faced with was my continuing role in the deacon program. Deacons within the Catholic church are permitted to be married. However, if they are not married at the time of their ordination they have to take a vow of celibacy for the rest of their life.

My ordination was just over fourteen months away. Finding Theresa was made even more imperative due to this deadline. I had to understand what had happened and what it meant for the future.

I recalled Father Steve prayed with me not long ago to have the perception to recognize the many blessings that would come with the storm that was upon me. My initial thought was an incredulous dismissal of his blessing. How could I be expected to find any blessing from a storm that threatened every part of my life?

As I was forging ahead toward Jekyll Island it dawned on me that Father Steve's prayer was inviting me to recognize my blessings during this difficult time because it is through my faith that I would be able to weather this storm. Father's prayer was a reminder that blessings abound when we allow ourselves to see them. We are not asked to drift aimlessly in the stormy waters of life but rather are reminded that when we keep our attention focused on the light and have faith, we will be led through even the darkest hour of the night.

This journey was undertaken to find Theresa. But what if I was not successful? Could God's presence be found in the realization the love of your life has left you forever? Maybe that was what this journey was about.

Maybe there would be a discovery that even in the mightiest of storms we can find God's blessing through a realization we have formed a closer bond with those who are most important in our life? A discovery of God's blessing through a recognition of the love and support from so many within our circle of family and friends? A renewed appreciation for blue skies, gentle breezes, waves rolling in on a sun-soaked beach, family picnics, a stroll through the park, birds singing and flowers blooming on a beautiful spring morning, the vibrant colors of a crisp autumn afternoon or the glow on a freshly fallen snow from a full moon.

Maybe the perception Father Steve was inviting me to recognize is all around me in the form of God's creation. Perhaps it is during these struggles that my ability to withstand the storm and find rays of light in the darkest of dark and peace in the midst of unbearable suffering can amplify the presence of God in my heart. Perhaps what Father Steve's prayer was really telling me was to resist the temptation to allow my suffering to swallow and overcome me, even if I am unable to find Theresa.

Chapter 10: Man's Best Friend

Whoever is righteous has regard for the life
of his beast, but the mercy of the
wicked is cruel

Proverbs 12:10

April 18, 2021

The *Waze* app was indicating I was only eighty miles from Jekyll Island as I merged onto *I-95 South* in Savannah. I wasn't sure what awaited me once I reached Jekyll Island but I knew I couldn't wait to get there. Theresa and I had always jumped at every opportunity to travel to any part of the East Coast. We loved the ocean and had travelled to many different locations up and down the Eastern Seaboard from Key West up to the Eastern Shore of Maryland. There was something mystical about the ocean that kept pulling us back. The rhythmic sound of the waves of the ocean rolling onto the beach, the smell of salt water in the air, a carefree atmosphere that was a relaxing getaway from our normal routine back home, the beauty of palm tress along the beach as we looked out over a seemingly endless ocean, allowing our minds to consider the world beyond the horizon.

Neither of us had ever been to Jekyll Island and to be honest I'm not sure either of us had ever heard of it before. Why Jekyll Island? I had no logical reason. I picked it from among hundreds of possibilities with the criteria being to go somewhere neither of us had ever been on the East Coast. I found out later that Jekyll Island had once been a popular summer destination back in the day for the Vanderbilts, Morgans, Pulitzers, and Rockefellers who summered at the *Jekyll Island Club Resort.*

I understood finding Theresa there would be like finding a needle in a haystack. I know it sounds crazy, and my family wasn't hesitant to suggest so when I announced I was going there to find her, but something in my heart was telling me that was where I would find her.

The drive down *I-95* was beautiful. Back home in Indiana spring was in the air and everything was bursting with signs of new life. The further south I had travelled the more it seemed summer had already arrived. This part of the drive was more rural than what a lot of my journey had been up to that point.

Outside of the metropolitan areas of Louisville, Nashville, Chattanooga, Atlanta and Macon I was able to see the beauty of a large part of our country as the changing topography took me from the rolling hills of southern Indiana, over the Appalachian Mountains to the coastal plains of Georgia.

Almost on que to emphasize this beauty, shortly after merging onto *I-95*, I spotted a bald eagle flying above the tree line just off the interstate. I had never seen a bald eagle in the wild. It looked so majestic as it floated effortlessly in the air with its wings spread wide. Such a beautiful animal. I wished Theresa was with me to see it.

To know Theresa is to know she was a champion of animals.

2010

Theresa's love for animals is legendary among our family and friends. We often joke Theresa loves animals more than she loves people. Of course, we know that is not the case because Theresa has never met a person whom she didn't love. But animals are definitely a close second. Theresa had two dogs when we first started dating. Ali, a strong willed but lovable boxer, and Sadie Jane, a beagle mix with a diva mentality. Theresa brought Sadie home from Tennessee as a puppy after learning some of her littermates had been swept up by hawks. She also had three cats, Cleo, MoJo (named after the monkey from the *Power Puff Girls*), and Caesar Henry Dude.

Theresa treats all of her pets as if they are her kids, even talking to them and, when someone else talks to them she responds as their interpreter. Oddly, one can easily find themselves engaging in conversations with the animal Theresa is speaking for as if it is really the animal speaking. It becomes quite comical when I start debating one of the animals sometimes forgetting for a moment it isn't actually the animal speaking.

In the early stages of our relationship, when we lived in separate cities and alternated staying at each other's homes, Theresa would load Ali and Sadie up in her *G37* and bring them with her to my house. It was a site to behold because it got to a point where anytime Theresa went to get in her car at her house Ali would attempt to jump in hoping she would get to come spend the night at my house. Eventually, Theresa realized her *G37* wasn't meant for hauling two dogs across southern Indiana so she traded her *G37* in for a *GMC Acadia*. It's funny how a love for our animals will often lead us to make major decisions in life (such as the type of car we drive).

Shortly after I started becoming a regular at Theresa's house Caesar started displaying unusual behavior. He stopped using his litter box and was doing his business at various places throughout the house. Theresa was bewildered and was worried about what might be the cause of the change in his behavior.

One evening, after a particularly long day at work, I went to Theresa's bedroom to take a short nap. When I woke up, I was distraught to discover that while I was sleeping Caesar had "done his business" on top of me. After that incident Caesar resumed using his litter box. Upon reflection, Theresa and I realized that those places where Caesar had been doing his business outside of the litter box were places I had been sitting. Apparently, Caesar was a bit jealous of the attention I was receiving from Theresa and needed to show me his dominance. I guess after my nap he felt he had made his point and no longer needed to mark his territory.

Theresa's love for animals doesn't end with dogs and cats. She is known to stop everything she is doing when she sees an animal she believes is in distress. There are many examples. Like climbing a hundred yards through brush on the side of a mountain in Tennessee (even though she is terrified of snakes and insects) to rescue a goat she thought was stuck. When she got to within a few yards of the goat she discovered it was not stuck as it took off running up the mountain. On another occasion she jumped out of her car alongside the road to scare a raccoon away from a nest of baby birds she had been keeping an eye on for several days. There was a farm near where we once lived that had pigs, cows and horses that routinely grazed in the pasture alongside the road. It was her practice to stop there and feed them apples she kept in her car for such occasions and of course carry on a conversation with them as she talked to them about their day. Another time we were leaving our driveway when she startled me by urgently demanding I stop the car. Quickly exiting the car, she went running into the yard flailing her arms and yelling. I gave her a quizzical look when she returned and she explained there were a couple crows near the eggs in the Killdeer nest we had been watching for a couple weeks and she was afraid they were trying to make a meal of the eggs.

But for sure, our dogs are her favorites. Since first meeting, Theresa and I have had several dogs. Of course, Ali and Sadie. Buddy, the dog I brought into the relationship. Roxie, a border collie mix we adopted from Kentucky. Doolittle, a goldendoodle we adopted. Coco, a goldendoodle puppy we stopped to pick up in Kentucky on our way home from our annual vacation in Myrtle Beach. We also adopted two pit bull / American bulldog mix puppies, Jack Sparrow and Jersey Girl.

Jack and Jersey's adoption makes for an interesting story in itself. Theresa saw on the internet that the *Brown County Humane Society* had a litter of dogs they were looking to find forever homes for. Over the course of a week or two she and I toyed with the idea of adding Jack to the pack of three we referred to as our kids. We looked at his pictures online several times a day eventually falling in love with him and decided to adopt him.

The *Brown County Humane Society* was a twenty-minute drive from our home so when the next Saturday came around, we drove there to meet Jack. Upon our arrival we were informed they didn't have a litter of pit bull / American bulldog puppies and suggested perhaps the *Brown County Humane Society* website we had been looking at was from another state. After logging back onto the website, we discovered the shelter where they were located was the *Brown County Humane Society* in Hiawatha, Kansas (a minor detail we had failed to notice when visiting their website previously). We were both devastated because by that time we had fallen in love with Jack.

As a surprise to Theresa, the following Saturday I drove to Kansas to get Jack. When I arrived, Jack was brought out to the lobby and he was as adorable as we had hoped. But there was a problem. He was whining excessively. When I asked if there was something wrong they explained to me there was another littermate he had become very attached to and he was probably whining because they had been separated. They assured me Jack would be ok after he was acclimated to his new home and our dogs.

I asked if the other dog would be ok also. Their response was not as reassuring. I was told Jack's sister, Jersey, was the last of the litter and no one had shown interest in her. She was the runt of the litter and her lower jaw had a slight defect so they were not sure she would be adopted. My heart sank leading me to make what Theresa and I called a 'unilateral executive decision' (decisions we make without first speaking to each other). I decided we would be adopting two puppies bringing our 'kids' to a total of five. Jersey grew to be anything but a runt and by the time she reached maturity was the alpha among all of our dogs. Jack and Jersey fit in well with the other 'kids' but the two of them remained inseparable, always finding a way to get into mischief together. Theresa refers to them as Frick and Frack.

True to form Theresa spoiled our dogs rotten and proved to be their staunchest protector. As a matter of fact, if she was forced to make a decision between them or me, I can't say with absolute certainty who would prevail. She is even known to stop at *McDonalds* on her way home from work for the sole purpose of buying cheeseburgers for the dogs as a special treat.

One night, when we lived out in the country, we let the dogs outside one last time before going to bed. While they were outside, we heard the familiar sound of coyotes. Although it was common for us to hear the coyotes, it was obvious on this particular night they were much closer to the house than usual. The dogs were barking and growling and it became clear there was a standoff occurring between the dogs and the coyotes in our backyard. Theresa yelled for me to hurry and get a gun but was not satisfied with the speed at which I retrieved it. By the time I reached the backdoor with the gun I discovered she had already exited the house and was running toward the commotion waving a broom. Her antics worked and the coyotes took off running and all were safe, dogs and coyotes.

Dogs, however, aren't the only animals Theresa has saved through adoption. Jeff was living in Virginia in 2020 and had purchased a home with his girlfriend in Lovettsville. As part of the purchase, they received several hens and roosters with their home. They loved their chickens … except for a rooster named 'Stu'. Anyone who has spent time around roosters knows they can be aggressive. Jeff and his girlfriend quickly learned Stu took the aggression to another level. Jeff reported to us during one of his calls that Stu chased his girlfriend one too many times and she was demanding stew be made of Stu. Hearing of Stu's pending sentence, Theresa sought clemency for him. After a passionate plea it was decided the only way Stu would be pardoned was if he was exiled to Columbus, Indiana.

Just like that we became chicken farmers with Theresa insisting we would also need to have hens with hopes of taming Stu's ornery behavior. Stu made his way to Indiana after we built a coop for the flock. We quickly learned the reports of Stu's aggressive behavior were not over-advertised notwithstanding his own flock to rule over. He would attack anything, animal or human, that invaded his area. On one occasion he fought off a hawk that was attempting to abscond with one of his hens.

For our part, anytime we interacted with Stu we had to carry a rake to keep between us and Stu at all times to avoid being attacked. Even with the rake in hand, if we turned our backs on him he would launch a surprise attack. Stu's exploits extended to all. Our priest visited us one day and hearing of Stu's behavior insisted he was not afraid of Stu, having grown up with chickens and roosters himself. He went outside to confront Stu and within thirty seconds was trapped in a corner by a very angry Stu who was ready to attack.

Another animal Theresa came to love was a dromedary located in a pasture on a hillside at the halfway point between her home and mine when I lived in Ellettsville. She named the camel "Humpty." When we were travelling back and forth between each other's homes we would always tell the other when we were passing by Humpty's house. Just as she did with the cows, pigs and horses near our home, it was not unusual for Theresa to stop and have a chat with Humpty and give him a treat on her way home from my house. Oddly, I suppose from the repetitive references to him as we traveled back and forth between our homes, Humpty became special to both of us and we had a picture of him set up at the reception for our wedding.

I say Theresa loves all animals. I guess that is not completely accurate. Her love doesn't extend to frogs and insects. I first became aware of her fear of frogs on a beautiful spring evening after we had experienced torrential rain for the previous twenty-four hours. We decided to take advantage of a break in the weather and took a drive through the countryside. Theresa was known for being horrible with directions. The running joke in the family was that for her to get anywhere in town she would have to first return home to go to a different location because the only way she knew how to get anywhere was from her home. On this particular spring evening Theresa didn't know exactly where we were in the country side but it was only a few miles outside of town.

As we were driving on the country road, we noticed something ahead covering the road. As we approached neither of us could comprehend what it could be but whatever it was covered about a thirty-yard section of the road from shoulder to shoulder. We had our windows down enjoying the evening and began hearing a noise that grew with intensity as we approached the covered section of the road. Shortly after hearing the sound, I realized the road was covered with what must have been thousands of frogs and the sound we were hearing was their croaking. It felt like a scene from an Alfred Hitchcock movie. When Theresa became aware of what was in front of us she demanded we turn around and for me to get us back into town immediately.

Ironically, about a year after the frog apocalypse, we bought our home out in the country. Theresa didn't realize it at the time but the home we were purchasing was only a half-mile from the scene of the frog apocalypse. Soon after moving into the home I discovered while mowing the grass the yard had hundreds of frogs in it. I was concerned that when Theresa learned we were living in frog country she would demand we sell our home. To her credit, she learned to adapt and miraculously grew to enjoy the songs of the frogs croaking in the evening.

The country living allowed us to take walks in evening on the county roads near our home. These roads were not heavily travelled and the little traffic one would encounter would be vehicles travelling at low speeds with drivers eager to wave hello as they passed by. *Hoosier* hospitality at its best. That's one of the reasons we enjoyed living in the country. Our walks encouraged us to slow down and enjoy God's creation. We learned during our walks that grasshoppers have a tendency to spend a lot of time on the country roads during the summer. A grasshopper, being a member of the insect family, was not Theresa's friend. Our walks had to be laughable for anyone who saw us because Theresa spent most the walk dodging and jumping out of the way of grasshoppers. Those watching probably thought Theresa was busting out some new Beyoncé moves.

But above all other insects, Theresa's nemesis in the insect family is spider crickets. A creepy little insect that appears to be a cross between a spider and a cricket. They are relatively harmless with an ability to strike an irrational fear in Theresa.

One evening while we were living in her home in town, she got up in the middle of the night to use the restroom. Just before turning the light off when she returned to the bedroom she thought she noticed a spider cricket on the floor and woke me up to catch it. After a "man look" for a few minutes, I offered there was no spider cricket in the room and suggested she had just imagined it in her sleepy state. Theresa was not accepting my theory and demanded I continue looking for the intruder. Thirty minutes later, after taking every piece of furniture out of the room, I finally found the offending monster hanging from the underside of the box springs of the bed. I shudder to think what would have happened had she accepted my initial evaluation and it crawled on her after she fell back to sleep.

During a trip to the *Smoky Mountains*, I discovered there was another animal that scared Theresa. We were taking a drive through *Cades Cove* and came upon an open field with a lot of cars parked alongside the road. We stopped to see what was so interesting to everyone who had exited their cars. We came up to a fence line and asked some onlookers what they were doing. They pointed to a spot across the field near a tree line, about one hundred yards from where we were standing. They indicated there were several bears which we could vaguely see when they pointed toward them. We had wanted to get some pictures of bears while we were visiting the park but hadn't been successful up to this point.

Figuring this might be the only opportunity to get some pictures I corralled a couple guys standing nearby and we crossed the fence line and started walking in chest high grass toward the bears despite Theresa's protestations as we moved through the field. About half-way across the field one of the bears looked up and stared at us intently. With the stares from the bear telling us our advance was not being well-received we reversed course and went back to the car where I was immediately greeted with a lecture about all the things that could have gone wrong, all of which for some reason hadn't crossed my mind until Theresa pointed them out to me. Upon second thought I agreed with her that my attempt to get a good photo op of the bears was not one of my brightest ideas.

April 18, 2021

Anatole France once said "until one has loved an animal a part of one's sole remains unawakened." I have never known anyone to love animals like Theresa. France's axiom has certainly never proven truer than it does with Theresa. She loves animals and they love her. I have also never met anyone whose soul is more awake than hers. She exudes a state of happiness and bliss and all who come in contact with her cannot help but come away from interactions with her in a similar state.

The journey I had embarked on at 5:30 this morning had been long. I had anticipated it would be a solitary drive, zoning out while listening to the songs on my playlist. It had been anything but that. The memories of the life I share with Theresa had been racing through my head for the entire drive. It was almost as if she was in the car reminiscing with me about our life.

My attention was brought back to the drive by the sound of my phone telling me the exit for *U.S. 17* was approaching. This next portion of the trip would be very short. I was nearing my destination.

Chapter 11: A Perfect Love Reaches Its Pinnacle

And over all these things put on love,
which is the perfect bond of unity

Proverbs 12:10

April 18, 2021

Only six miles remained before reaching the causeway to drive onto Jekyll Island and then another six miles on the causeway before reaching the island. It had been a long day reflecting on the life Theresa and I share. The one consistent throughout my reflections is how much I love her.

Over the years I tried my best to make sure she always knows that. After she left I went back through my laptop to try to find the love letters I had written her. Much to my dismay I wasn't able to find most of them but I transferred the ones I found to a single document and downloaded them onto my phone thinking they may be useful at some point on this journey. Committing a cardinal sin as I was driving, I opened my phone to re-read what I downloaded.

November 10, 2015

I remember when I first stared into your eyes as we sat under our special gazebo. Even then I felt the concerns and worries of my world vanish while I was with you.

These past five and a half years have been the happiest and fullest of my life. My world is a beautiful place because of you and the love you have given me.

Thank you for loving me unconditionally and remaining endlessly patient with me (I am indeed a work in progress). The knowledge that even when I stumble and fall, you are there to pick me up, brush me off, and hold me close (and yes, even when you tell me to suck it up buttercup), is undoubtedly one of the loveliest gifts ever given to me. Thank you for supporting me and pushing me further than I think I can possibly go. Thank you for walking hand in hand with me on the spiritual journey God has placed before us. Thank you for being you.

Truly, as Maya Angelou once wrote, in all the world, there is no heart for me like yours. In all the world, there is no love for you like mine.

Love...I wish there was a word more descriptive than 'love', for by itself it does not seem to convey all that I feel for you. My extraordinary love for you my dear is simply immeasurable and indescribable.

October 15, 2017

Six years ago you made me the happiest man alive by becoming my wife. In reality though I became the happiest man alive the first day we met. I have never understood how someone as wonderful as you fell in love with me but I thank God for your love every day. When we met it was as if I was born again because that is when I started to live. That's when I believe I started developing into the person God created me to be. That's when I finally understood how to love someone with all my heart. That's when I felt a complete love from someone else. As we celebrate our sixth year of marriage, I renew my vow to always strive to love you with all my heart and to never let you doubt that for the rest of my life. You are the Good in my Good Morning, the Happy in my Happy Birthday and the Love in my I Love You. Happy anniversary to the woman who is the essence of my life. Happy Anniversary!!!

June 5, 2018

First Date Anniversary. WOW, 8 years!!! Where has the time gone? It seems like only yesterday when we first met yet it also seems as though I have known you a lifetime. From our first conversation sitting in the gazebo in Nashville until this moment I have always known what a truly special, amazing, genuine and completely beautiful person you are. Soon after, if not during, that first meeting I knew I was in love and dreamed of spending the rest of my life with you. Now, I could not imagine the rest of eternity without you. The saying goes that when you find the right person, they will complete you. This could never be more accurate than in our relationship. Reflecting back to where I was 8 years ago to where I am today, I have experienced dreams fulfilled, goals achieved, fears conquered and a solid relationship with God established and growing. I have seen an empathetic and caring side of myself blossom and new aspirations, goals and direction set that were previously either thought unattainable or unimaginable. Most of all dear I have experienced love like never before in the form of a love shared with God, the love I receive from you and the love I have for you and our children. All of which is fostered by your love, encouragement, motivation and support. I love you with all my heart. You truly are my better half.

October 15, 2018

Happy anniversary baby. We have had many special days together, from the moment we met to this very day. In reality though each day has been a special day because we are together. But today, on our anniversary, I celebrate our marriage because it represents how you changed my life and brought happiness back into it. This day reminds me that God really does love me, for He gave me the most wonderful person in the world and chose her to be my lifetime partner. There are not enough words to describe how deeply I love you. You are my love and my soul. Days have passed on, years have gone by, and my love for you has grown stronger with each passing hour. I will always love you. As you know, I love the sappy love stories. To me, every love story is beautiful, but ours is my favorite and it will continue to be until the end of time. When we first met, I would have never imagined all that we have done or where we are today and the direction we are heading but I knew from those first moments I would be the luckiest man in the world if I could spend my life with you. We have plans and goals for the future with God at the center as our guide and only time will tell where He leads us. However, days like today invite us to reflect on where we have been. Happy Anniversary dear. I love you.

October 15, 2019

It has been almost a decade since we began our fairytale by spending an afternoon together in 'our' gazebo getting to know each other. When we met that day, I was shocked by your physical beauty. Sure, I had seen your pictures but they did not prepare me for how truly beautiful you are. Now, almost ten years later, having gotten to know the inner you as well as I know myself, I understand the beauty I saw on that first day radiates from your core. I've never known a person who is as compassionate for others as you. Who always intuitively knows what's right and just. Who has a burning desire to help others and give back to the community. Who I can trust with my heart and know you will always have my best interests in mind, even when I may disagree with what you know is in my best interests.

When we went our separate ways that first day we met, I had an odd sense I had known you my entire life and felt an eager anticipation to see you again. We connected immediately and became best friends overnight. Today, as we celebrate the 8th anniversary of our wonderful wedding day, I still experience that eager anticipation to see you every time we are apart. Although I have not actually known you my entire life, eight years after we pledged our eternal love to each other, I know our fairytale will be one of living happily ever after for the rest of our life. I love you.

September 8, 2020

We first gazed into each other's eyes on June 5, 2010. We sat for hours talking and laughing at each other's stories falling into a comfortable rhythm, as if we had known each other forever. Some say love at first sight is not possible. They are wrong. I knew on that first date I had met the love of my life. Before I met you, I had prayed that God would lead me to someone I could love with all my heart and who would love me the same in return. I had no idea God's answer to my prayer would be beyond anything I could have imagined on my own. His answer was you. The perfect person for me. My soulmate. My best friend. My partner. My advisor. My hero.

The old cliches say you complete me and you are my better half. You, my dear, are the reason those cliches exist. The life we share together and the person I am today have only been possible because of who you are, your inspiration, your encouragement, your faith in God and your confidence in me.

Last night I was looking back at pictures of some of the special times we have shared together over the years. Although we may have not known each other for our entire life, we certainly have packed a lifetime of memories into the time we have been together. You encourage me to spread my wings and fly and together we do just that.

I can think of no better day to reminisce about all of those wonderful times than the day God blessed our world with your birth. God sure works in mysterious ways. A girl born in Baltimore and raised in Virginia Beach and a boy raised in a small town in Indiana were, as the song goes, put on broken roads that would lead us to each other, proving that even in the darkest of storms God's radiant light is shining beautifully on the other side as a beacon for hope in even the most difficult of times.

So, on this most special day, my dear, know that you are the love of my life and I cherish you and us. You may not have been my first love but you are my forever love. I love you!!! Happy birthday and a salute to all the memories we will make in the years to come.

October 15, 2020

9 years! It seems like just yesterday but yet it seems as though we have lived a lifetime together. It seems as if I have known you all my life. It seems as if somehow you are a part of every memory in my life, even before we met. Paraphrasing Dickens, we have shared the best of times, we have experienced the worst of times, it has been a season of light, there has been a season of darkness, our marriage is my spring of hope, we have witnessed a winter of despair. One thing, however, has remained constant dear. There has not been a moment when I haven't cherished our marriage with all my heart or a day that has passed when I didn't love you more than the day before. Through the mostly ups and the occasional difficult times, I always consider you my blessing from God through which I am working toward becoming the person He

intended me to become. I love you. Happy Anniversary!!!

February 14, 2021

On this Valentines Day there is no better time to tell you how deeply I love you.

Regardless of where life has taken us baby you have been there by my side. Even when we met online and you didn't see a picture of me, you gave me a chance. Even after tricking you into believing I was the health conscious, chain smoking, biker in leathers with a girlfriend beside me when we first met at the Speedway gas station, you gave me a chance. Even after your son warned you of me when he doubted I was who I said I was because he didn't approve of my car or dress attire, you gave me a chance. Even after I told you we were going to marry someday long before you were ready, you gave me a chance. Even after I gave you a book (*The Choice*) to read telling you that my love for you was like Travis' love for Gabby (knowing Travis almost killed Gabby), you gave me a chance. Gosh, now that I look back on all of that, I was kind of creepy.

You have been there at my side during all the great times we have shared together. All the family Christmases and Thanksgiving gatherings. RCIA. Easter Vigils. My baptism and our communion. Sharing confirmation together. Sharing our faith together. Birthday celebrations. Our family Sunday brunches. The Halloween parties. The pool parties. The family cook-outs. Our annual outings to the state and county fair. Our nightly diners out. Bayview on Mackinac Island and Schooner in Myrtle Beach (both of which became our homes away from home). Our love for the sounds of clip clop, clip clop, clip clop on Mackinac. Hawaii. The Outer Banks. Gatlinburg and ziplining through the Smokey's. Cancun. Chichen Itza. Honduras. George from Uruguay. Our balloon ride over the sugar cane fields in the Dominican Republic. Washington DC. The royal wedding party. Stranded at sea on a cruise ship, our other cruises and my eloquent (not) proposal. The surprise Las Vegas trip. The X birthdays. The surprise Chicago trip and all of our other Chicago weekends. Pictured Rocks and being chased by the fog bank on Lake Superior. Lambeau Field. Virginia Beach. Baltimore. Hershey and Reading, Pennsylvania. Cleveland. Dallas. Jacksonville. Philadelphia. Miami. Tampa Bay. St. Augustine. The pizza tours. The *Yankees, Cubs, White Sox* and *Orioles* baseball games. Our Sunny and Cher duet. The Colts football games (even if you were cheering against them). The Pacers basketball games. IU football and basketball games. The traveling Easter Bunny. *Phantom of the Opera* (both times). *Wicked.* Blue Man Group. The Barry Manilow / Red Hot Chili Pepper ticket exchange. Mellencamp. Chesney. McGraw. Elton John. Lady Gaga. Trans-Siberian Orchestra. *Indianapolis Indians* baseball games. The luaus. Fourth of July Fireworks. Taking the grandkids to *Apple Works* every fall. Pumpkin pie and cookie baking days. Bonfires and s'mores in our backyard. Watching *White Christmas* every year. Cheer Fund delivery days. Calling the grandkids the first day of school every year to sing 'School Days' to them. Taking the grandsons to Saturday morning kid's workshop at *Menards*. Sharing some of life's hardest moments in the loss of parents and fur babies. Sharing some of life's greatest moments such as our children's graduations and the births of grandchildren. Swimming in the Atlantic and Pacific together. Kayaking on *Lake Huron*, a river in Hawaii and much smaller lakes and rivers in Indiana. Swimming together in Lake Monroe on New Year's Day in below freezing temperatures. Descending into the depths of the *Hoover Dam* and taking a boat ride on the Colorado River in the Grand Canyon. Making friends together from across the globe to those living in our own town. Hiking to water falls in Tennessee and on Maui.

Watching the sun rise over the Atlantic and while atop Haleakala and watching it set in the Gulf of Mexico, the Caribbean and the Pacific Ocean. Visiting lighthouses from Michigan, to Florida, to North Carolina, to Virginia, to Hawaii. The great pity party of 2016 when my "I don't feel like myself" comment was followed up with your "Suck it up buttercup" response. The great diving incident from the upper deck of the pontoon boat on Lake Monroe. Nicholas Sparks and Mitch Daniels congratulating us on our wedding. So many great memories. We truly have had a lifetime of memories ... always supporting each other during happy times and sad times ... for better or for worse.

I only wish I could go back in time to be able to do a better job at showing you each day how much I am truly in love with you. You are my Gabby!!!

I love you. Happy Valentines Day my love!!!

March 23, 2020

Ushering in the beginning of one of the eeriest periods of our lifetime, we received word that on March 23, 2020 Indiana would be joining the growing list of states 'shutting down' because of the COVID pandemic sweeping across the world. Reports of the rapid spread of the virus and rising number of deaths were paralyzing our country with fear. Not much was known about the virus, how it spread, or how to treat it. We were receiving daily reports on the news about the virus and how seemingly healthy people were contracting it and dying almost overnight. To make matters worse, Theresa was a nurse practitioner in an ear nose and throat office which put her at an increased risk for exposure.

I was relieved when the doctors at her office decided to shut the office down. At almost the same time I received word that my field of employment would be shutting down and going virtual for the quarantine. Even though there were many uncertainties about finances during this time (all of which worked themselves out in short order), Theresa and I strictly complied with the quarantine and remained home exclusively but for a quick weekly trip to the grocery. Our personal quarantine lasted for approximately six weeks but even after that we tried to stay to ourselves for most of the summer of 2020.

At first, even though relieved Theresa would not be exposed to the high risk of contracting COVID at work, I was not excited by the prospect of being confined to home. We lived an active lifestyle and were constantly on the go. We were active in the church. We ate out every night. We travelled a lot. We volunteered. We enjoyed going to concerts and ballgames. Literally, the lifestyle we knew ended overnight.

But for us there were some very good unexpected consequences from our quarantine. Maybe because of fear of the unknown, we started seeing God everywhere. Every time we turned around we saw and heard Him. We saw Him in the brilliant blue sky and felt Him in the warmth of the sun. We heard Him singing with the birds as they played in the trees and built their nests. We saw Him playing with our dogs as they tumbled over each other while playing in the yard without a care in the world and felt Him moving with the gentle breeze as we went about our day. We heard Him talking with the frogs that were awakening from their long winter nap. We saw His grace as the blue heron spread its wings in our field in preparation for flight. And as if to emphasize the wonderful days we were experiencing together we saw His beautiful artistry in all its glory in the setting sun.

Another consequence was we slowed down. Selfishly, I had Theresa all to myself. There had been times on vacations when I had her all to myself but even then, it was for short periods of time and we were on the go. The quarantine was much longer than a vacation and we would be home with little to do but spend time with each other. We did puzzles together. We played Scrabble endlessly. We watched all of the episodes of *Yellowstone*, *The Crown* and *The Chosen* together. We did projects around the house together. We had marathon sessions of watching reruns of *The Andy Griffith Show*. We watched *Big Bang Theory* religiously. We took daily walks together. We talked for hours. We connected like never before and our love grew to depths greater than ever before.

Even so, we began missing our regular contact with family and friends with the quarantine stretching on without seeing them. Easter was April 12. As *Holy Week* approached Theresa suggested we modify our quarantine for Easter. She was concerned the quarantine would ruin Easter for our grandchildren, the children of her sons' girlfriends, and the children of some of our friends. She proposed we order an Easter Bunny costume and spend *Holy Week* making sure they all had a visit from the Easter Bunny, practicing social distance in the process of course. How she comes up with her ideas is beyond me but I thought it was a wonderful idea. It was a perfect example of how Theresa is always thinking of the welfare of others.

Luckily, she was able to find a company online from which we could order a costume, notwithstanding the quarantine, so she placed the order and it arrived before *Holy Week*. The pure joy we saw on the children's faces when the Easter Bunny visited their homes was priceless. After weeks of quarantine it was a pleasure to bring some form of normalcy back to their life, not to mention ours. The Easter Bunny completed its rounds by Good Friday and then Theresa suggested another idea. Would I be up to travelling to Virginia to allow the Easter Bunny to visit Jeff and his girlfriend's daughter? Why not, I thought. It wasn't like we had anything else to do.

Seeing Theresa being the Easter Bunny's surrogate during the quarantine is a memory I will never forget and added to the long list of Theresaisms that I will always cherish in my heart. Although COVID was a tragedy for so many, the quarantine was a blessing for our relationship. We connected like never before and that connection continued until the day she left me. We were at the pinnacle of our love affair, so it seemed.

April 18, 2021

I drove onto the *Jekyll Island Causeway* after what was supposed to be an eleven-and-a-half-hour drive listening to the playlist on my phone turned into a fourteen-hour marathon reflecting on my life with Theresa. I couldn't help but think that my life with her had been a fairytale dream unlike anything I had ever known.

An east coast woman brought to Indiana under less-than-ideal circumstances meets a midwestern man, each having recently experienced the darkest periods of their life. We fell in love when we were both least expecting it. We worked through issues to ensure our love would endure. Two lives joined together making one. Two families joined together making one. Making a lifetime of memories. The places we visited together. The activities we enjoyed together. The faith we shared together. The community involvement we participated in together. Too many memories to remember to speak of here. But most importantly, the time spent with each other and the love we shared.

I was not prepared to lose all that we had nor the promise of the future yet to come. It was time to face whatever the next seven days would bring ...

PART 2

Chapter 12: The Beginning

Come to me, all of you who are weary and carry heavy burdens, and I will give you rest. Take my yoke upon you. Let me teach you, because I am humble and gentle at heart, and you will find rest for your souls. For my yoke is easy to bear, and the burden I give you is light.

Matthew 11:28-30

August 13, 2020

We both took the day off from work and were up by seven getting ready for the day. We had a full day scheduled. We would be going to Theresa's doctor appointment for an endoscopy and colonoscopy hoping to get some answers to why her hemoglobin levels had dipped and why she had been feeling lethargic. Her lethargy had been an issue for some time along with some intermittent shooting pain into her jaw. Initially, it was thought it might be heart-related so she had some cardiac work-ups to determine if that was the issue but the tests came back negative. When her hemoglobin levels dropped, however, her primary care physician wanted to check her digestive system. There was some concern she had possibly developed an ulcer and he wanted to check it out.

After the tests we would have lunch and then go shopping in Indianapolis. I was thankful for the opportunity to spend the day with Theresa, a continuation of the new connection we had established since the beginning of the pandemic.

We arrived at the hospital for the tests at 8:30 a.m. After a short period in the waiting room, a nurse came out and called Theresa's name to take her back to prepare her for the procedures. I was instructed to remain in the waiting room as they prepared her after which I would be called back to her room where we would meet with her doctor before the procedures began. While I was waiting, I checked in with my office to see how things were going and then called my son to see if he would be interested in meeting us for lunch after the procedures were completed.

It wasn't long before I was called back and Theresa and I discussed where we would go shopping after lunch. Dr. Waxel, her primary care physician who would be performing the procedures, came into the room and explained the procedures in detail and asked if we had any questions. Over the years Theresa and I had developed a jovial relationship with Dr. Waxel, no doubt aided by the fact Theresa was a provider herself. Dr. Waxel explained the procedures would take about forty-five minutes to an hour and that he would call me back after the procedure to tell me how it went.

With that I went back into the waiting room and watched the morning news filled with reports of the COVID pandemic's current status. Anyone who has been in the waiting room of a hospital while a loved one is having a procedure performed knows time seems to stand still while waiting. My concern for Theresa's well-being combined with the monotony of hearing about the COVID updates on the television and eagerness for lunch and shopping had me checking my watch every few minutes trying to anticipate when I would be called back to Theresa's room. Almost on schedule the nurse finally called for me and told me they were ready for me to come back.

When I arrived in Theresa's room she was already there, sound asleep from the anesthetic. After another short wait, Dr. Waxel came into the room. Gone, however, was his usual carefree demeanor. With her still asleep he began explaining the procedures. He performed the endoscopy first and indicated it didn't show anything out of the ordinary. That was surprising because that is where we thought we would find the ulcer.

He then began to explain the colonoscopy. Theresa had a routine colonoscopy about three years ago so there weren't any expectations it would reveal anything either. Those expectations proved to be wrong. Dr. Waxel explained he was not able to go far into the colon because he found a large mass shortly after beginning the procedure that prevented him from going further. I had no idea what that suggested but immediately thought of the possibility of a tumorous cancer and asked him if that was a concern. Anticipating a rebuttal, my world came crashing down when he replied he was not sure but wanted to refer Theresa to Dr. Sneed, an oncologist, for further testing and that he had arranged for us to meet with her later in the afternoon.

I couldn't believe what I was being told. We woke up this morning believing Theresa was going to have a few quick routine medical procedures to develop a plan on how to treat an ulcer and then have an enjoyable day together eating lunch and shopping. Now I was being told instead we would be meeting with an oncologist because Theresa might have colon cancer. Dr. Waxel ended his de-briefing with an apology, cementing for me that he suspected more than he had revealed.

He left the room and I was left there with the love of my life sleeping, unaware herself of the results of the procedures. The walls of the room were contracting on me. I could not breathe. My mind was spinning and I instantly had a raging headache. I was confused. I was lost. I kept thinking I must be in the middle of a horrible nightmare but try as I might I could not wake up. I felt so lonely sitting by Theresa's bedside holding her hand with no one to speak to as I tried to process what was happening. I desperately needed Theresa to wake up to explain to me what was going on and to tell me it all would be ok. She was the medical professional after all and she would be able to tell me that as usual I was being a drama king and overreacting.

Not getting any quick answers I turned to my phone to do some impromptu research on colon cancer. What I found was terrifying. The median survival rate of colon cancer patients is five years with only a fifty percent curable rate, and only if the cancer is localized to the colon. This couldn't be happening, I thought. There has to be a mistake somewhere. Theresa, I need you to wake up!!!

With Dr. Waxel's words and my research weighing heavy on my mind and no signs Theresa would be waking up anytime soon I stepped out of the room to make a few calls for emotional support and spiritual guidance from Father Steve and Deacon Mark. I was able to reach them and they both offered to drop everything they were doing to come to the hospital but not knowing how much longer we would be at the hospital I thanked them for their thoughtfulness and told them that was not necessary.

Knowing what to say to someone who just dropped news like this on you is always difficult but they somehow knew exactly what I needed. They reminded me Theresa and I would be coming home later in the day and that we didn't yet know what the diagnosis and prognosis was. They explained what was important right now was for me to breathe, take things one step at a time and adapt as we discovered more, be present and in the moment for Theresa and, most importantly, pray.

Theresa eventually woke up but, in my self-pity during the whirlwind thirty-five minutes I waited for her to wake up, I had not stopped to think I would have to be the one to tell her the results of the procedures. How do you tell the love of your life she may have cancer? A cancer with a high mortality rate. I knew she would understand that herself without the research I had to do.

I decided to tell her in the same manner Dr. Waxel had told me, straight facts about what we knew with no editorializing. Probably out of a concern for how I would react and her medical experience, Theresa took the news calmly and replied, "Ok, well then, the next step is to see what Dr. Sneed has to say." It was almost as if she had been expecting this news, making me think that perhaps she had been keeping her expectations from me in hopes of protecting me from unnecessary concern.

With our plans for shopping cancelled we decided to go ahead with lunch while we waited for the appointment with Dr. Sneed. I called Brent to tell him what was happening and that we would need to take a rain-check on lunch with him. Needless to say lunch was subdued while trying to avoid the topic of the elephant in the room. We finished lunch and once we arrived at Dr. Sneed's office didn't have to wait long to see her.

Dr. Sneed was an upbeat and positive person. She was reportedly one of the best oncologists in the Indianapolis area. Dr. Sneed got straight to the point. Theresa did in fact have a tumorous cancer in her colon. So much for there being a mistake. The process at this point was to determine what kind of cancer and whether or not it had spread beyond the colon before determining a treatment plan. Further testing would be required and she had scheduled that for the following Monday. It was Thursday. It was going to be a very long weekend.

August 17, 2020

Monday could not come soon enough. The results of this upcoming test would tell us a lot about treatment and, more importantly, how successful the treatment would be in curing the cancer. The four days waiting for Monday to arrive were filled with crying, sleepless nights, a lot of time holding each other closely and a ton of prayers. It didn't make sense to us how this was happening. Theresa led a healthy life. She didn't smoke, seldomly drank alcohol and was health conscious with her diet. Cancer wasn't prevalent in her family so it didn't appear it was hereditary either. We led an honest life devoted to serving God and others. "Why?" kept running through my head. Why Theresa? If it had to be one of us, why not me?

Theresa's wasn't vocally saying "why me?" but I can't imagine her not feeling that way subconsciously. We had reached a point in our life where we were happy and settled. Our children were starting to have children of their own which we looked forward to spoiling. We had the rest of our life to share together. Family gatherings, vacations, the love of our life in each other, so many more memories to make together. We had always talked of growing old together and sitting on a porch in our twilight years holding hands and remembering the life we enjoyed together. Now, we were faced with the real possibility all those dreams were in jeopardy. I know for my part I kept asking myself why.

The procedure Dr. Sneed scheduled would be performed in the hospital and would require an overnight stay. I scheduled off work Monday and Tuesday to spend the night with Theresa in the hospital. When we arrived at the hospital, we were directed to the oncology floor. I recall feeling awkward going to the oncology floor thinking we didn't belong in that part of the hospital.

After checking into the hospital, we were visited by Father Steve who performed the Sacrament of Anointing the Sick on Theresa in her room. He also performed it on me encouraging me to look for blessings that may be difficult to recognize during these difficult times. I couldn't imagine what blessings there might be in this situation but incredulously agreed I would look for them.

I had planned on staying the night in the hospital but Theresa asked me to go home to take care of the dogs and chickens, assuring me she would be ok and just needed to sleep. I suspect what she was really needing was some alone time to help her process what was happening. I had been doting over her since receiving the news the prior Thursday so she hadn't had any time to herself. Everything was happening so quick our emotions were having trouble keeping up. She asked me to come back first thing in the morning so I would be there when Dr. Sneed came in to tell us the results of the test.

Reluctantly, at the close of visiting hours I went home. That night would be the first time I hadn't slept in the same bed with Theresa in years. Operating on autopilot I fed the dogs and chickens before settling in for the night. I was in a daze and it felt as though I was having a terrible dream from which I couldn't wake. I went to bed that night crying myself to sleep. I suppose in hindsight I too needed some alone time.

I awoke the following morning with a heavy heart scared of the road that lay before us and the news we would be receiving from Dr. Sneed later in the morning. As I was sitting at our dining room table trying to eat a breakfast which provided me no interest, I was staring out the window contemplating how to go forward. In a remarkable sense of timing, and a miraculous feat of bravery with our dogs looming outside, a dove landed on a chair just outside the window and seemed to be looking directly into my eyes with such intensity I felt as though it was touching my soul.

While sharing this moment with the dove, Father Steve's prayer replayed in my mind and I could not help feeling this dove was the Holy Spirit descending to provide me with a blanket of peace, comforting me with a knowledge that God is in control. A sense of calm spread over me that I hadn't experienced since the morning of the previous Thursday. I recalled reading once what Jan Richardson had written about blessings. She wrote something to the effect that she had come to see with greater clarity that a blessing is at its most potent in times of adversity. When God's protection and care seem most difficult to find, a blessing helps us to perceive God's grace that interacts with us, helping us to forge ahead. This must have been what Father Steve was trying to help me understand. The dove was one of those blessings.

I arrived at the hospital bright and early expecting Theresa to still be asleep. To my surprise she was wide awake joking with one of the nurses when I walked in. She never looked more beautiful. She reported that she had a good night's sleep and was feeling positive about what Dr. Sneed would be reporting on the test results. Her calm and reassuring demeanor soothed my soul adding to the calm the dove had provided earlier in the morning. One thing I had come to learn since meeting Theresa was she always had that soothing effect on me.

Dr. Sneed had a smile on her face when she entered the room later in the morning. I was hoping that was a good sign. She proceeded to give us the results in medical terms but after she was finished, she and Theresa dumbed it down so that I could understand what was said.

Essentially, the bad news was the cancer was stage IV, having spread to her liver. The good news was the type of cancer Theresa had was responsive to treatment. The plan was to treat the cancer with chemotherapy to reduce the size of the lesions on the liver and once they had shrunk to have surgery to remove them from the liver and colon. When questioned why not have surgery now to remove the tumor from the colon Dr. Sneed replied surgery on the colon would require a recovery period before starting the chemotherapy. Reducing the size of the lesions on the liver was the priority at this point and that required chemotherapy.

That seemed backwards to me but who am I to disagree with professionals. Dr. Sneed then told us chemotherapy would begin the following day on an outpatient basis. She explained the chemotherapy would cause little to no hair loss but might cause nausea. The plan was to have four treatments every other week and then have more tests to see how the cancer was responding. Dr. Sneed ended our meeting saying she was changing Theresa's diagnosis from palliative to curable and that she was releasing Theresa to go home.

The discharge paperwork that needed to be completed for Theresa to be released seemed to take forever but as soon as she was released we walked to the car, got in, and with a tear running down my cheek I asked Theresa, "Did I hear Dr. Sneed correctly, she said curable, right?" With her own tear running down her cheek she looked back at me with a big smile on her face and said, "Yes." The tears started flowing freely for both of us and then turned to outright sobbing with a long embrace. It had been five days of pure torture not knowing what was before us but we had finally heard the word we were praying to hear ... curable.

The road ahead would not be easy with chemotherapy and surgery. But ... curable. With that one word the weight of the world's problems was lifted from our shoulders. Our prayers were answered. Our dreams saved. Our future together secured. The forty-five minute drive home from the hospital was filled with phone calls to our children, my mom, our siblings, Father Steve, Deacon Bill and some friends. With each call excitement, relief and tears of joy filled the conversation.

The burden we had been carrying was heavy and we were weary. As Matthew's Gospel teaches us, in such times we are to give our burdens and weariness to God for we will find rest in our souls through Him. The past five days had been filled with prayers. On my behalf, my prayer was for God to work His will through us, whatever His will may be. Certainly, our will was for Theresa to be cured and for us to return to our wonderful life loving each other and serving Him. But we never know ahead of time what God's will is. With one word, curable, Dr. Sneed provided solace that perhaps our will was God's will.

Chapter 13: Progress

Answer me when I call, O God of my righteousness!
You have given me relief when I was in distress.
Be gracious to me and hear my prayer!
Psalm 4:1

August 19 – October 29, 2020

We arrived at Dr. Sneed's office the following day apprehensive of the unknown. Theresa's specialty was not oncology and to my knowledge I had never experienced anyone undergoing chemotherapy. We took comfort in what Dr. Sneed had told us about hair loss and there being a possibility of nausea (which we took as there also being a possibility there wouldn't be nausea). Those two symptoms are probably two of the most commonly known side effects of chemotherapy. But beyond that, we didn't know much else. The treatment, which was intravenously, went smooth enough and Theresa said it was painless.

She didn't feel much different for the next twenty-four hours but felt a little nausea after that and it lasted for about forty-eight hours. She was scheduled to have a treatment once every two weeks. The next three treatments were pretty much the same with the nausea becoming a little more severe and lasting a little longer with each successive treatment. After each treatment she also experienced a loss of appetite, sensitivity to cold especially in her hands and slight neuropathy in her fingertips, all of which likewise became a little more severe and lasted a little longer with each successive treatment. But the symptoms always seemed to dissipate after about forty-eight hours. Thankfully, the blood work they did before each treatment was positive and she was only losing minimal weight.

By this time Theresa's office had opened back up even though COVID was still a significant risk. She wanted to return to work notwithstanding my protestations. Dr. Sneed had told us the chemotherapy would compromise Theresa's immune system. With the reports we were continuing to hear on the nightly news about the potential severity of COVID, even in the healthiest of people but especially those with compromised immune systems, I could not understand why she would be willing to take the risk.

Theresa explained to me that she had to have some semblance of normalcy in her life for her mental health. The cancer threatened to take so much from her life, even life itself. She had to feel she was winning the battle for her own sanity and returning to work would be a victory toward that goal. I understood why it was important to her but still my worries were not alleviated. The doctors Theresa worked for had always been ideal employers and treated everyone who worked with them very well. They shared my same concerns about unnecessarily exposing Theresa to COVID but also sympathized with her need to return to work.

Accommodating both concerns the doctors arranged to allow Theresa to work from home providing telemedicine to her patients. They had never offered telemedicine in the past. Telemedicine, however, had become prominent in the medical field out of necessity during the early stages of the pandemic. So, shortly after starting chemotherapy Theresa returned to work ... from home. She was a stalwart, even on the days following her chemotherapy when she was not feeling well. She was bound and determined to continue on with her normal life and to not let cancer get the better of her.

October 29, 2020

After her fourth treatment on October 29, Dr. Sneed announced it was time to perform another CT scan to determine how the cancer was responding to the treatment. The scan was scheduled on November 2, the following Monday, with an appointment with Dr. Sneed later in the afternoon to go over the results. Anxiety built over the four days we had to wait for the scan and reached its crescendo after the scan while waiting for Dr. Sneed to enter the room to tell us the results.

When she walked into the room, Dr. Sneed had a giant smile on her face and held up her hand to Theresa to give her a 'high-five'. This had to be a good sign as we interpreted it to mean there was good news. Dr. Sneed sat down in a chair and told us that the scan showed the lesions on Theresa's liver had been reduced by fifty percent. That certainly sounded good and we asked her what does that mean going forward. She announced with glee that it means it is time for Theresa to be referred to an oncology surgeon to discuss surgery to remove the rest of the lesions on the liver. She also said chemotherapy would be suspended until the surgeon determined if it was time for surgery.

When Theresa and I left her office and got into our car we again cried together and gave each other a big hug. Finally … finally … we were seeing a light at the end of this never-ending nightmare. Not only was she being referred to a surgeon to take out the remaining cancer but the chemotherapy was also being suspended. While the chemotherapy treatments were continuing and the side effects were worsening and lengthening, we were starting to wonder if the chemotherapy was possibly worse than the cancer itself.

Because the world was still under COVID protocols to some degree, the appointment with the surgeon was scheduled virtually, just as Theresa provided to her patients. Mercifully, Dr. Sneed scheduled it for Thursday, only three days away. The surgeon was Dr. Fletcher. We were excited to meet with Dr. Fletcher in hopes of having the surgery scheduled as soon as possible. Theresa's cancer was our enemy and getting it out of her body could not happen soon enough. We logged on to the virtual appointment early not wanting to delay the doctor unnecessarily. He entered the virtual appointment promptly at the scheduled time.

After the initial introductions Dr. Fletcher got right to the point. He could not operate. There were too many lesions spread over Theresa's entire liver and to get them all he would have to cut away too much of Theresa's liver. We were devastated. We asked what this meant going forward. He explained further chemotherapy most likely but that would be up to Dr. Sneed. We asked how much more the lesions would have to shrink before he could perform surgery. In a moment of blunt honesty, he replied more than was likely to occur.

Just like that our hopes were shattered. Eight weeks of tortuous chemotherapy combined with an emotional roller coaster, only to find out that even with a fifty percent reduction in the size of the cancerous lesions the surgeon was telling us it was all for nothing. After our meeting with Dr. Sneed three days ago we were convinced we were making progress in the battle against the cancer and victory was near. Now, with Dr. Fletcher telling us it was unlikely he would ever be able to operate, even with more chemotherapy, it appeared the cancer had progressed to the point of no return. We were at a loss for words after the meeting ended and just stared at each other. Fearful that this news could have unspeakable ramifications we hugged each other tighter than we had ever done before as we sobbed uncontrollably.

What do you say to the love of your life when she is told all of the agony and suffering she has endured for the past several months in a battle for her life hasn't been enough? Recalling Father Steve's words to search for blessings especially in the most difficult of times, try as I might I could not find any in this news. For the first time I saw despair and doubt in Theresa's eyes. More than that, however, I saw fear.

Theresa had always been the one person capable of calming me during my times of distress – the stresses of our wedding week, the multiple surgeries I had during our marriage, and even upon first learning of her diagnosis, just to name a few. As one would expect, it was clear from her reactions to this news, she had reached her limits emotionally. It was time for me to attempt to be the calming support in our marriage.

I suspect Theresa had always been successful with her calming demeanor because she was a nurse. Those of us who have family or close friends who are nurses know they have something in their DNA that makes them extraordinarily compassionate. They have a natural ability to reassure others in times of need and Theresa excelled with this characteristic. I, on the other hand, had always excelled in what Theresa called being a "drama king." Seeing the immense suffering my dearly beloved was enduring, both physically and emotionally, flipped a switch in my psyche. It was my turn to be the compassionate, reassuring, positive caregiver in our marriage.

We met with Dr. Sneed again. The eternal upbeat, positive, optimist. She had a plan. The treatments were working, she reminded us. We would continue with four more treatments with an increased dose on a more frequent basis and re-evaluate after those treatments. Theresa was deflated. I was deflated. The previous treatments were beginning to take a toll on her. She couldn't imagine doing four more treatments at increased dosages and frequency. But we had no other choice I reasoned with her. She was going to beat the cancer, I reminded her, and this was how it had to be done. Easy for me to say not being the one being subjected to the chemotherapy. Unsure how she could endure four, more aggressive treatments, Theresa reluctantly agreed to proceed with Dr. Sneed's recommendation.

As expected, the next four treatments were significantly more difficult. Fatigue was becoming a major factor. Her appetite was all but gone. The nausea was much more severe. The sensitivity to cold was exacerbated. The neuropathy in her fingertips was becoming almost unbearable. She started having sores in her mouth. She also started having what the doctor termed 'chemo brain' causing her to be forgetful and in a foggy daze. She began having pain in her abdomen which had been mostly non-existent previously. Also, during this next group of treatments her blood work was slowly going in the wrong direction and she began losing weight at an alarming rate.

We were scared. We didn't know if the acceleration of the symptoms was being caused by the increased dosage of chemotherapy or the progression of the cancer. We were soon to find out.

December 17, 2020

After the fourth treatment, Dr. Sneed scheduled another CT scan for December 17. This time, after the scan was completed, Dr. Sneed walked into the room with a far less animated demeanor. She sat down in her chair and began the appointment by saying she had some bad news. The lesions on the liver had grown since the last scan. Not only had they grown, they were now larger than they were at the time of her initial scan. Stating the obvious, she confirmed the cancer was no longer responding positively to the treatment.

Dr. Sneed told us this was not the end however. There was another form of chemotherapy that could be administered that had shown good results for the form of cancer Theresa had (which for me begged the question why hadn't this stronger treatment been used from the beginning – although I kept that thought to myself). This other chemotherapy was much stronger, however, with far more severe side-effects. She wanted Theresa to start it immediately. We were just a week away from Christmas and the way things were progressing we were starting to wonder how many Christmases were left. Theresa asked if Dr. Sneed would mind leaving the room for a moment while she discussed the options with me. Understanding the significance of the decision to be made the doctor readily complied.

After our meeting with Dr. Fletcher, I had seen despair, doubt and fear in Theresa's eyes. When Dr. Sneed stepped out of the room, for the first time since hearing the news of her cancer, she expressed defeat. She told me she feared this would be her last Christmas and New Year and if it was, she didn't want to experience it with the side-effects of chemotherapy that would be more difficult than what she had experienced with her last round of treatment. She wanted her last holidays to be as enjoyable as possible.

I wasn't prepared to give up. I wasn't prepared to think about the possibility of losing Theresa. I reminded her that Dr. Sneed said she needed to begin the new treatments immediately. Theresa looked me in the eyes and said "Baby, this isn't going to end the way we want it to. I will do whatever you want me to because I love you but you need to start preparing for a result neither of us want. I will do the treatments if that's what you want me to do. But if that's what you want I would prefer to start them after the first of the year so that we can enjoy the holidays as much as possible."

Since the first day we met, Theresa was my Gabby. Like Travis, I knew I would do everything I could to hang on to our love. Now, like Travis, I was being asked by the love of my life to let go. I had always proclaimed if I were ever in Travis' position I would make the same choice he did with Gabby by refusing to let go, even when there was only the smallest sliver of hope. Theresa was telling me her wishes but like Gabby did with Travis, she was putting the decision in my hands. I recalled Theresa had told me in a similar situation she had to talk to her father about letting go when her mother was dying. But Theresa was my Gabby. Dr. Sneed knocked on the door and entered the room.

"Have you made a decision on how you would like to proceed?" she asked. Theresa looked over to me. "Doctor" I said "Theresa would like to proceed with the new treatments ... after the first of the year." I expected the doctor to protest by saying it was imperative the new treatments start immediately. But her acknowledgement that she understood and felt that was the best course of action at this point was all I needed to hear to convince me we had made the right decision.

Scripture tells us God hears our prayers and answers them. I had been praying for God to do His will with the belief His will was also my will. In the past month it had become increasingly apparent my will was not aligning with

His. Just four months before this most recent meeting with Dr. Sneed we would have never considered the possibility of this being Theresa's last holidays. We thought we had decades of holidays left together. I think we both also assumed that when the time came for one of us to pass on, it would be me to go first. If it were to truly be Theresa's last holidays, she needed them to be as 'normal' as possible … who am I kidding, I and the rest of our family needed them to be as "normal' as possible.

Chapter 14: Family Time

Dear Heavenly Father,
All good things come from you.
Bless our family with peace and love.
May our family stay strong through difficult
times and rejoice in good times. May our
family be a support to one another and always
look to you for guidance and direction.

Author unknown

December 24, 2020

Following the appointment with Dr. Sneed, Theresa and I tried our best not to dwell on the road ahead choosing rather to live in the present. We were determined to make the most of the Christmas and New Year season and enjoy it with family the best we could under the circumstances. The week following the appointment with Dr. Sneed was filled with preparations for Christmas. Customarily, we would be hosting a Christmas Eve party for family and close friends consisting of a light meal and games. On Christmas Day we would travel to my sister's home for Christmas dinner.

Partly as a result of the pandemic but mostly because of Theresa's condition we would be scaling down the Christmas Eve celebration. The Christmas Eve party would go on as usual but with fewer in attendance. We would be staying home on Christmas Day. Our children would be celebrating with us and Jeff and Stephanie would be staying with us at our house through the new year.

Theresa began to feel a little better as Christmas approached now that her chemotherapy had been suspended after the appointment with Dr. Sneed. 'Better', however, was a relative term when referring to how she was feeling. The cancer was not better. She was not better. In fact, she continued to lose weight and her fatigue was not improving. She was starting to have shortness of breath with even the smallest of physical activity. She would never admit it but I sensed she was in much more pain and felt far worse than she was telling me. But at least the nausea was improving as were the cold sensations and neuropathy in her hands and fingertips. Thankfully, the chemo brain was also going away allowing her to be more present to her surroundings. It seemed as Christmas grew closer the Theresa of old was returning, even if it was only in small parts.

The family knew Theresa had put her chemotherapy on hold. They also knew the last scan revealed the cancer was growing at an alarming rate. We all could see how much she had deteriorated in the past six weeks. I'm sure each of our unspoken thoughts were that there was a real possibility this would be her last Christmas.

Christmas Eve and Christmas Day came. Our conversations consisted mostly of reminiscing about the past, telling funny stories of Theresa's childhood, and talking about her extended family. It was a subconscious effort by all to recount as much of Theresa's life as possible in hopes of securing it in our memory banks. At the end of the festivities on Christmas Eve and Christmas Day the hugs were tighter and longer, the 'I love yous' were said more earnestly said, the good byes were extended ... and the crying after everyone left was uncontrollable.

We had never been ones to go to parties on New Year's Eve. Over the past several years we had been going to a local art store that offered 'wine and canvas' lessons on New Year's Eve. We would attend, paint our masterpiece (always Christmas themed) and then hang our masterpieces on the walls the following Christmas season. Our paintings would be of the same scene and we always hung them next to each other and quizzed family which they liked best. Theresa's was always chosen, without exception. This New Year's Eve we skipped the wine and canvas and stayed home with Stephanie, Jeff and his family. Theresa was a champ and stayed up to watch the ball drop despite her extreme fatigue. She was determined not to miss this New Year's Eve.

2021

Soon after the beginning of 2021 Theresa began the new regiment of chemotherapy. It was horrible, undoubtedly worse than the cancer itself. She quickly started declining and it immediately became apparent the new chemotherapy was giving her no quality of life. After a couple of treatments, she had another heart-to-heart conversation with me. She wanted to discontinue the treatments. They were our last ray of hope and we both knew what discontinuing them meant for her prognosis.

The hope had been that they would extend her life for a year or so. Jeff and Ben were both planning their weddings for late summer and early fall and it was her goal to attend both of their weddings. We spoke to Dr. Sneed about how long she would have left if the treatments were discontinued and Dr. Sneed estimated four to six months.

Even though she wanted more than anything to attend the weddings, she also knew she could not survive the new treatments if they continued. Her weight was already a major concern and she was spending all of her time in bed. She did not want to live the time she had left sleeping and sick in bed from the chemotherapy. After telling her I would support whatever decision she made, Theresa discontinued her treatments.

Theresa didn't want Jeff and Ben to change their wedding dates because of her sickness. I had other plans. Unbeknownst to Theresa, I contacted Jeff and Ben, their fiancées and their fiancées' parents to ask a favor. Would they be willing to have small intimate marriage ceremonies at our house as soon as possible to allow Theresa to attend her sons' weddings? I suggested they should keep their scheduled wedding dates and have the weddings they had already planned.

Everyone was so gracious in agreeing to this plan. We scheduled Jeff's wedding for Saturday March 6 and Ben's for Sunday March 7, over Theresa's less than earnest objections. In her heart I knew she was grateful for everyone's willingness to arrange for her to be a part of these special occasions.

January 21, 2021

Theresa had not eaten for the past four days. Regardless of how much I prodded her to eat she just simply could not hold anything down and stopped trying. I was becoming quite concerned with how long this could continue and was telling her if she couldn't get anything down I was going to have to take her to see Dr. Sneed. It wasn't as if she was refusing to eat. She just couldn't.

At 5:46 on the morning of January 21 my phone buzzed. A very strange hour for me to be receiving a call. I looked at my phone and saw it was Rae calling. Even stranger that it was my sister calling at this hour. Not wanting to wake Theresa I got out of bed and took my phone to the living room to answer the call. Rae informed me she was at our Dad's house. She told me that Dad had called her about an hour earlier because he wasn't feeling well and needed her help. Rae told me that by the time she got to his house he was unresponsive. She told me I needed to get there as soon as possible because she wasn't sure he was going to make it. He lived in Bloomington, about an hour away from our home.

I rushed getting ready and then woke Theresa up to tell her what was happening. When I was able to wake her it was obvious she had taken a turn for the worse herself. She needed to get to the hospital. I was torn on which direction to go. I called Ben and Scott, both of whom lived near us, to see if either of them could come over and take their mom to the hospital. Ben didn't answer (undoubtedly

256

sound asleep). Luckily, Scott did and readily agreed to take care of his mom while urging me to rush over to Bloomington.

As I was pulling out of the driveway to head over to Bloomington after Scott arrived at our house I called Rae to tell her I was on my way. She told me to hurry because Dad was dying and she wasn't sure how much time he had left. Try as I might I could not get there quick enough and when I was about ten minutes from Dad's house Rae called and told me Dad had died.

I hung up and called Scott to see how Theresa was doing and he told me nothing had changed and they were pulling up to the entrance of the emergency department of the hospital. The rest of the morning was consumed with waiting on the coroner to come get Dad, visiting the funeral home to make arrangements for Dad's funeral and many telephone calls to Scott to see how Theresa was doing. Scott eventually told me his mother was being admitted to the hospital. I assured him I would come to the hospital as soon as my Dad's arrangements were completed.

When I arrived at the hospital in Indianapolis, Theresa was awake and alert looking better than she had in days. The IV hydration they were administering was restoring some of her energy. As I came into the room she motioned for me to come over to her beside and gave me a big hug, told me how sorry she was for Dad's death, cried with me and apologized profusely for making this day more difficult for me because of her condition. That was Theresa, always thinking of others. I assured her it was not her fault and what I needed most from her was to do everything she could to work on getting well enough to come home.

Theresa remained in the hospital for eleven days during which time I spent every moment with her except attending my dad's funeral. Long before his death my Dad asked me to give his eulogy when he died. So those first few days after his death I worked on preparing his eulogy while sitting at Theresa's beside in the hospital. It was a surreal time having to work on my Dad's eulogy because of his unexpected death while sitting at my wife's bedside in the hospital while she was in a fight for her own life.

When it was time for Dad's funeral, I knew under the circumstances there was no way I could give the eulogy I had prepared. I was thankful Father Steve and Deacon Mark attended the funeral. Father Steve gave the opening and closing prayers and Deacon Mark read the eulogy I prepared. Theresa was able to watch the funeral online. Dad had always loved Theresa and always jokingly told me I was overachieving by marrying her. Theresa likewise loved my Dad.

On the day Theresa was released from the hospital we were surprised by a knock at the door after we had settled in at home. It was Jose, one of my classmates in the deacon class. He was carrying a vase of hyacinths. I had mentioned in one of our deacon classes one of Theresa's favorite flowers was hyacinths. His wife had a greenhouse in their home in which she grew hyacinths. From that day forward Jose would bring a vase of hyacinths to our home each week for Theresa. A beautiful gesture highlighting the heart of a deacon (soon to be deacon in his case).

February 1, 2021

Upon hearing of their mom's hospitalization, Jeff and Stephanie rushed back to Indiana from their homes in Virginia and Florida. Theresa was released to come home on February 1. She was determined to make it to that first weekend in March to be there for her sons' weddings.

Her condition continued to deteriorate however with the fatigue worsening and weight loss accelerating. Jeff and Stephanie were a Godsend in helping me care for their mother.

On February 15 we again had to rush Theresa to the hospital. During this hospitalization stay Dr. Sneed recommended that a feeding tube be used to help Theresa receive nutrition. Dr. Sneed told us the feeding tube could extend her life by several months. Theresa agreed because she was unable to eat otherwise and she was going to do everything she could to make it to the weddings of her sons. She remained in the hospital this time until March 1, being released just in time for the weddings.

March 6-7, 2021

The weekend of the weddings couldn't come soon enough. Theresa was barely hanging on. We set up a make-shift wedding venue on our back deck. Jeff and Ben had asked that I prepare and perform the ceremonies. Father

Steve and Deacon Mark attended and Father Steve again gave the opening and closing prayers. Jeff's fiancée's parents attended virtually because they lived in Virginia and Ben's fiancée's parents were able to attend in person because they lived nearby. Stephanie, Scott and his daughter (Theresa's granddaughter) attended as did Ben's step-children. Considering the circumstances, the weddings were nice intimate affairs and, most importantly, Jeff, Ben and their wives were able to have pictures taken with Theresa on their wedding days.

March 10

When we awoke on March 10 Theresa's condition had again taken a turn for the worse. In what was becoming an all too familiar routine we rushed to the hospital. This time was different. She wasn't bouncing back like she had in the previous hospitalizations. I called her sisters to let them know now was the time for them to come to Indiana. They each arrived within days and stayed at our house.

Theresa was in the hospital for fourteen days this time. The day before she was released we met with Dr. Sneed. To my surprise, Theresa asked Dr. Sneed about the consequences of taking the feeding tube out. Dr. Sneed stated the obvious, Theresa would not receive any form of nutrition thereby significantly shortening the time she had left. In a scene strikingly similar to our appointment just before Christmas, Theresa asked Dr. Sneed if she could step out of the room to allow us to talk. As soon as Dr. Sneed left the room I turned to Theresa and said "Baby, you know you can't live without nutrition. We can't take the feeding tube out."

She replied, "Baby, it's time. I made it through the boys' weddings. You know that was my goal. Yes, I would give anything to be here to see them have children but we both know it doesn't matter what we do, I'm not going to be here long enough to see that day. I'm tired of being in pain all the time. I have no quality of life. I don't want to live like this. I can't live like this. I don't want you to live like this. I have nothing left to give. I've had a great life. You and the kids are the reason for that and I am so thankful you all have given me the life I have had. But I am suffering now and it's not going to get any better. You are only going to see me get worse and I don't want to extend that suffering for you any further than necessary. I know you are in pain seeing me like this. I can feel it. I don't want you to hurt like you are hurting. I want you to be able to live life. This feeding tube is only extending my suffering and your pain. And for what? I want you to make me a promise."

"Baby" I replied "I'm not in pain. I have you. That's all I need. I don't care things aren't the way they use to be as long as I have you. Please don't give up. I need you. I'm nothing without you."

With tears running down her cheeks she responded, "It's time. I need you to promise me something."

"What?" I said absent mindfully.

"I want you to drop out of the deacon formation program."

Startled, I replied "why would you want that? That is our dream, to serve others."

"Because," she said "staying in the program would mean you could never fall in love again. You could never marry again and I don't want that for you. I want you to love again. I want you to feel what we have again. You deserve that. You are the most loving, generous, affectionate and compassionate man I have ever known and I love you more than you will ever know."

"No way" I insisted. "There is no way I could ever love anyone like I love you."

"In time you can" she retorted. "You are full of love and I want you to find someone to give that love to. Please don't close your heart to it."

There was a long pause.

"Do I have your support to have the feeding tube taken out?" she asked again.

"Baby, I don't want to lose you. But I don't want you to suffer either. I know what you are asking is probably harder for you than it is for me. I have always supported you and I always will, even if it's not what I want and even if it's the hardest thing I will ever do."

"Thank you," she said. "Please ask Dr. Sneed to come back in."

When Dr. Sneed came back in Theresa told her she would like to have the feeding tube removed. Dr. Sneed shook her head in agreement and placed an order for it to be removed. The doctor then told us it was time for Theresa to begin receiving hospice care. The following day we returned home and a hospice nurse visited our home.

March 26

The Last Love Letter

Over the eleven years of our love affair, I had written a countless number of love letters to Theresa. Try as I might I never felt any of my letters adequately expressed how much I loved her. By March 26 it was becoming painfully clear I didn't have much time left with her. I still had one last opportunity to get it right. I watched her read it as we both released the floodgates of emotions that had been building up in us for the past seven months.

Baby,

While you were sleeping, I have been sitting here next to you writing this note. I was distracted many times, however, because I kept glancing over at you in disbelief. The very first time I looked at your profile picture before we met, I was so amazed by the beauty I saw in the pictures. I etched them in my mind before we ever spoke to each other. Those pictures depicted the most beautiful woman I had ever seen. I have to be honest though, that is not true today.

No, today, the most beautiful woman I have ever seen is the one laying next to me as I write this note. You have never been more beautiful than you are at this very moment.

I was forty-six years old when we first met. I had been through a twenty year marriage, raised kids to adulthood, established myself professionally, travelled some, and I had fallen in love a couple times. But it was not until we fell in love that I began to live ... truly live. And that is because the love you and I share is beyond anything I have ever had. It's beyond anything I even knew was possible. We hear of fairytales and living happily ever after. Baby, our love is our own fairytale and because of it I will live happily ever after knowing we are united for the rest of eternity.

There is not a day ... not even one ... that I haven't thought I was the luckiest man in the world to have you as my wife. During the good times (which has been almost all of our time together) there is no one other than you I want to share them with. But that applies to the difficult times too. You are my compass in the stormy times and the rudder steering me in the right direction during those times. You are the sail keeping me moving forward when I don't think I can do so myself. No one but you can sooth my soul when it is most needed. You once told me you couldn't help but think I got a raw deal when I fell in love with you. You haven't been wrong often in our marriage but you were so wrong about that. God gave me the greatest blessing he has ever given me when you came into my life. A blessing that continues to this very day.

I would give anything for our situations to be reversed, for me to be sleeping while you write this letter, but that apparently isn't God's plan for our love story. Although the situation in which we find ourselves is not our plan I am still blessed He has given me a love like I have never experienced. A love I cherish and am thankful for with each passing day and will continue to be for all of eternity.

During the eleven years of our love affair, we have made memories that many take a lifetime to make. Memories that I will carry in my heart for the rest of my life. So many I dare not attempt to mention them all here. But they are secure in my heart and I will treasure them forevermore.

What stands out most in all those memories, however, is how deeply and utterly in love I am with you. Our love has been so natural, never having to force our feelings for each other and never doubting the love we share. Without question, my dear, you have completed me by encouraging me to be the person I was intended to be.

Through you I have come to have the relationship with God that I sought my entire life. You have led me to a life of service that allows me to be the person God intended me to be. You have encouraged me to do things, like learning how to fly, that I have always dreamed of doing. You have given me a family that compliments the family I already had.

We have shared an intimacy like I have never known. Our souls have become one. Your thoughts have become mine and mine yours. We have shared dreams and disappointments. Successes and failures. Goals and setbacks. Good times and bad. Throughout it all you have given me your unconditional love. A love I have never doubted or taken for granted. And throughout it all I have always wanted nothing but the best for you and have strived to make sure you have it.

I was sitting out on the deck yesterday as a group of Sandhill Cranes flew over the house to destinations unknown. In the days, weeks and months ahead we too don't know where destiny will take us. What I do know is you are my Gabby and like Travis I will never let you go. Fate may require us to be separated for a time here on Earth but it is only temporary and in God's time *we will be together once more for all of eternity, that I have no doubt.*

You have given me a life far greater than anything I could have ever imagined myself. You have given me a perfect love that will forevermore be unmatched. Please know baby I love you more than I can ever put into words.

When she finished reading the letter I looked at her and said, "You asked me to make you a promise. I'm not sure it's a promise I can keep but I want you to promise me something."

"Please don't ask me to stay baby because you know I can't" she pleaded.

"I know you can't. It's not that" I said. "Please promise me that when you leave you will send me signs so that I know you are ok and are still by my side."

She gave me a weak smile and said "I will see what I can do."

March 29

I awoke around 7:30 a.m. and turned to Theresa to see how she was doing. She was awake but didn't respond to my greeting of good morning. I looked into her eyes and could tell that she knew I was there and what I was saying but she couldn't respond. She had a look of concern in her eyes that spread across her face. We both understood the end was near. I held her tightly for a long time and then pulled back and looked into her eyes again and said "You are so beautiful. I love you more than I can ever tell you." She couldn't respond but I knew she heard me when I saw her slightly shaking her head in the affirmative with tears running down her cheeks while trying to mouth she loved me. Later that afternoon she closed her eyes for the last time.

April 1

4:37 a.m.

Holy Thursday arrived at the strike of midnight. The day commemorating Jesus' last day with his disciples prior to his crucifixion. I had been up all-night stroking Theresa's hair and holding her hand. Shortly after 4:00 a.m. I noticed her breathing slowing dramatically and becoming more labored. Around 4:25 a.m. I summoned all of her children and sisters to the bedroom knowing the end was near. At 4:37 a.m., while holding her as if there was no tomorrow, Theresa took her last breath with her family at our bedside.

Chapter 15: Mourning

Brothers and Sisters.

We do not want you to be uninformed about those who sleep in death, so that you do not grieve like the rest of mankind, who have no hope. For we believe that Jesus died and rose again, and so we believe that God will bring with Jesus those who have fallen asleep in him.

1 Thessalonians 4:17-18

April 1, 2021

Just seventy days after spending the day making arrangements for the funeral of my father, I found myself repeating the same thing for my beloved Theresa. If I had been told less than eight months earlier, I would be doing this today I would have thought it inconceivable. I could not wrap my head around how much life had changed in such a short period of time.

I always envisioned I would be the one to die first never considering it would be the other way around. I don't think Theresa even considered she would be the one to leave first. In fact, it had only been a few years since she convinced me to get life insurance, no doubt having the same thoughts herself.

This had to be a nightmare. I was hoping to wake up anytime to prove it was.   In the days, weeks and months to come it became all too apparent it was in fact a nightmare, but one that was real.

Jeff and I went to the funeral home later in the day to make plans for her arrangements followed by a visit to the church to plan her services with Father Steve and Barb. We set April 5 as the date of her service to allow time for the rest of Theresa's family to arrive from the East Coast. Later in the day I received a call from the archbishop of the *Indianapolis Archdiocese* giving me his condolences for Theresa's passing.

The kids agreed to take on the task of putting together a set of pictures and a video presentation to display at the funeral home for her showing. I wanted to write her eulogy, with Deacon Mark agreeing again to read it at the service since I knew there would be no way I could get through it in an intelligible manner. I offered each of Theresa's sisters and children the opportunity to provide me with information for material to include in the eulogy. Over the course of the next several days I began writing what I considered to be the most important document I had ever written.

April 5

The day of Theresa's service arrived. The last day I would see Theresa's face in the flesh. I arrived at the church early to be able to spend as much time by her side as I could before she was taken away to be cremated after the service. Slowly the church filled. I was pleased that so many people

270

attended. Evidence of the person she was and how much she was loved by all.

Family and friends, far and near. Co-workers from the places Theresa had worked over the years. Classmates from her time in school. The men and their wives from the deacon program. Several current deacons throughout the archdiocese. On the altar platform there were four priests and four deacons presiding over the service. The service began and in time Deacon Mark rose to give the eulogy on my behalf.

Theresa always told me to get to the point when telling a story and that she wanted the *Reader's Digest* version, not the long-winded attorney version. Well, anything about Theresa is my favorite subject, so this eulogy is probably much longer than what she would consider appropriate. So, my apologies from the beginning.

As I began writing this, I was having trouble concentrating or typing the words because I couldn't stop crying and the tears were clouding my vision. After an extended period of this self-pity I was suddenly startled by a distinct, familiar voice in my head saying .... "SUCK IT UP BUTTERCUP AND STOP BEING A DRAMA KING!!!" Sound familiar?

I am sure her son Ben will think so after being told this when his mom made him go to school even though he was sick only to discover later, after being admitted to Riley Hospital, he had bi-lateral pneumonia with a collapsed lung.

I know her daughter Stephanie remembers being told this when she cut the tip of her finger off with a chain saw and, rather than rushing her directly to the E.R., Theresa put a cloth on her finger to slow the bleeding so Theresa would have time to clean up before heading over to the E.R.

I know I certainly witnessed my share of "suck it up buttercup" moments over the years, but one in particular stands out. I had an accident at the lake that resulted in my small toe coming dangerously close to being amputated and me probably losing close to 10 pints of blood. This was met with Theresa's infamous "suck it up buttercup" admonishment while she was driving putting her make-up on while taking me to the hospital and sewing my toe up in her bikini in the E.R.

We laugh at these stories now but they are perfect examples of one of Theresa's core values as a person. I am not going to go into detail about her past because that was something she kept private but what most already know, for a significant part of time while her children were young Theresa was a single parent raising her four children on her own without any financial support.

But Theresa was not the kind of person to dwell on her difficult circumstances. She was the type of person to rise above any obstacles placed in her way to provide a better tomorrow for her children. She completed her bachelors and masters degrees while working three jobs and raising her children. You can only do that when you have that "suck it up buttercup" mentality.

So, a toe dangling from a foot was just a bump in the road for Theresa. It certainly wasn't worthy of all the drama I wanted to make of it. On second thought, after Theresa suggested I was possibly overreacting, maybe the cut on my toe only required a few stitches and maybe there was only minimal blood loss.

Theresa is a blessing to all who know her, and to many who did not. Sometimes you are not aware of the lives you touch.

That was definitely the case with Theresa. For most of her illness, Theresa didn't want to make her diagnosis public. However, toward the end I started giving more and more details about her diagnosis publicly. As her diagnosis got out, I started hearing from many of the people whose lives she has touched. A common theme was that Theresa has touched so many lives over the years. I relayed these praises to her as I received them and Theresa was deeply touched by all the wonderful things people were telling me about her.

What is so amazing about Theresa is that even though she touched all those many people in so many ways, she didn't even realize she was doing it because of how humble she was. To her, the acts of love and kindness were not anything extraordinary. It was simply Theresa being Theresa, acting through a genuine love for others, changing the lives of so many as she always encouraged others to do, one kind act at a time. One thing is for certain. If the world was comprised of nothing but Theresas, just imagine what a wonderful representation of heaven the world would be today.

Scott .... Ben .... Stephanie .... Jeff. The four of you are your mom's pride and joy. There is NOTHING your mom wouldn't have done for each one of you. She was so proud of each of you and she loved each of you more than anything in the world. She has always wanted the best for each of you. I learned very early on in our relationship that the four of you were the number one priority in her life and I was either on board with that or I would be thrown overboard.

I spoke to the four of you privately as a group before your mom passed and I'm going to repeat what I told you then. Your mom loved the four of you more than you will ever know. What she wants more than anything is for each of you to find true happiness. She wants each of you to remain close and take care of each other and never let anything or anyone come between your relationship with each other. And she wants each of you to open your heart to the possibility of building a vibrant relationship with God. My prayers ... your mom's prayers ... are that you each do your best to fulfill your mother's wishes.

Individually, neither Theresa or I were perfect .... although Theresa was much closer to it than I. But our love was perfect. Our souls matched. We were meant for each other. I believe that what Theresa and I shared is what is meant when someone tries to describe love. She will always be my Gabby. Together we found true love. More importantly, however, together we found a Godly love. A love that we not only shared with each other but one we also sought to share with God, family, friends and strangers. It was through that Godly love that our love for each other grew stronger with each passing day. It was through Theresa that I have grown closer to being the person God created me to be. A person through whom God seeks to extend his love to others.

I would be remiss if I failed to also mention how much Theresa loved animals. So much so that over the years we have assembled our own united nations of animals. We have five dogs that we have picked up from Tennessee, Indiana, Kentucky and Kansas. We also have a cat, a rooster we acquired from Virginia and eight hens.

It doesn't matter what kind of animal, Theresa would try to protect it. We were in the Smoky Mountains once and she saw a goat in some deep brush on the side of a mountain. She thought the goat was stuck so she climbed through the brush (even though she is scared of snakes and insects) up the side of that mountain to try to help the goat. Last year there was a killdeer nest in our front yard that had several little eggs in it that Theresa and I had been keeping an eye on for several days. As we were leaving the house one day, she urgently had me stop our car and she hopped out and went running over to the nest with her arms flailing. At first, I wasn't sure what she doing until I saw two crows flying away and realized she was trying to protect those bird eggs.

Her love for animals was legendary and so genuine that it was her goal to build a rescue center for animals behind our house when she retired. As a side note, Theresa asked me to be sure to mention she would prefer there be no memorial contributions but if you are so inclined, please make them to the *Bartholomew County Humane Society*.

As it became evident over the past several months that Theresa's battle with cancer wasn't going to end how we wanted, I asked Theresa to show me signs after she passed to let me know she was OK and was watching over me. Yesterday, I was mowing grass around a tree when something on the ground caught my eye. When I took a second glance, I saw that it was a bird egg and above it in the tree within reach was a nest that, given my proximity, surprisingly still had the brooding momma bird in the nest. After I placed the egg back in the nest, I had a sense of calm and peace come over me telling me Theresa was OK and I broke down in tears of happiness.

I want to believe that bird egg was the first of many signs to come from Theresa. For those of us who have a special place for Theresa in our hearts, I would urge you to look for Theresa in all you do, as I will continue to do, because she is there wanting to share her love for and through us. I know I will be closely looking for those signs in all I do for the rest of my life.

As I mentioned at the beginning of this eulogy, Theresa would think I've went well beyond the length of what is appropriate so I should probably bring this to an end at this point. But as I conclude, I will say one last thing. This won't be the last time I write or speak at length about Theresa because I will be talking about Theresa in one form or another for the rest of my life, not only because she is the love of my life, but also because she is a testament to a holiness on Earth we all should strive to emulate.

I love you Theresa with all my heart and soul. And to each of you out there mourning Theresa's passing ..... Suck it up Buttercups, wipe those tears off your face and stop being drama kings and queens. Welcome home baby.

The kids, sisters and I hosted a cookout and celebration of life at our home following the service. I was pleased to find that a large number of people attended, again a testament to how much Theresa was loved. A few stayed well into the night and we sat outside telling therapeutic stories of each of our memories of Theresa. But eventually the celebration was over. The next day the sisters left to return to their homes on the East Coast and Jeff went back to Virginia. For the first time in well over a month the house was quiet. Stephanie remained but we were both in mourning and didn't interact much.

Personally, I was in shock and depressed. I didn't know what to do with myself or how to respond to the death of the love of my life. I did not know how to grieve. Yes, my dad had passed away not too long ago but I hadn't allowed myself to grieve his loss. I was incapable of processing it with Theresa's rapidly declining health. It seemed as though I was able to deal with dad's loss effectively by keeping him out of my thoughts so I think subconsciously I thought I could deal with Theresa's loss the same way. I attempted to return to life immediately, as if nothing had happened. I stayed busy at work. I stayed busy at church. I kept busy around the house. I did everything I could to keep Theresa out of mind.

The weekend following the service was a deacon retreat weekend. The director of the program contacted me to let me know I was excused from attending that weekend but I insisted I was ok and that I would be there. When I arrived I think most of the men in the class were surprised to see me there but they were very supportive, gave their condolences and tried the best they could to make it a 'normal' weekend.

The last event for each of our deacon retreats is Sunday morning mass. On Saturday evening I was approached by Deacon Greg. He told me he would be giving the homily at mass the next morning and he had a question he wanted to ask me about his homily. The deacon formation program had reached a point in formation where we were encountering a couple of weekends of challenging topics. Deacon Greg explained the purpose of his homily would be to give us some words of encouragement to help us tackle those subjects. He wanted to know if mentioning Theresa in the homily would upset me. I told him he was welcome to mention her, having no clue what he would say about her.

As I entered the chapel the next morning I had put my talk with Deacon Greg out of my mind, until he stood to give his homily. As he approached the pulpit to give his homily apprehension spread throughout my body not knowing what he might say. Deacon Greg then gave a Knute Rockne homily giving us a pep talk encouraging us to continue strong in our formation program. As he was nearing the end of his homily it appeared as though he had decided not to talk about Theresa and my tensions began to ease until he ended with "in the words of St. Theresa of Columbus … suck it up buttercups."

I almost burst into tears right there in the chapel. Overwhelming feelings of guilt flooded my heart. Here I was trying my hardest to keep Theresa out of my mind while others were looking to her for inspiration. It was then I realized what I really wanted more than anything … what I needed … was to think about her every second of the day. I became paralyzed by a fear that I would start forgetting details of our life together if I continued to try to keep her out of mind. I realized I had to stop trying to avoid my emotions. I needed to face them head on. I had to find Theresa again to assure I would always remember the details. I had to go away for a period of time to be in solitude to think about her and put my thoughts down on paper so I would never forget.

As soon as I returned home from the deacon retreat I logged onto my laptop to find a place to go to spend time away in solitude. Far enough away I wouldn't be tempted to return home early and somewhere I wouldn't be in a touristy area that would cause distractions. I wanted to be alone with nothing to do but think and write. Somewhere I had never been, especially with Theresa, so that I could focus on the past from memory rather than seeing things from our past vacations. After an hour or so of researching I settled upon Jekyll Island, Georgia. I then did a quick search for hotels and booked a room for a week at the *Holiday Inn Resort*, beginning April 18.

Chapter 16: Jekyll Island

But you, when you pray, go into your inner room,
close your door and pray to your Father who
is in secret, and your Father who sees what
is done in secret will reward you.

Matthew 6:6

April 18, 2021

I was not prepared to lose all that we had nor the promise of the future yet to come. It was time to face whatever the next seven days would bring ...

As I came off the causeway onto Jekyll Island the sun had already set and it was dark. One of the first things you encounter when coming onto the island is a round-about with a sign welcoming you to Jekyll Island. As I approached the round-about my attention was focused on the *Waze* app to determine which way I needed to go to reach the *Holiday Inn Resort*. Just as I entered the round-about I glanced up and noticed the Jekyll Island sign in the middle of the round-about and saw it was decorated with flowers. Very nice I thought as I began to circle the round-about.

Luckily, there were no cars behind me because almost as a reflex to a startling stimulus, I slammed on my breaks bringing my car to an abrupt stop. At first it didn't register in my mind but as I refocused my attention, I couldn't believe what I was seeing. Those flowers around the Jekyll Island welcoming sign weren't just any flowers ...

they were the most beautiful flowers I have ever seen in my life.

Hyacinths. Hundreds of them. In full bloom. A array of colors of red, pink, yellow, and white vibrantly welcoming me to Jekyll Island. I couldn't believe what I was seeing. Theresa's favorite flower welcoming me onto the island. Theresa promised me she would try to send me signs to tell me she was ok and by my side and here it was, clear as day, as if to say "Welcome baby. What the hell took you so long." She was telling me I had come to the right place to find her.

After circling the round-about several times to view the prettiest flowers I had ever seen I continued on my way to the resort. Driving toward the resort I noticed the whole island was decorated with hyacinths. They were everywhere. I smiled big with a tear in my eye and said aloud "Ok baby, I see them, I'm not doing a man look. Love and miss you."

I spotted a small grocery store just before reaching the resort. Thankfully, it was still open. I stopped and purchased enough provisions to last me through the week. My intention was to stay in my room the whole week writing. I didn't intend to leave the room for anything. I knew when I returned home free time would be at a minimum after having taken so much time off from work during the last several months. I had to get as much down on paper as I could while it was still fresh in my mind. I checked into my room after stopping at the grocery. I put the groceries away and laid down on the bed exhausted physically from the long drive and mentally from my life the past eight months.

I woke the next morning just before sunrise. I made breakfast and went out onto the balcony of my room to eat it while watching the sun rise over the Atlantic Ocean. After breakfast I retrieved my laptop and brought it out onto the balcony and started writing. I began by just writing about any memory of Theresa that came to mind. I wasn't trying to think chronologically. I wasn't trying to write in a logical order. The only thing that was important was to write about whatever came to mind to preserve my thoughts. My emotions were all over the place. I would laugh at some of the memories and while writing about the same memory cry so hard I had to stop because I couldn't see the screen.

I was hearing Theresa in my mind as if she was sharing the memory with me. I was remembering things that had been buried in my mind for years, as if Theresa was sitting next to me saying, "oh do you remember when ..." My thoughts were flowing freely and I couldn't type quickly enough to keep up. Because it was so quiet outside, I was able to write on the balcony most of the morning until it got too hot. It must have been an off season on the island as evident by very few people being outside by the pool under my balcony.

As the week progressed, I started putting what I had written into a more organized prose. The idea of writing a small book about Theresa and our love affair began to formulate in my head. The more I thought about it the more I began to convince myself to do it. I thought writing a book preserving our life together would be a wonderful gift to give to our family and a few close friends in remembrance of Theresa and as a way of showing them my appreciation for all the help they gave Theresa and me.

The days passed in pretty much the same fashion each day, full of nothing but writing, stopping only for quick breaks to eat or to use the bathroom. Never once did I hit the proverbial 'writer's block.' I was writing about Theresa which meant I could write effortlessly and endlessly. I wrote from sunrise until well past sunset each day for six consecutive days.

By late evening of my last full day on Jekyll Island I had tired of eating the same thing every day. While checking into my room upon my arrival I had noticed there was a restaurant called the *Beach House* just across the parking lot. I decided I would go there to eat dinner for a much needed break from the monotony of the hotel room. I reasoned that if I took my laptop with me and made it a working dinner, I would not be breaking my pledge to spend the whole week doing nothing but writing. The evening dinner rush must have ended by the time I walked into the restaurant because there were only a few people there eating. I asked the hostess at the front desk if they were still open and she confirmed they were for another hour and invited me to take a seat wherever I wanted. The hostess told me a waitress would be at my table in a few minutes.

I looked around and had a seat by a window with a view of the ocean. There was an outdoor seating area and a nice indoor bar that suggested the *Beach House* was the place to be during the tourist season. After sitting down in a booth and opening my laptop to resume writing, a young waitress, probably in her mid-twenties, came to my booth, introduced herself as Brie, and asked me if she could get me something to drink. I ordered a *Dr. Pepper* and she said she would be back with my drink in a few minutes.

For the past couple hours or so before coming to the restaurant I had been writing about an emotional part of my relationship with Theresa that I particularly wanted to make sure came across as I intended. Looking back down at the screen of my laptop I picked up where I had left off.

As promised, Brie returned with my drink after a couple minutes. Not hearing the southern accent I had noticed with the receptionist at the resort, the clerk at the grocery and the hostess when I came into the restaurant, I asked Brie if she was from this area. She indicated in fact she was not. She was from Norfolk, Virginia. She told me she and her husband had moved here about six months before when her husband's uncle offered him a foreman's position on a construction crew. I mentioned I was very familiar with the Norfolk / Virginia Beach area which led to an extended conversation about common areas of interest in that area. I found Brie to be very charismatic. As our conversation came to an end she asked if she could take my order and after doing so, off she went and I resumed my writing.

A short time later Brie was back with my order and politely set it on the table. I mentioned the restaurant was slow tonight and asked if it had been busier earlier in the evening. She replied it had been slow since her shift had started and offered that it was an off season and she had been told tourists would be filling the place in a few weeks. Brie then asked how long I had been on the island and I told her. Glancing down at my laptop she then asked if I was here for business. I told her not per se. I explained I was here to write a book. She raised an eyebrow and said that's interesting. She asked what kind of book and I replied a love story. She said she loved reading love stories and then seeing that my drink was empty picked up my glass and said she would be right back. While she was gone I had a wild idea. No one had read what I was writing. For all I knew it was gibberish nonsense. Maybe Brie would be interested in reading this part I had been writing about for the past couple hours.

Brie returned with my drink and I asked her if she had a few minutes to spare. She replied there was nothing urgent for her to finish up since I was now the only patron remaining in the restaurant. I asked her if she would be interested in reading what I had been working on for the past few hours. She quickly plopped down in the booth in the seat across the table and said she would be delighted to read it (attempting to put a southern accent to her reply). Taking one last look at my work I turned the laptop around and slid it toward her and said enjoy. I started eating my dinner as she began to read.

Every so often I would glance up at Brie to see if I could gauge her reactions to what she was reading. I would see her smile occasionally. I saw her bite her lip a few times. She arched her eyebrows. But for the most part I was having trouble discerning what she was feeling or thinking so I decided to focus on my dinner. After several minutes Brie slowly pushed the laptop back to me and as I looked up to her I saw tears rolling down her cheeks. She wiped at her eyes, smearing her mascara, quickly stood up and excused herself. Well, that was interesting I thought. I guess that means she either liked it or thought it was a horrible mess I reasoned.

After several minutes passed I started wondering if she would return. I had finished my dinner and was waiting for the check. Several more minutes passed before Brie returned, much more collected than when she had abruptly left. She laid my check on the table and asked me if she could ask me a question. I said sure. Brie asked "Who is Theresa?" I confessed she is my wife. Brie responded, "Did Theresa die?" I told her yes and explained when and how. Brie started crying again and left the table as she told me the checks are paid at the hostess desk.

I finished my drink, gathered my laptop, left a generous tip and went to the hostess desk to pay my check. While walking to the door after paying my check Brie rushed over to me and asked me if I would do her a favor. I said certainly. While handing me a piece of paper she asked me if I would send her a copy of my book when I was finished because she wanted to read more about Theresa and our love affair.

As I opened the piece of paper that had a name and address written on the inside my jaw dropped as I read the name ... Gabby. I looked up at Brie with what was obviously an expression of shock on my face. Brie asked what was wrong. I replied "Gabby?" She explained to me that her real name is Gabriel but her friends and family call her Gabby. Looking down at her name tag I said "But you told me your name is Brie. Your nametag says your name is Brie?" Gabby then explained she only goes by Brie at work. While tucking the piece of paper in the front pocket of my jeans and with the biggest smile imaginable that was almost breaking out into a giggle I said "Gabby, you will be the first person who receives a copy of the book when it is finished. You have no idea how happy I am to have met you. Good night."

I returned to my hotel room and rather than continue to write I began packing. I knew my journey to Jekyll Island had been a success. I found Theresa. I found Gabby.

Afterward

A life full of love is a life that extends beyond time.
Although we cannot be together right now the love we
share transcends time and place.

Blue skies, gentle breezes, waves rolling in on a sun-soaked beach, family picnics, a stroll through the park, birds singing and flowers blooming on a beautiful spring morning, the vibrant colors of a crisp autumn afternoon or the brightness of a full moon after a freshly fallen snow. Sometimes through the beauty of His creation the presence of God is recognizable all around us if we allow ourselves to look. But dare we look for God's presence during the storm, during the darkest hours of the night or when all seems lost. Can God's presence be found in the death of a loved one? Perhaps it is in the moments of our personal suffering that our greatest moments occur as God makes Himself known to us. Just perhaps it is during these struggles God's presence is most felt in the ability to withstand the storm and to find rays of light in the darkest hour of the night and peace in the midst of unbearable suffering. God's gift of grace is always present when we resist the temptation to allow our suffering to swallow and overcome us.

I have always been one who loves having my emotions moved through music. Since Theresa's passing I have adopted as my own personal ode to Theresa the song *Everything I own* by *Bread*:

You sheltered me from harm
Kept me warm, kept me warm
You gave my life to me
Set me free, set me free
The finest years I ever knew
Were all the years I had with you

And I would give anything I own
I'd give up my life, my heart, my home
I would give everything I own
Just to have you back again

You taught me how to love
What it's of, what it's of
You never said too much
But still you showed the way
And I knew from watching you

Nobody else could ever know
The part of me that can't let go

And I would give anything I own
I'd give up my life, my heart, my home
I would give everything I own
Just to have you back again

Is there someone you know
You're loving them so
But taking them for granted?
You may lose them one day
Someone takes them away
And they don't hear the words you long to say

I would give anything I own
I'd give up my life, my heart, my home
I would give everything I own
Just to have you back again
Just to touch you once again

I was asked recently, how are you emotionally and are you angry. I understand the first question but was caught off guard by the second. Admittedly, with the passing of Theresa and my dad so close together, each life-changing events in themselves, the days were a blur for a long time and seemed overwhelming at times.

It is an age-old question. Why do we have to endure suffering? More to the point, why does God allow us to endure suffering?

Theresa was the kindest and most compassionate person I have ever known. She had a heart of gold, always searching for ways to help others. She brought out the best in those around her and was an inspiration to those with whom she came in contact. She had a deep faith in God which she shared with me, serving as a catalyst to a deeper formation of my own faith. If the world was comprised of nothing but Theresas we would live in a society much closer to a representation of heaven than what we have now. Why then did God allow his faithful servant to suffer in the manner that Theresa suffered?

I love my Dad and wish he was still with us. There are so many things left unsaid that I wish I could say to him. But Dad's health was not good and, although his death was not totally unexpected, its timing was. From a selfish point of view, why now? Why God, did dad's death occur when the cross was already so heavy? Although I am not perfect, I try to serve you, God, the best I know how. Why then was the suffering so great?

So, with this in mind, yes, I understand the question about how I am emotionally. As I said, at times it was almost overwhelming. But those times were the exception. The days of Theresa's sickness and death and Dad's death passed as if I was in a surreal nightmare from which I couldn't awake. I don't know if I've finished grieving their deaths. I suppose in ways one never truly finishes grieving loved ones. Grief, after all, is the reflection of the love we have for those we grieve and I will never stop loving Theresa and my Dad. But overall, I am at peace and generally I feel as though I am in a good place. More on that later.

But what about that second question, the one that caught me off guard ... am I angry? My initial thought when asked this question was, why would I be angry and, for that matter, angry at who? Certainly, the road was difficult. But who am I to think we are entitled to a life without suffering? When God himself endured the most unimageable suffering for us, who am I to believe my life should be void of suffering? And to whom should an anger be directed? No one caused Theresa's death. No one caused Dad's death. The timing of both is unfortunate but is there ever really a good time for either?

Should I be angry with God one might ask? Why on earth should I be angry with God? It was through God that I was blessed with a dad that loved me and that I loved. It was through God, in some of my darkest hours, that I was led to the love of my life. I am not angry with God. Rather, I thank and praise God for his many blessings in my life, Theresa and Dad being at the top of those blessings.

Still, some may ask, God is the creator of the universe so why does he allow suffering? God says in *Isaiah 55:8-9* that His thoughts are not our thoughts and neither are our ways His ways. He goes on to tell us that just as the heavens are higher than the earth, so are His ways and thoughts higher than our ways and thoughts. In other words, we don't know why God allows suffering because it is not something we are capable of understanding.

I heard a talk by Bishop Robert Barron recently describing this scripture passage as follows (paraphrasing): When we take our dog to the vet to receive vaccinations our dog doesn't understand the trauma of receiving the shot is actually something good for him because he doesn't have the capacity to understand things as we do. Similarly, when we take our children to the dentist to have dental work performed, they too don't yet have the capacity to understand the trauma of the dental work we are forcing them to endure is for their own good. All the dog or our children understand is the suffering we allow, and sometimes cause, them to endure. Similarly, we too aren't capable of understanding that the suffering God may allow us to endure can lead to a greater good.

What good can come from Theresa's death? What good can come from my father's death? What good can come from these heavy crosses being placed on me simultaneously?

Quite frankly, as Isaiah tells us, we can't understand. I do know, however, that I have been much more in tune with the daily blessings bestowed on me. I recognize what a blessing it was to have Theresa as my wife and my dad as a parent. I am cognizant of the blessing of knowing that so many of our family and friends were ready and willing to give us support in whatever way we needed. I am aware of the blessing of knowing that there is so much good in the world as evident by the fact that even people who didn't know us were praying for us and reaching out to inquire about helping. I am blessed by the knowledge that God was with us every step of our difficult journey. It was a blessing seeing God in the routine activities of daily living during our suffering. I am blessed that Theresa continues to give me signs that she is ok and is by my side.

Perhaps God's way is meant to bring these many blessings into focus. Perhaps God's way is a means of bringing reassurance and blessings to those who are suffering in similar ways by witnessing my response to my own suffering. Perhaps God's way is allowing others who have not accepted God's calling to see his love in my response to my suffering and seek the same love in their own life. The point is, we are not capable of understanding God's reasoning for allowing suffering but there is good that can come from it. Just as the dog and child can't understand the greater good, we too cannot always understand God's plan.

If left to me, I would have taken the suffering from Theresa. If given the option, I would have accepted the suffering in Theresa's stead. But it was not left up to me. So, I accept God's plan, whatever that may be, accepting that His thoughts and ways are not my thoughts and ways and that His thoughts and ways are much greater than my own. It is only through this acceptance that I say I feel at peace and generally in a good place.

In one of our last conversations, Theresa asked me to promise her I would drop out of the deacon program to allow myself the opportunity to find love again. When I resisted making the promise to her, she asked me to at least consider it. In my mind, there was no way I would drop out of the program. It was a five-year program and there was only fourteen months left before it would be completed and my class ordained. Although it hadn't been a lifelong dream it was one that had been stirring in me since beginning *RCIA* in 2014.

As I have grown older, I have reflected more and more on the purpose of life, why am I here? I've heard others express similar thoughts as they age so perhaps my reflections are not out of the ordinary. In my humble opinion I have come to understand the purpose of life is fulfilled when one opens their heart and listens to what God is asking of them and then strives to become God's best version of that person (always remembering that our own thought of the best version of ourselves is far inferior to God's best version of us). I am also of the humble opinion that in my case God's best version of me ultimately places me in communion with and in servitude to others.

Through this communion and service, I have learned it is not about a duty or obligation. Rather, it is about being part of the human race. It is about being part of a community. It is about helping each other out whenever and wherever we can. It is about trying to help each other live their best possible life. It is simply about loving each other and having an impact on each other's lives. Thomas Merton once said we will not find the meaning of life by ourselves alone – we will find it with one another. Theresa's interactions with others and her dedication to making other's lives better any way she was able, one small act of kindness at a time, epitomized Merton's guide to finding the meaning of life.

But Theresa asked me to drop out of the program that would best position me to serve others. Why would she ask this of me? Because, as she stated, she wanted me to fall in love again. It was easy to refuse this possibility with Theresa staring into my eyes. However, several months after her passing, living alone with only my dogs and chickens to keep me company, I began to feel lonely. I had lived with either Tina or Theresa for over thirty-three years, all but three years after receiving my undergraduate degree in college. I was starting to question if I would truly want to live alone the rest of my life. I was also starting to understand why Theresa wanted me to find love again. I didn't know if I ever would or if I would ever want to but following through with the deacon program to ordination would not give me the option. If I decided to end my deacon formation, I reasoned there were many other ways I could serve God outside of the diaconate.

I decided I had to have more time to search my heart before making a vow of celibacy for life. So, in August, just prior to the beginning of the last academic year of my deacon formation program, I made a call that just one year before I never imagined I would make. I called the director of the program to inform him I would be dropping out of the program, fulfilling the promise Theresa asked me to make. For his part, the director was understanding and offered to give me some extra time to discern my candidacy for the diaconate. But I didn't want to put any artificial timelines on a decision and declined the gracious offer. Ten months later, however, when my classmates in the program stood in front of the archbishop for ordination, I sat with their families giving them my full support.

I fulfilled Theresa's request to drop out of the deacon program and open my heart to loving again. Conversely, Theresa fulfilled her promise to give me signs she is ok and by my side. If nothing else, Jekyll Island taught me the importance of looking for those signs, or at least the importance of not intentionally trying to avoid them.

As long as I'm not trying to avoid her, I have learned Theresa will make sure her signs are noticed, even for her loving husband known for his man looks. As a matter of fact, it seems her signs come when I'm least expecting them, just as we initially found each other when we first met. I am finding Theresa everywhere these days but there are a few instances that are particularly noteworthy.

As the first Halloween after her passing was approaching, I decided I would not decorate for the occasion. The Halloween season was the unofficial beginning of the holidays in our household and I was not looking forward to the holidays without Theresa. Our home had a main level with a walkout basement and an unfinished attic with dormers in the front of the house. Coming home from work one evening in early October I was preparing to pull my car into the garage when something told me to look up to the window in one of the attic dormers. To be honest, in the entire time we lived in this home I'm not sure I had ever looked up at these dormer windows. I was startled when I looked up because there appeared to be a man standing in the window. I got out of my car, walked toward the window, refocused my eyes and discovered what I was seeing was an old window decoration of a stalker Theresa had put there a few years earlier as a Halloween decoration. We had clearly forgotten it was there when putting decorations away and it had remained there ever since. But to me, it was a sign Theresa was with me. I would have never looked up to that dormer window had Theresa not been trying to send me a sign.

Theresa told me once that one of her favorite memories of her childhood was of a music box her father gave her that would play "*You Are My Sunshine*" when opened. There have been occasions since her passing that I would go into states of melancholy while thinking of Theresa. Its uncanny how many times I would hear "*You Are My Sunshine*" during those times. It might be the song playing on the radio, a commercial on the television or an ad on social media for a necklace that would open and play the song. No matter in what form, it seems Theresa would find a way for the song to be played for me, often times when I needed it most. Regardless of how I am feeling, when I hear the song, it brings an immediate smile to my face and brightens my mood.

Another sign that brings an instant smile is when I see a rainbow. Shortly after I asked Theresa to send me signs, we were looking out the window in our living room and saw a vibrant rainbow. Theresa turned to me and said when you see a rainbow in the future I want you to think of me. Today when I see rainbows Theresa is the first thing I think of, again often times that being when I'm melancholy and least expecting them. I always look up to the rainbow and say aloud "Hi baby, you are looking beautiful today. Love and miss you!" When I see a double rainbow, I like to think it is Jesus accompanying her and I will greet them both.

Theresa and I had a favorite restaurant in Columbus, *Riviera Maya* ("*Maya*"). We would frequent *Maya* for dinner two or three times a week. We were 'regulars' and became good friends with the staff over the years, even having them to our house for our pool and Halloween parties. They came to know us so well the waiters knew our orders without asking. After Theresa's passing, I continued to have dinner at *Maya* but not at the same frequency. I usually ate there alone. One particular evening while eating there alone I was missing Theresa more than usual (as if that is possible) with the one-year anniversary of her death approaching. I started scrolling through the pictures on my phone reminiscing about some of the times we had shared together. I was experiencing one of those pity parties that Theresa was always able to end with just a few words. The pictures were bringing smiles to my face remembering some of the great times we had shared but they were also making me sad with the knowledge those days were over. I was in no hurry to leave but I was falling deeper into my self-pity with each successive picture.

After about an hour I figured it was time to leave. I paid the bill and exited the entrance of the restaurant only to find a group of people standing just outside the door talking, partially blocking my exit. I excused myself, side stepping a woman standing with her back to me. As I squeezed past her, I glanced down at her back. I got by her taking three or four more steps and then stopped dead in my tracks. Something written on the back of her sweatshirt had caught my eye that didn't register at first. I turned around and went back to her and asked if I could take a look at the back of her sweatshirt. She must have thought this strange man wanting to look at her back was creepy but she complied. In big bold letters her sweatshirt read "Suck It Up Buttercup". And just like that Theresa sent me a message telling me to get my act together. Her love reaching out to me from beyond. Another one of those signs I asked her to send to me.

One of the best vacations Theresa and I ever shared was a two-week trip to Hawaii during the spring of 2019, visiting Oahu, the Big Island, Kauai and Maui. The first week of the trip was a cruise aboard the *Pride of America* with our children and grandchildren. The cruise portion of the vacation was our 2018 Christmas present to the kids. For the second week of the vacation we sent the children home and Theresa and I flew to Kauai and Maui spending three days on Kauai and four days on Maui.

While in Kauai we took a sunset cruise to the Na Pali coast and were mesmerized by its beauty. We loved it so much we decided to take a drive through Waimea Canyon the following day and then on up to hike along the ridge of Kalalau Valley on the Pihea Trail to the Pihea Vista to view the Na Pali coast from above. We arrived at the trailhead in the early morning with a full day on the southwestern part of the island planned for the rest of the day. Unfortunately, when we arrived a rain storm was approaching and we were in heavy clouds as we reached the parking lot (which was at an elevation of four thousand feet). We were very disappointed when we decided the hike was probably not a good idea and turned around and left. Not seeing the Kalalau Valley from above was our only disappointment during the entire vacation.

After leaving Waimea Canyon we drove to *Polihale State Park*, to spend the day at the beach. The park is located in an extremely remote area on the western shore of Kauai. Because of its remoteness we found it to be almost deserted.

Several miles of beach practically all to ourselves. We laid out on the beach, sat in our beach chairs, watched the surf crashing on the beach, and took a couple long walks along the beach holding hands. We engaged in small talk while solving all of the world's problems. We were able to unwind like we had not done in a long time, captivated by each other's company. It was one of the most romantic times I recall ever having with Theresa.

As the sun was racing toward the western horizon we reluctantly decided it was time to pack up our belongings and head back to civilization, neither of us wanting the day to end. On the way back to our resort we stopped in Eleele for dinner at *Kauai Island Brewing Company* adjacent to Port Allen. Despite the inauspicious beginning to the day above Kalalau Valley, it was one of the best days Theresa and I would ever share together.

In late April of 2022 I felt Hawaii pulling me to return and asked Brent, Misty, Scott, Ben, Stephanie and Jeff if they would like to join me. Only Jeff and Stephanie had the ability to get away for an eleven day trip on the spur of the moment. We visited Oahu, Kauai and Maui. One of the highlights I had planned for the trip was retracing the steps Theresa and I took on our memorable day on Kauai.

This time, I prayed, we would be able to hike the Pihea Trail and see the views of the Kalalau Valley down to the Pacific Ocean. When we arrived at the Pihea Trail trailhead it started to mist and clouds were rolling in off the Pacific Ocean just below us in Kalalau Valley preventing us from seeing anything below the ridge we were on. We were disappointed and Jeff and Stephanie questioned whether we should begin our hike.

Something (or someone) was telling me we should take the hike. A portion of the trail goes along the ridge of Kalalau Valley so I reasoned with Jeff and Stephanie that if we hiked the trail we might come to an opening in the cloud cover. They hesitantly agreed to the hike. It was a difficult hike made so not because of the terrain but rather by the extremely muddy conditions. We hiked away from the trailhead for about a mile with the clouds becoming thicker along the way. As we continued on the clouds started to slowly work their way up the valley toward us. As we were walking, I lagged a few yards behind saying a prayer to Theresa ever so often to intervene on our behalf with the powers that be to open the clouds for just a few moments to allow us to see the view that she and I had so desperately wanted to see and for what I brought Jeff and Stephanie to see.

With the mist starting to turn into rain and the clouds beginning to overtake us Jeff and Stephanie insisted we turn back. I have to admit, the deteriorating conditions were starting to worry me also so I agreed. But I didn't stop praying to Theresa to give us even a small glimpse of what we came to see. The hike back seemed to take even longer because of the worsening conditions but finally we were able to see the trailhead ahead of us. I figured one last prayer couldn't hurt so I mentioned to Theresa it was now or never.

We took another few steps and then saw a crowd of people gathered together near a rail at the edge of the ridge pointing out to where we assumed the valley was so we went over to the rail to see what had caught their attention. As we reached the rail we looked out and saw the clouds slowly separating until we had a clear view of the valley below and the ocean beyond. My heart swelled with love knowing Theresa had answered my prayers and was with us at that very moment.

Tears were rolling down my cheeks as we stayed glued to our spot along the rail for about fifteen minutes observing the view becoming clearer and clearer allowing us to take numerous pictures of what is probably one of the most beautiful areas in all of Hawaii. Realizing the time was much later in the morning than we had planned to be here we walked back to the parking lot beyond the trailhead and as we were taking off our muddy clothes it started pouring rain.

As we continued retracing that wonderful day Theresa and I had on Kauai, we made our way to *Polihale State Park*. We parked the Jeep we had rented and made our way to the beach. As expected, it was almost deserted. We laid out towels on the beach and sat down. Jeff and Stephanie were restless, however, and after a few minutes wanted to jump in the ocean and invited me to join them. I declined and encouraged them to enjoy the surf but cautioned them to be careful because the waves were big. Jeff and Stephanie were in the water for a long time and as they came back onto dry land they motioned for me to come with them on a walk down the beach. I shook my head no and off they went. What I didn't mention to them was I was feeling Theresa's presence while sitting in solitude on the beach and didn't want anything to interrupt our time together.

As the sun began its downward trek across the western sky, I saw Jeff and Stephanie returning and figured we should probably start packing up our belongings because we still had a couple more stops to make. The plan was to have dinner at *Kauai Island Brewing Company* as Theresa and I had and then go watch the sunset at Kehaha Beach, known for being the best place to watch the sunset on Kauai. After the sunset we planned to throw a lei into the ocean in honor of Theresa.

The drive back to Eleele took an hour which was a little longer than anticipated. On our drive there was a heavy rainstorm coming in from Waimea Canyon and a torrential downpour started just as we walked through the doors of the restaurant. With sunset rapidly approaching we assumed the arrival of the rainstorm ruled out the possibility of seeing a beautiful sunset but agreed we would still go to Kehaha Beach after dinner for the lei ceremony. Dinner was nice and leisurely. When we exited the restaurant we were surprised to discover the rain had stopped. Not only that but when I looked up to the sky, I noticed the clouds were clearing and a beautiful rainbow was visible off in the distance. "Well, hello baby. You are looking beautiful today. Love and miss you."

We had not hurried in the restaurant thinking we weren't going to be able to see the sunset but now it seemed as though we might be able to get a glimpse of it if we could make it to the beach in time. We had to hurry though because Kehaha Beach was about a twenty minute drive from the restaurant. We jumped in the Jeep and drove as fast as traffic would allow us. Fortunately, we made it with several minutes to spare but to our dismay discovered we weren't the only ones with this idea. The parking lot was full. We pulled back out onto the road searching frantically to find a parking space as quickly as possible because time was running out.

By this time, it was obvious it was going to be a stunning sunset because somehow there was not a cloud in the sky. Where the clouds went is still a mystery to me. With time running out we decided we had no choice but to park alongside the road and found a spot that seemed as though it would not create an obstacle to vehicles travelling on the road. We hurriedly got out of the Jeep and ran across the road to the beach just in time to see the most beautiful sunset any of us had ever seen. It was postcard perfect. After the sun dipped below the horizon and darkness started to settle in, we made our way to the ocean and said a prayer thanking Theresa for the wonderful day and told her how much we missed her with tears clouding our vision as we laid the lei in the ocean and watched the waves take it out to sea.

It had been a long day but the most enjoyable one of the vacation. Personally, I had felt Theresa's presence all day with her sending me signs of her presence throughout the day. We sauntered from the beach, crossed the road and started getting in the Jeep. I was driving and the driver's door was on the road side. I opened the door and started to sit in my seat when I heard Stephanie yell for me. She was walking around to the passenger side door. I quickly got back out of the Jeep and went around the back of the Jeep which is where it sounded she was. As I turned the corner around the back of the Jeep I saw Stephanie standing facing away from the road holding her phone up with the flashlight on pointing toward something. Stephanie instructed me to look. I looked in the direction of where the flashlight was pointed and read a sign that said *St. Theresa's Catholic Church* and beyond that I saw the church itself ... Theresa putting an exclamation point on her presence and love.

There are some who do not believe our loved ones can send us signs from beyond. Theresa has made it abundantly clear to me that she can in fact send me signs, as long as I am receptive to recognizing them. She will always remain in my heart and soul. She will always be a part of my identity. She will always be in my memories. She will always surround me with signs of her nearness. I know for the rest of my life I will be finding Theresa wherever I may be.

I love you Theresa

Now and Forever

You suggested your arrival was approaching. Vigilantly, we fought your advance. The battles were fierce. There were victories. There were defeats. Our emotions were heightened, our nerves exposed. Our attention was focused. Your presence demanded no distractions. When all seemed lost, the unexpected provided hope. Then you struck. Just when victory seemed to be upon us, your attack was brutal. We were surprised and shocked. How were we caught off guard? We knew the battle was to come, but misjudged the battleground. A valiant adversary you proved to be. Refusing to play by the rules. Creating confusion and imbalance before your advance. Our attention was diverted and divided. We were weakened and vulnerable to all of your attacks. Our total defeat was upon us. All was thought to be lost. But your confidence ... your strength ... was your weakness. Our humbleness ... our weakness ... was our strength. We knew our limitations were great and your superiority insurmountable. But alone we were not. Death may be your spoils, but eternal life is our glory. You are powerless. Your destruction is complete. Your defeat final. Although your efforts may have separated us temporarily, we know in time we will forevermore live together. We offer our praise for our Lord's glory and our deepest gratitude for His ultimate sacrifice.

Acknowledgments

The only names I did not change in the body of this book are mine and Theresa's. All other names were changed for privacy purposes.

It has been a long-time dream of mine to write a novel. Like so many other things in my life, I am blessed to have Theresa in my life as an impetus to fulfilling this dream. The wish/need to preserve our special bond for memory's sake and to explain to family and friends the amazing love Theresa and I shared was a consuming motivation for completing this book. So, as with so many other things in my life, thank you, Theresa, for being the force behind the fulfillment of my dreams. But even more, thank you for being you and for the love you brought into my life. I hope the preceding words help the reader understand what a truly remarkable person Theresa was and the saint she is to a countless number of people, especially me. Love and miss you, baby.

During Theresa's illness and after her passing, I leaned on many people for emotional support. It is impossible here to list everyone who provided me comfort during the difficult times, but please know your kind words, listening ears, and prayers are appreciated more than I can ever express. Thank you.

Spiritually, I'm particularly indebted for the guidance, prayers, and availability of Fr. Chris Wadelton, Fr. Jeff Godecker, and Deacon Bill Jones. You were there for Theresa and me every step of the way.

My brothers in the diaconate formation class and their wives were like family to Theresa and me. Thank you for your prayers and support: Dcns Kerry Blandford, Pat Bowers, Jorge Sanchez Leanos, Dave Urbanowski, Jerry Besler, Kevin Daily, Tim Elder, Mark Henry, Elvin Hernandez, Tom Hosty, Nick Martin, Neil May, Mike Nygra, Jim O'Connell, Chris Rainbolt, Mark Schmidl, and Jim Wood.

Our family was there by our side throughout, helping out in so many ways. I am sure I will never know the full extent of everything they did behind the scenes because of their efforts to allow me to keep my focus entirely on Theresa. I love each and every one of you. Thank you from the bottom of my heart for being there for us: Brittney Thrash, Logan Thrash, Travis Thrash, Derrick Thrash, Mary and Bill Muir, Dorothy Canoles, Kathy Phillips, Pat and Kevin Keppley, Debbie Ernest, Ryan Baugh, Shelby Baugh, Becky Baugh, and Pam and David Adams.

Theresa and I had many friends who assisted us, both during her illness and after her passing. I thank each and every one of them for their support. I would like to mention a few by name here: Angie Megerle, Denesha Megerle, Daija Megerle, Beverly Money, Leigh Hancock, and David and Michael Wilkinson-Wheatcraft.

I had no idea what I was getting into when I began writing this book. Naively, I had a belief I would complete the book while I was in Jekyll Island, Georgia, for a week. It is now two and a half years since I visited Jekyll Island, and I am just now wrapping up the whole process (admittedly, I took an extended break from writing when I reached Part II of the book because I wasn't ready to write about Theresa's illness). I have discovered the process of writing this book – the memories that have been recalled, coming to terms with the events of the past thirteen years, and the thought-provoking reflections that have come from these events – has been a cathartic process that has allowed me to experience a cognitive insight into the emotions from the loss of Theresa (and my dad).

As I have reached these final stages of copy editing and proofreading, I have relied heavily on several individuals and would like to thank them for their invaluable guidance, input, and encouragement: Jessie Roth Goyne, Carmen Pike, Shauna Synder, Shelby Baugh, Rose Baugh, Becky Baugh, and Margie Clouse.

The artwork for the cover of the book was painted by Anna Fagin Larimer. Her painting is an excellent work of art representing the two times I found Theresa and thus bringing the theme of the book full circle … from when I first 'found' Theresa during our talk in the gazebo on our first date to finding her again when I was greeted by the hyacinths on Jekyll Island upon first arriving … a sign from Theresa that I had come to the right place to find her again. Thank you so much, Anna. You did a wonderful job capturing the essence of the book.

I also want to thank the team at *Amazon Publishing Agency* for their professionalism and guidance in bringing this project to fruition. Once I completed writing, copy editing, and proofreading, I quickly discovered transforming my work into a publishable book and the marketing necessary to get the book to the reader to be a daunting task.

The team proved to be very attentive to my ideas and eager to help every step of the way.

A special thanks goes out to Jennifer Woods. Thank you for your acceptance of Theresa, the love we shared, and her family, who will always be a part of my family. Thank you for your patience as I have completed this project and your understanding of my need to finish this book. It takes a special person to give the support you have provided me in this process. I know at times, it couldn't have been easy, especially when I would become melancholy and deeply engrossed with writing. I know Theresa would have loved you as much as I do, and I can't help but believe you are the one she knew I would find one day.

About the Author

Finding Theresa is the first book written by Paul Baugh. Paul was born in 1963 and received a degree in Law and Public Policy at Indiana University - Bloomington in 1987 and a Doctor of Jurisprudence at Indiana University – Indianapolis in 1990. He was an associate attorney with the Law Office of Gary Kemper in Madison, Indiana, from 1990 to 1993. Since 1993, he has been a sole practitioner in his hometown of Bloomington, Indiana, focusing his practice in the fields of family and criminal law. *Finding Theresa* is based on actual events, texts, emails, and conversations from his love affair with Theresa. Names of those mentioned in the book have been changed, other than his and Theresa's, to protect their privacy. Paul and his dogs recently moved from the home he shared with Theresa in Columbus, Indiana, to his hometown of Bloomington to be closer to family and his office.

Printed in the USA
CPSIA information can be obtained
at www.ICGtesting.com
LVHW051418180124
768653LV00023B/1103